THE GRACE'S WAR

TIDES BOOK THREE

R.A. FISHER

ACKNOWLEDGMENTS

Thanks to Joe, for again finding the things I missed, Jane for inspiring me, and Tomomi for putting up with me.

For Taiki. I hope you can read this one day and be proud.

PROLOGUE
BLACKVINE

"We need to kill the ones who refuse Heaven. At least until we can reinforce the caravans enough that they no longer present a threat," regret tinged Major Rohm's voice.

Colonel Heine nodded and swept a hand across his pitted face, scratching an insect bite beneath his long mustache. His brown eyes looked sad, but then, they always looked sad.

"Yes," he agreed. "Or at least driven to the edges of the valley until we can secure the farms. Are the saplings through the tunnel yet?"

Major Rohm shook his head. "We haven't gotten any word yet. It shouldn't be long, now."

It had been easier than Colonel Heine dared hope. In fact, he'd expected disaster to come at any moment, but it seemed the traitor General Albertus Mann had indeed broken these people when he'd come to this valley over three years ago. There'd been no resistance when Heine had led his paltry force of marines and farmers down the ropes, still dangling abandoned from Mann's incursion. He wondered why the people here hadn't just left after a way out had been presented to them. If he could ever get one of these barbarians to speak N'naradin, that was the first thing he would ask them.

He looked up at the grotto. A messenger had begun his descent, over-cautious, clutching at cracks in the obsidian cliff as he edged down the old rope. It had supported the fifty-five men who'd already come down; he didn't know why this lone, scrawny man was so worried about it breaking now. Idiot. He chewed on the end of his mustache.

Their journey across the Yellow Desert had been easy too. The desert tribes had either seen their debt with the N'naradin Empire settled or not viewed Heine's little gathering of marines and farmers a threat worth their time. Either way was fine with Heine, and Rohm had shown visible relief when they'd arrived in the foothills un-harassed. Mann's mistake had been bringing his army all at once. In groups of fifty here, a hundred there, the former General would have been able to cross with the regular caravans just as he had. If Mann had bothered asking for his advice last time, he would have told him as much.

Once within the valley, there'd only been one lone skirmish, in which the Grace's forces had driven off their attackers of teenagers and elderly with ease. Rohm said they'd killed all the able-bodied adults their first foray here, thanks to the wisdom of Cardinal Vimr, whom General Mann had murdered with a knife in the back. Coward. Rohm had shown his spine by reporting that blasphemy to the Grace Herself after they'd returned. It had earned him a promotion. Whispers were he'd become the Grace's General after they returned home from the Black Wall and Heine joined the clergy. It was a shame Mann had escaped the Pit with the help of a few pirates. Heine hoped the old man was rotting now, wherever he was.

After what seemed like hours, the messenger finished his descent and trotted over to Colonel Heine and Major Rohm. Behind him, more farmers had begun their long descent, with,

Heine noted, more courage and speed than the messenger had displayed.

"Colonel," the young man wheezed as he stopped in front of them with a flaccid salute. "The plants are through the tunnel, and the caravan is prepping them for their return to Fom. Commander N'fallis says the safest route will be to follow the foothills north, then skirt the Dry Mountains all the way to The Piers, rather than risk crossing the desert again. Not because of the nomads, she says. Nobody knows how those brambles would fare in the heat, but she says since they grow way up here, they probably won't do well in—"

"Yes, yes," Heine cut in, annoyed. "I suppose there's wisdom in that. It will add a month or more to her trip back to Fom, but it can't be helped. Tell her I approve any action she sees necessary. I will do my best to rendezvous with her in Great Spring once I am confident things are settled here. But make it clear she is not to wait more than a week. Who knows how long the Grace will be able to keep the Upper Great Road secure if Tyrsh makes another go at it? The added security will mean nothing if we're under siege the whole way through the wastes."

He turned to Rohm, who'd been watching the exchange with a poorly concealed smirk, guessing Heine's thoughts. "Major, I'm sorry to reward your service with such a miserable task, but you're the only one I trust to oversee our settlement here. Besides which, you've had some dealings with these people before. Limited, I know, but it's still more than anyone else can say. I trust you have no complaints at staying behind. If Mann had allowed me to accompany you into the valley last time, I'd do it myself."

Rohm saluted and bowed. "None at all, Colonel. This climate suits me."

"Good. Start with that first farm. The one a few hours from

here, due south. Don't worry about the others until we know if all this will be worth it."

"The Grace thinks it is, Colonel."

"Indeed, she does, and she's rarely wrong. We've supposedly learned how to shape these miserable brambles. Now we just need to see if it actually works." He watched the continued descent of the farmers and soldiers before turning back to Rohm. "With a little of Heaven's luck, these bushes will both survive the trip back to Fom and grow once they get there. Then we can leave this Heaven-forgotten chasm to whatever wretched barbarians remain."

"Yes sir. May I be dismissed, sir? I'd like to begin defensive preparations at the first farm as soon as possible, in case the defenders find their spines."

"Of course, Major. May Heaven guide you."

Colonel Heine watched the departing back of Rohm, mind on N'fallis's task of getting the bushes back to Fom alive. He pulled out the smooth, black, wooden knife the Grace had given him before he'd departed and examined it again. Taken from some vagabond a patrol had found in the mountains east of Fom, filed away and forgotten by idiots who didn't recognize its significance. That vagabond had been from this valley; one of the last defenders pursuing Mann across the continent to get back whatever the traitor had taken. He'd been thrown in the Pit, only to escape with none other than Mann himself before anyone realized who he was. Heine wondered where that man was now, and whether he'd ended up killing the general after they'd escaped. He hoped they'd ended up killing each other.

Still, through the mercy of the Heavens and the wisdom of the Grace it had worked out in the end. When the Grace had taken Myrion's Revenge, the occupying forces had come across detailed notes in the ruins of the government house describing this substance—this blackvine. How they worked it into knives and roof tiles and everything else they used here in this forsaken valley. Wood that could cut through bronze as if it were a hard cheese.

The civil war had become a bloody stalemate. The Arch Bishop had suffered a major blow with the destruction of Eheene and the loss of the never confirmed but long suspected aid of the High Merchant's Syndicate, but he still had far greater numbers than the Grace of Fom. Neither side had gained advantage since that explosion had reduced the Skalkaad capital to ashes and an ever-burning naphtha fire.

Maybe, if they could master the use of this blackvine, Fom would find the upper hand the Grace needed.

1

PIRATES

"I said starboard old man! You got crabs in your ears? You'd better—"

A wave forty hands high crashed over the deck and drowned out whatever else Ves was yelling, but Mann got the gist. He banked the wheel one last time hard to the right and tied it with the dripping rope dangling from a hook on the ceiling, flapping in the gale despite its sodden weight. He dove out of the open wheelhouse door across the copper deck, wrapping his arms around the cowl vent as the Heaven's Compromise tipped into the next trough. A few shards of glass from the shattered bridge windows skittered past him and disappeared into the churning waters of the Sea of N'narad.

There was a crack, almost unheard over the driving rain, and a second later, the rail and a chunk of the aft deck blew apart. The ship shuddered.

Below, the engine growled and sprang to life, and the Compromise heaved itself up the next swell.

Ves charged, skid, fell, and slid into the door, which was opening and slamming closed again with a life of its own on the last unbroken hinge. He untied the wheel and spun it madly to the left. The Heaven's Compromise groaned and plunged into the next trough. Through the squall, Mann glimpsed the third N'naradin ship banking, trying to line up its deck cannons for another volley, before the swells hid it again.

There was another cluster of cracks. Six geysers exploded in the boiling waves to the starboard, but none found their mark as the Heaven's Compromise gained speed.

Mann regained his footing in time to see the other two N'naradin warships falling behind on either side, banking away from each other to avoid collision, the Compromise momentarily forgotten. Anger swelled in his gut and he groped his way back to the bridge where Ves still clung to the wheel. The pirate was laughing.

"You idiot," Mann wheezed as he slammed the door behind him. It bounced open again and continued its mad, flapping dance. "You went *between* them?"

"Goddamn straight, I did." Ves glanced over at Mann and saw the anger on his face. "What?"

"We're faster. We could have run." Mann had regained some of his composure and moved to stand next to Ves, following his gaze out the broken window, squinting against the rain driving into his eyes. He wiped at his face uselessly. The Compromise pitched and rolled, but she'd evened out enough that the threat of capsizing had passed.

"Maybe. In this weather, who knows? They might have had a fourth ship creeping up behind, assuming they knew that's what we'd try."

"You ran us towards three ships that wanted us at the bottom of the sea. We couldn't even see where they were until we were between them."

"Goddamn straight," Ves said again. "And they couldn't see us either. I knew where they were. More or less. We weren't going to hit them, if that's what's got your dick in a knot. Worst would have been if they'd hit us with their broadsides as we were going through. That would have been the end, for sure. Best would have been if they'd blown each other apart when they tried." He clapped Mann on the back. "We got somewhere in between."

"They did hit us," Mann said, voice weak. The need to argue the point had fled him.

Ves glanced over at the old man, grinning. "Just once. And a graze at that. We'll get it patched up, no problem. What you might call 'cosmetic damage.' As long as Saphi can keep the engine going until we can get to a port somewhere, we'll be fine. That is, if we can find our way out of this fucking storm and figure out where we are."

Mann sighed, defeated. "I'll go check on her." He turned to the ladder in the back of the room that led to the aft hold and the engine room below it.

"You forgot to call me Captain, old man!"

"Fuck you." Mann closed the hatch behind him, cutting off the sound of Ves' laughter.

————

Three years ago, as he'd stood on the deck of a naphtha tanker and watched a pillar of white fire two thousand hands high consume the city of Eheene, the former General of N'narad Albertus Mann had considered swimming back to the Foreigner's District, walking into those flames, and falling to ash. But Vesmalimali had taken him by the arm and led him away.

The N'naradin tanker had taken the refugees it had gathered from the flames to Pom, but only the ones who could either prove their citizenship or swear fealty to Heaven and the Arch Bishop. Even then, only those prepared to pay a thousand

Three-Sides in Salvation Taxes had been allowed to disembark. Mann had stayed below with Ves, afraid someone would recognize him and turn him in as the traitor who'd murdered Cardinal Vimr and escaped the Pit of Fom. The Arch Bishop would be even less forgiving than the Grace for stabbing his advisor, and she'd thrown him in the Pit to die.

Funny, Mann thought later, how fast his desire to sacrifice himself for his failures had turned into a fierce will to live so he could try to make up for a fraction of them.

The tanker had turned back and deposited the rest of them along the Upper Peninsula, where most had made their way to Maresg. For months in the tree city, Mann and Ves spent their days wandering from bar to bar, drinking to forget and failing.

Ves eventually turned his business sense and reputation again to the delezine trade. The drug wasn't illegal in Maresg—almost nothing was illegal in Maresg—but shipping it to Fom and Tyrsh was frowned on and therefore profitable. Mann helped, the last of his moral convictions hammered into him by seventy years in the Church burned away by the fires of Eheene. He realized that somewhere between the Pit and the Foreigner's District he and Ves had become friends, but with that thought came memories of Pasha and his sister, and the need for another drink.

In just under two years from when the sky fell over Skalkaad, they'd saved enough for a steamship. "A real fucking ship" as Ves called it, even if it was small by steamship standards. The former Corsair scraped up a crew of nineteen in less than a week, and when he offered Mann the position of first mate, the old general didn't see any reason not to take it.

And they'd been at sea ever since.

Five years, Mann thought. It took five years to fall from General Mann, servant of the Church, his soul bound for the

Heaven of Flowers, to the infamous pirate Whitehook's ancient first mate.

———

Mann found Saphi cursing and kicking at the overflow valve in the back of the engine room. She glanced at him as he climbed down the ladder, gave one more vicious kick, picked up a bronze wrench as long as her arm, and whacked it one more time with an overhand swing before tossing the wrench back on the floor and giving Mann a little wave.

"Hi old man."

"Hello Saphi." He dropped down, skipping the last two rungs, gave a grunt of regret when his hip almost gave out, and wobbled as the Compromise lurched over another swell. "Problems?"

Saphi insisted she was twenty, but didn't look over fifteen. Ves said she'd been one of the best mechanics in Maresg before he'd scooped her up from the shop she'd apprenticed at. She was swarthy under the layers of grease, with a thick wedge of a nose, skeletal cheekbones, and a small mouth. The girl claimed to be next in line for chief in one of the karakh tribes, but had run away because, as she put it, she couldn't imagine a life "trapped on the Upper Peninsula, telling a bunch of goat riders what to do." She had a knack for machines, and Ves made sure they put it to good use. Better use than lubing pulleys, which is how she'd described her job before she'd joined Ves' crew. Mann didn't know if she was being metaphorical when she'd said that, and he'd always been afraid to ask.

"Not anymore," she answered. "Overflow valve got stuck again. That's why we stalled. Bad timing. I heard the deck get hit. Is it bad?"

Mann shook his head. "No, not bad, I don't think. Nothing that Ves can't fix, anyway."

"We're gonna need fuel soon."

"Ves knows. He says we're almost to a Ristroan smuggling route, as long as we can make our way out of the storm. Shouldn't be long before we find an easier target than a trio of N'naradin warships. After that, we can find port somewhere for a week or two and get things fixed up."

"Three of them? How'd we get away?"

"Ves ran between them."

Saphi laughed. "*Between* them? That asshole. No wonder the deck got hit. Wish I was up top to see it."

A bell sounded from above.

"You were saying?" Saphi smirked as she turned to cut the engines. "It figures as soon as I get her going, I've got to shut her down again."

"See you soon," Mann said as he started up the ladder back to the wheelhouse, where he could hear Ves shouting something over the sound of the crashing sea. His hip growled in pain. *I'm too old for this.*

———

Kaleb and Edge had done a commendable job flooding the lowest three port compartments. The Heaven's Compromise leaned at a dangerous angle, precarious on the diminishing waves from the squall now churning to the west. A few glints of the morning sun peeked through the grey in the east.

Ristro had grown cautious since the Grace's rebellion. Smaller, faster boats, almost always alone and hard to notice. They'd turned to smuggling supplies to both sides of the war. Since the destruction of Eheene and the Merchant's Syndicate, the naphtha shortage had made raiding N'naradin freighters less worthwhile, and the use of the firepacks had become almost nonexistent as fuel shortages spread. With the rise in demand for Ristro goods—tarfuel engine and dirigible parts, mostly— their smuggling lanes had grown busy, but they'd grown careless too. Neither Fom nor Tyrsh attacked Ristro vessels these days, unless they knew for certain the Corsairs were bound for the other side. Even then, neither the Grace nor the Arch Bishop seemed too eager to burn their own bridges with the last reliable smugglers on Eris.

Ves hadn't been a Corsair in over twenty years, but he still knew their old routes and how they operated. They wouldn't be able to resist a ship foundering near their lanes, though after the third time the Heaven's Compromise sprung their trap, Mann suspected the trick would wear thin, if it hadn't already.

The sky had cleared to a few streaks of clouds streaming after the black shadow hanging in the west before a Ristro cruiser came into view. Ves called Mann over, smiling.

"See?" He said. "I told you it would work. One more time, at least. Corsair captains are always competing. Can't resist easy prey. Not until the Astrologers pass it down that the prey might not be easy as it looks. Best we're careful after this one."

Mann frowned, but didn't press. With Ves, there was no point. He took his place at the wheel, while Ves went below to prep with Kaleb and Edge.

He didn't need to feign fear when the Ristroan grapples clanked onto the deck, caught the rail, and grew taut. One of these times they'd be boarded by pirates who'd call Ves' bluff, or worse, have firepacks of their own that really had fuel. Three times was already too lucky in Mann's opinion.

Five grapples found home. A few seconds later, five Corsairs appeared at the edge of the deck, cautious but confident. They wore the long-faced masks of the firethrower crews, but as had been the case before, their backs were empty of the bulky fuel packs. Ves had told them after the first time that the Corsairs only continued to wear them for intimidation. If there was so little naphtha that Tyrsh had resorted to buying tarfuel engines from Ristro to convert its navy, there was little fear of the Corsairs having enough to fill their weapons. Mann wasn't fond of the thought that the big pirate was betting their lives on that guess every time they lured another Ristro ship, but he'd been right so far.

Ves, with the timing of a dancer, erupted from the hold just as the fifth Corsair set her feet onto the deck. Kaleb and Edge flowed after him. None wore masks, but all three brandished salvaged firepacks. Ves had bought them on the black market in Maresg. Of those, only one functioned at all, and Ves had only found enough fuel for it to fill a N'naradin naphtha lantern. So far, they hadn't needed more, but once they used up what they had, they'd need to change their tactics. Ves reasoned if the other two stayed in the back, nobody would pay too much attention to them after Ves showed off the one that worked. So far, he'd been right about that too.

"Stand down, you wretched assholes!" Ves shouted at the stunned Corsairs in Ristroan. "You know who I am. I can tell by the looks on your sniveling faces. Relax, have a seat on the deck, and you might just live long enough to fuck your mothers again!" He punctuated his speech with a short blast from his firethrower, off the deck and to the side, where the thin, thirty-hand stream of blue flame cascaded into the still-rolling sea like a snake of blue magma, where it continued to burn.

The Corsairs sat. Kaleb and Edge tied them, while Ves lowered himself down onto their smaller ship.

Mann stood at the wheel, watching through the shattered window. Nobody noticed him, and he was fine with that.

———

Later, Mann sat with Ves in his "Office," as Ves called it, which was just a small cabin next to the captain's quarters where Ves had put a Brobdingnagian desk he'd spent the last of his delezine tin on. "Important people have big fucking desks," he'd declared to Mann, who'd watched with some amusement as the four dock men struggled to get the hideous thing down the gangway and through the door. "And I'll be the most important goddamn person on the Sea of N'narad."

Ves refilled their glasses with clear, slightly salty rum and leaned back. "Not much more than one, maybe two demonstrations left in the firepack," he announced. "Maybe just as well. I don't expect we'll get away with doing that more than once or twice more anyway. Four times in five months is a good haul though. After next time, we should get enough to settle down for a spell. Long enough to come up with a different strategy."

Mann sipped his drink. "Is that your way of telling me I was right when I said this couldn't last?"

"Hah! Hell, I never said it would last. You need to think like a pirate instead of a general."

Mann frowned into his glass, but managed to make the expression friendly. He took another drink. "What does that mean?"

"Think about *now*. Then think about tomorrow, maybe the day after. And don't give a shit about anything after that, because even if you're alive by then, everything will be different."

Mann snorted a little laugh. "Where were you forty years ago? I could have used advice like that when the Grace promoted me to General."

Ves paused. "This...what we have going on now, it would probably have lasted longer if you hadn't stopped me from killing the crews. Even spread out across Eris like the Corsairs are, stories spread when there're survivors. I might be making you hard, but you're making me soft."

The old man shrugged, ignoring Ves' inuendo. "Maybe. Or maybe Ristro would have sent out a half-dozen cruisers to hunt us down by now because their smuggling crews kept winding up massacred."

Ves gave a grudging nod, but before he could say anything, Mann changed the subject. "You said you found something on that ship? Are you planning on telling me about it? I thought that's why you invited me in here."

"I invited you in here because I like your company for some reason. But yeah, I found something. A few somethings." He filled their glasses again and sat back. Mann sipped his rum and waited.

"Got the usual. Tanks were half full, plus barrels on reserve. That should keep us in tarfuel at least another month or two. Got a load of parts too. Good ones. Bronze, even some iron and steel. Someone in Tyrsh paid a literal boatload of tin for that. They won't be happy when it never comes. Ha!

"Also found some messages in the captain's quarters, after he was nice enough to let me in and show me around. Some interesting intelligence." He paused again, grinning.

Mann sighed. "Go on."

"First, this was their last trip to the Island. Maybe just this crew, but I got the impression the Astrologers were cutting off the Arch Bishop. Interesting, yeah? Second, after this delivery to Pom, they had orders to head up to Skalkaad. Didn't say what for—only a few names given—contacts in New Eheene who would already have their orders. My guess is they're looking at taking over some of the abandoned naphtha refineries, or maybe some kind of recon into the ruins."

"New Eheene?"

"It's what they're calling the shanty town of drunks, squatters, and shit-suckers that's sprung up in what used to be the Foreigner's District. Anyway, I'd bet my fucking boat the first and second are related. Not the first rumors we've picked up that a few of the refineries are back in business, though whoever's operating them is anyone's guess."

Mann thought a minute. "Anything else?"

"Not much."

"Can I see those orders? Might be something between the lines."

Ves let out a little chuckle and pulled some papers from the top drawer of his desk. "Sure. Didn't know you learned how to read Ristroan, since you still speak it like shit."

Mann's hand wavered and fell where he'd been reaching to take the papers from Ves. The big pirate laughed again and put them away. "Anyway," he said, "Don't need you to read between the lines for me."

"Oh?"

"I read between them just fine: things are about to get fucked. Let's get some sleep."

Mann drained his glass and stood to stumble towards the door. He hadn't realized how drunk he'd gotten until he'd tried to stand. At least his hip didn't bother him now.

"Remember, old man."

Mann turned in the doorway, eyebrows raised.

"Think like a pirate, because next week we might be dead."

2

GRIEF

"It was a Kalis, and fuck off if you don't believe me. My cousin swears it. Reckons they're hiring themselves out now. Bodyguards an' shit. Foot soldiers for the Arch Bishop even. Grace, too, I'd say. I mean, why not?" The speaker, a balding, rotund man with a blotchy, red face, took another swill of his glogg and gave the table a thump with his free hand. "Says they needed to blow the entire ship to get rid of her. Would have took back Myrion's Revenge for the Arch Bishop, otherwise. All by her goddamn self."

His companion, a dark, equally round woman with a crooked nose and black, curly hair hanging in mats past her shoulders let out a forced guffaw. "Yer cousin's full ah blovey wine and karakh shit. No such thing as Kalis. For fuck's sake, Manch, Eheene goes and blows itself up and everyone starts seeing goddamn ghosts everywhere. Didn't know you was so stupid as to believe 'em."

"There's Kalis, awright," the man sitting a few seats down the bar chimed in. He was short and wiry, dressed in filthy Tidal Works coveralls. The skin of his face was saggy and rough, but his green eyes were sharp under the haze of alcohol. He gripped his own mug of glogg with his left hand, mutilated with burns and missing the little and ring fingers. "There's Kalis. I's seen 'em. Seen 'em myself," he nodded as if confirming his own statement. Then he coughed once and took a long drink, eyes never leaving the rough grain of the unpolished bar.

The woman wheeled around to face him, unsteady. "Mind yer business little man. Nobody talking to you."

He looked up from the table to blink at her. "But I'm talking t'you. You say there's no such thing is Kalis. I say there is. I seen 'em myself. If you and your fat ass doesn't believe me..." He paused, swaying in little circles on his stool. "Well, you should."

The bald man stood and walked over to sit on the other side of him, frowning. "You better bug off now, 'fore someone gets hurt."

The little man twisted around, almost falling off his stool. "Wha's your problem? I'm on your side."

"I don't need anyone on my side. 'Specially not a little Tidal Works slug. We was having a nice conversation, and it didn't involve you. Mind your own business and fuck off."

"Enough of this shit," the woman grumbled and reached out to grab the little man's arm.

He spun around in a blur, launching his forehead against her nose with a wet crunch. She grasped at her face with both hands, coughing, blood flooding down her chin onto her filthy blouse.

"Hey!" The bald man shouted, but before he could say anything else, the smaller man had spun back to him, thrusting his elbow into the larger man's gut. He doubled over, wheezing.

The little man stood, still unsteady, and looked around the bar. It was crowded, but a space had cleared around the altercation. No one spoke.

He glared around at the staring faces, then reached across his body to peel the flesh away from his forearm above his mutilated left hand, revealing a swirl of tattoos their eyes couldn't focus on. "Told you there were Kalis. Now you've seen one too. Tell your friends, if you got any. Nobody's safe. Nobody ever was."

He—she—plowed through the silent crowd and out the door as they scrambled to get out of her way.

———

Syrina stumbled into the night, swerving through alleys and busy streets, before stopping in a crooked doorway halfway down a dead-end lane. She wiped the pouring rain from her face.

"I suppose it's a good thing you keep doing things like that or I never would have found you. Kalis Syrina, I presume?"

She jumped at the voice and spun around, seeing nobody. Then, outlined in the rain, the shape of a woman a little taller than herself. Brown eyes blinked at her.

Syrina dropped into a fighting stance and felt her heart slow as she dug through her mind for the entrance to the Papsukkal Door, failing to find it.

"Relax," the other Kalis said. "You realize if I wanted to hurt you, I would have just done it. I've been looking for you for a long goddamn time. Like I said, I'd still be looking if you hadn't made it so easy to find you. You of all people know how hard it is to find a Kalis who doesn't want to be found."

Syrina stood straight, but her mind still scrambled to find the door. She took a deep breath to clear her head, but that failed too. "Why?"

"My Ma'is sent me. Why else?"

"There aren't any Ma'is anymore."

"There are a few still. The destruction of Eheene didn't get them all. Unfortunately. But my Ma'is doesn't like me calling her that anyway. Not anymore. Lifetime of habit, I guess. You met her once a while back, and made quite an impression on her."

"Ka'id."

"I'm glad the years of alcoholism and regret haven't dulled your mind."

"How did you find me?"

The other Kalis shifted. The rain fell harder, and she stood out in the darkness like a waterproof shadow. "I'm Kirin, by the way. Do you have somewhere out of the rain we can talk, or does it suit you more these days to get wet when you're not picking fights in bars?"

Syrina gave a reluctant sigh. "Yeah, there's a place close to here. Wouldn't call it nice, though."

Kirin shrugged, the gesture almost invisible even outlined in the downpour.

Syrina led them a half-span through the winding streets to an alley much like the one they started in, pulled up a manhole cover concealed by a layer of greyish-green, sticky mud, and gestured for Kirin to go first.

"Still think I'll try to kill you?" Kirin asked, but she started down the ladder, her brown eyes glittering.

"I've got trust issues." Syrina waited until Kirin was almost to the bottom before going down, pulling the cover closed after her.

The chamber was small and square, twenty hands to a side. Brass pipes ran along three walls, tarnished with age. The fourth wall was bare limestone brick, more recent than the rest of it. A lone, flickering glow globe sputtered high in one corner, and mangy rags and discarded clothes covered half the floor. Empty rum and glogg bottles lay toppled against the lone bare wall, and a smaller stash of full ones lined the pipes opposite.

Kirin looked around. "Been keeping yourself busy, I see. How did you find this place?"

Syrina slumped down among the full bottles, selected one, and took a long drink before offering it to Kirin, who shook her head. "Luck, I guess," she answered. "Without Ormo's tin, I needed to dig around for a place to stay, and I came across it. Don't know why they walled it up. I bet nobody else does either. Not anymore." She paused. "Fuck knows why anyone does anything."

"You could have stayed in Ristro."

"Ah. That's how you found me."

Kirin laughed, hesitated a moment, then gestured for the bottle. Syrina handed it to her and Kirin took a sip before passing it back. "Ugh. I guess you couldn't afford the good stuff."

Another shrug. "Don't drink it for the flavor—you'll be disappointed. It does the trick."

Kirin settled down on the mass of dirty blankets. "The Astrologers are how I found out you were in Fom almost two years ago. Been here looking ever since, minus a few trips back to check on Ka'id."

"An Astrologer told you I was in Fom?"

The vague shape of Kirin shifted. "He told me you showed up a while after Eheene went up to give your report. 'A corpse-filled lifeboat with no oars' was how he described you. You know how they love to be poetic. He said you were somehow responsible for what happened to Eheene. That some of your friends got caught in the middle and didn't make it out. According to him, after you gave your report, you spent two months drinking, then caught a smuggler's ship headed to Fom. No one's heard from you since."

Syrina studied the bottle in her hand. "Friends. Yeah."

Kirin eyed her, but Syrina wouldn't meet her gaze. "I figured there was more to it than that. I was hoping you'd enlighten me."

Syrina stared at the bottle for a long time, silent. Then she sighed and took another long drink before passing it back to Kirin. "They say anything else about me?"

"He said a long time ago, Ormo gave you a pet bird—an owl—then had it killed and it woke up some kind of voice in your head. You offered to work for them instead of Ormo because you wanted revenge. Revenge for an owl. Not that I'm one to judge."

Syrina gestured for the bottle and took another drink. "That's the short version, or close enough. Turns out if I stay drunk, that voice doesn't talk."

"Is that good?"

She stared at the bottle in her hand again and didn't say anything for a minute. "I don't know. It is what it is. So why does Ka'id want to see me so bad she'd send one of her Kalis all over Eris to find me?" She handed the bottle to Kirin again and sat back.

"I'm her only Kalis these days, which might tell you how bad she wanted to find you. And I'm here because things are bad, and they're getting worse."

"Yeah, tell me about it."

"I'm trying."

"Fine." Syrina made a show of pressing her lips together and gestured for Kirin to continue.

"As far as Kavik can tell—or I guess I should call her Ka'id, since you know who she is, and there's a new Kavik now. Old habits and all that." Kirin reached over to pass Syrina the bottle again.

"Just get on with it," Syrina took another long drink. This time she didn't hand the bottle back.

"Sorry. So as far as Ka'id can tell, there are five or six High Merchants left. Some ronin Kalis have tracked them down to offer their services, on top of the ones they managed to keep."

Syrina nodded. "I suppose that makes sense. I might have done the same, six or seven years ago."

"Me too."

"Alright, go on."

"And as far as we can figure, the surviving High Merchant moved to Tyrsh. That's where Ka'id went too, after the Storik incident, so you can see how the others showing up there might make her nervous."

Syrina arched her eyebrows. "That's odd. Why would they go there? Ka'id I could see, since she's N'naradin, at least supposedly, but the others?"

Kirin moved a half dozen empty bottles out of the way to lean against the bare wall. "So, you don't know. I didn't either until Ka'id told me."

"Know what?"

"The High Merchant's Syndicate created the Church of N'narad."

Syrina stared at Kirin for a few seconds, but then she nodded and put the empty bottle down. "Influenced, even controlled, I had a hunch. But created? Still, I guess it makes sense. Get everybody worked up enough about going to Heaven, nobody looks at what's going on down here. Not to mention the revenue stream. It would explain the war too. I'm guessing the Grace of Fom started taking the Heaven thing a little too seriously to watch her erstwhile boss keep selling out to the heathens in the north."

"That's Ka'id's guess too, in so many words. So yeah, that's why they went to Tyrsh. But there's more."

Syrina gestured for her to continue while she groped around for another bottle.

"The Arch Bishop is getting naphtha again. We can't figure out who's supplying it, but somebody up north got control of a refinery, and they're supplying Tyrsh, just like before. Not as much. Not even close. Still, it's concerning."

"Huh."

"It gets better. there're rumors about the Grace. She sent people east to the Black Wall. Found some thorn bushes or something that can be sculpted like clay and fired to be harder than steel. Some say they've been there and back again, while others say they all died in the Yellow Desert on the way there. But for the past year, strange black weapons have been showing up along the Great Road and in Valez'Mui, so I suspect...Syrina?"

Syrina's eyes had grown distant and sad as they stared at a point somewhere past Kirin, the fresh bottle forgotten, half-opened in her hand. At her name, she blinked. "Sorry," she said, her voice soft. "I'm listening. Go on."

"One last thing. About six months ago, some spies from Tyrsh were caught in Fom and got themselves publicly executed."

"I remember hearing something about that."

"Ka'id suspects they came here looking into the Tidal Works. She thinks the Arch Bishop's plan to break Fom is to disrupt, maybe even destroy it. Or rather, that's the Syndicate's plan, and they're getting Arch Bishop Daliius to go along with it."

Syrina had managed to pull the cork out of the new bottle, but she put it down again without drinking. "You're sure?"

Kirin shrugged. "I'm not sure of anything, and neither is Ka'id, but I trust her and she's worried about it. I thought, since

Fom seems to be the place you've chosen to drink yourself to death, you'd want to know."

Syrina stood and leaned against the warm pipes, swaying while Kirin talked. "You don't know how bad that would be, do you?"

Kirin frowned. Syrina couldn't see it but she could hear it in her voice. "No, I guess not."

Syrina staggered over to the ladder, focusing a part of her mind to get her tattoos to purge the alcohol from her system. It had been years since she'd done it, and it was harder than she remembered. It gave her a headache. "Ka'id does. An inkling, anyway, if not all the details. Okay, I'll go see her. Take me."

But Kirin was shaking her head as she stood to follow Syrina up the ladder into the rain. "There are a few other things I need to do first, but there's a Ristroan ship on the Lip. Ka'id's been hiring them to wait for you there, in case you ever turn up. I think it's cost half of what was left of her fortune. Can you remember an address in Tyrsh if I tell it to you?"

Syrina scowled a look over her shoulder as she clambered out of the manhole, but didn't answer.

"Fine. Just thought I should ask. Seems like it's been a while since you've done much. I need to make sure you're all there."

"I'm not," Syrina said as Kirin climbed out of the hole and turned to face her. "But I can remember an address."

"Great. Looks like maybe we'll be working together, so I'll see you soon, yeah?" Kirin's voice trailed off. She was again just a shape in the rain. A second later, that was gone too.

"Yeah," Syrina said to herself. "See you soon."

Then she turned and moved through the darkness toward the lip, peeling her clothes and skin off as she went, until she, too, had disappeared.

3

REUNIONS AT SEA

"WHERE THE HELL DO YOU THINK THEY'RE GOING?"

Ves handed the lens to Mann, who swallowed and peered through it again. "It's only one ship, smaller than ours. They probably heard about us and don't want to take the chance. You said word would get around."

He watched a moment longer. The Ristro ship skimmed over the waves, so low it was almost hidden by the gentle swells as it headed into the setting sun. In a few minutes the glare off the water would hide it completely, save for the streams of black tarfuel smoke wafting from the pair of low stacks.

Ves looked thoughtful. "Maybe. But they're going due west. They're not on any of the normal routes, and they're not heading to one either. Anyway, that's a reconnaissance boat, not a smuggler."

Mann frowned, wondering what the difference was, and handed the lens back to Ves with a sigh. "I'm sure they must switch up their routes sometimes, or people would catch on. Right?"

"Mm. They used to do that, back when N'narad had a

policy of sinking every Corsair on sight. But since the war started, Ristro's been smuggling to both sides. It's only been a few weeks since they stopped their runs to the Island. I doubt the Arch Bishop's figured out yet that Ristro's cut him off."

"Unless the Astrologers told them."

Ves shook his head. "Not their way. Too confrontational. No, they'll just keep sending apologies and excuses to Tyrsh until Daliius or someone working for him figures it out on their own. Anyway, nothing east of here but Fom. So why is a Ristro ship sneaking across the Sea of N'narad from Fom to the Island?"

"Spies?" But Mann didn't sound like he believed his own idea. It didn't explain why Ristro would be hauling spies between Fom and Tyrsh, whichever side they were spying for. Ves didn't bother to answer.

Without the lens and against the setting sun, the Corsair ship was invisible. They were lucky they'd spotted anything more than a pair of exhaust trails. Then again, Mann didn't know how lucky it was.

"Well," Ves grumbled. "We could use more fuel, as always. We're faster than them. And I'm just too goddamn curious to let it go. That's a sign of intelligence you know, curiosity." He winked at Mann and stepped into the wheelhouse. A moment later, the engines growled to life, and they began their pursuit. Mann shook his head, knowing there'd be no point in arguing but feeling the need anyway. "You said we needed to come up with a different strategy, now that the firepack is empty."

"You're still not thinking like a goddamn pirate, General." Ves laced the title with sarcasm. "Anyway, this *is* a different strategy. We're not going to lure them—doesn't look like they'd stop if we tried. Nah, we'll just run the fuckers down and see what all the fuss is about. And I didn't say the firepack is empty. I said it was *almost* empty. Clean your ears."

But he said the last with no small amount of affection, and Mann just shook his head again and followed Ves into the wheelhouse.

At least, he thought, they'd fixed the windows.

———

Syrina was lying in her cabin, wondering when and if the voice in her head would come back now that she'd cut down on the rum, when she felt the ship slow and begin to turn. She was naked. It was strange, riding on a ship as an invited passenger, undisguised. Ristro was getting used to having Kalis around, and she didn't know if that was good or not. Not when everyone else was getting used to it too.

She got up from her bunk and slunk up the gangway to the deck.

The unnamed Ristro ship was tiny. Crewed by six, with a sloping bow. It resembled a normal boat capsized, wood covered in cobalt-painted copper, and low enough in the water it would be hard to see just a span away on the open ocean. Unfortunately, since the shortage, the naphtha engines had been converted to tarfuel, and the short stacks in the aft that jutted above the narrow-windowed wheelhouse coughed lines of black smoke.

And that, she saw, had been their downfall. A small steamship groaned towards them. It sported a pair of broadsides on each side and one bronze grappling cannon on its bow. Not a N'naradin vessel—not with the name "Heaven's Compromise" painted in crude lavender letters on either side. The color reminded her of a barge called the Flowered Calf she'd given Ves in Valez'Mui a lifetime ago. The memory strummed a pang in her chest, but she pushed it aside. These were just scavengers, but they were faster.

There was no way the Corsair's little crew of six could defend against whatever was coming, so it was a good thing Syrina was there. She climbed back down the hatch and closed it behind her but stayed at the top of the ladder, listening.

A minute later, she heard the growing grumble of the larger ship as it closed, and a second after that, her own ship shuddered with a wooden *crack* and a metallic *thunk* as the pirates' grapple embedded itself into the hull at the rear of the vessel.

Syrina coiled, ready to spring.

They picked the wrong ship, a voice in her head said, as if speaking just behind her where she wasn't looking.

"Oh, for fuck's sake," she said out loud.

———

"Something is wrong. They're not coming out." Mann frowned down at the Corsair ship from the deck of the Heaven's Compromise, rubbing the stubble on his chin.

Ves shrugged. "They're just doing what I would do. We're attacking them. If they stay in there, they only need to fight us one at a time, while we jump down into the meat grinder."

"Okay. So, what's your plan?"

Ves pointed. "That hatch on the deck is the only way in or out. Can't see anybody on the bridge, at least from this angle, which means they're all down below, waiting for us to come to them. But our harpoon cracked their rudder, so they can't go anywhere. We can either wait it out or storm in."

"And?"

"We've got a bigger crew. Might as well go in."

"The firepack is almost empty," Mann reminded him.

Ves shook his head. "Nah, I wouldn't want to use that and risk torching anything we can use ourselves. We'll go in the old-fashioned way."

He turned to call into the open hatchway, "Val! Seran! Get your asses out here. I'm too fat to go first!"

Mann was still frowning. "They might have firepacks too."

But Ves shook his head again. "They might, but I doubt it. Ship's too small to carry them, even when times were good— like I said, it's recon, not a pirate ship. Nowadays I'd be even more surprised. Even if they did, they wouldn't use them below any more than we would, for the same reason."

Mann still looked unconvinced, but he nodded. "If you think you know what you're doing, I'll leave you to it."

Ves laughed. "That's the spirit. Go wait by the wheel, just in case we've got to leave in a hurry for some reason. Tell Saphi to be ready too."

"Aye, aye, Captain." Mann's voice oozed sarcasm as he stepped into the wheelhouse, past Val and Seran, who were just coming out.

Ves only smiled. "There you go! Not that hard, now, was it?" He waved the two recent arrivals over. "Come on. I need you to go in before me, so if there're any surprises they'll kill you first."

Valenashalan and Seranalafan, Ristroan twins only a little smaller than Ves, were used to their captain's comments and responded with smirking nods so in sync that Ves suspected they'd choreographed it ahead of time. They led the way down the tethering rope and across the small deck to the closed hatch in its center. Val glanced into the wheelhouse window, then looked back at Ves and gave a quick shake of his head.

Fine, Ves thought. They all want to hide below, let them. He gestured to Seran, who nodded once to his brother and flung open the hatch, ceramic long knives drawn. Val dropped through a second later.

Silence dragged on.

"Val? Seran?" Ves edged over to the opening, a bronze cutlass in each hand, and peered down.

There was a blur of motion, and he felt himself plummeting face first, the sanded, copper-plated bamboo of the inner hull rushing to meet him. He thrust both arms out, swords turned away, and his palms scraped against the floor a split second before his face smashed into it, his swords skittering across the metal sheeting to clatter against opposite walls. His hands broke his fall enough to save his neck, but not his nose, and blood cascaded from it and his split lip, making the floor in front of him slick. He spit out a chip from his tooth.

"What the fuck?" he groaned as he scrambled for his swords. He saw Val and Seran laying on either side of him, wheezing and unmoving.

"Ves?" A familiar voice.

He sat up, swords forgotten, wiping at his face. "You've got to be fucking kidding me. Fuck. You."

A blurry form he couldn't focus on picked up both swords and held them out to him, hilts first. "Holy shit," it said. "What are you doing here?"

Val and Seran were both slowly clawing their way up to sitting positions, confusion written on their blunt faces.

"Me?" Ves growled, taking his cutlasses back. "What the fuck are *you* doing here?"

An indistinct hand reached out and helped Ves to his feet. "Good point," Syrina said. Her green eyes panned to the twins. "Sorry about that. I didn't know you were friends of Ves'." She looked back at the pirate captain. "I'm not hiring myself out as a mercenary guard for Ristro, if that's what you're thinking."

"It crossed my mind."

"I'm getting a lift to Tyrsh."

Ves raised his eyebrows.

"And since it looks like you broke my ride, you'll need to get me there instead. It's important."

"It's always important with you."

"Nature of the job, I guess." She looked down the hall, where a few of the Ristroan crew stood watching the exchange. "You guys can go home. Sorry about your boat."

They didn't move, faces unreadable, and she turned back to Ves. "Not really the chatty types. Glad you're here—to be honest, I'll be happy to have someone to talk to."

Ves gestured to the twins, who both scuttled up the ladder and back to the Heaven's Compromise. A few more of the Ristroan crew had gathered at the end of the gangway, watching with the others. That they were aware they were transporting a Kalis was more unnerving than Syrina being there in the first place, and Ves wondered what Mann would think, but then the thought of his first mate reminded him Syrina might still hold a grudge. "I should let you know, Mann is still with me. My first mate now."

"Oh," Syrina said as she followed Ves back up to the deck. The pirate still seemed unsteady, but he got to the top without falling on her. "I never would have bet on you two getting along so well."

"Going through enough shit together will do that."

"I guess so."

Ves hesitated on the deck of the crippled Corsair boat, and Syrina waited. "Mann... he blames himself, I think. For Pasha. You might blame him too. I don't know what happened in Eheene, but the old General didn't take it very well. Neither of us did." He gave the indistinct shadow of Syrina a meaningful look.

Syrina turned away so he couldn't see her eyes. She was quiet a long time. "Whatever happened to Pasha," she whispered. "It wasn't Mann's fault."

Ves nodded. "I guess you know more about that than we do. But you'd better tell him that." He pointed up the rope still linking the Ristroan vessel with the Compromise. "Lead on, Kalis."

Syrina followed Val and Seran up the tether. Ves, still woozy, climbed after her.

———

Syrina stared at the table a long time. She'd covered her face with some lightly scented white powder Ves had found somewhere so they could see her better, but she couldn't meet their eyes. The engines grumbled as they pushed west, after siphoning enough tarfuel from the Corsair ship to get the rest of the way to the Isle of N'narad. She'd insisted they leave the Ristroans enough to at least limp their way to a smuggling route so someone could either pick them up or fix their rudder, and Ves, unwilling to cross her, had agreed, though he complained about it plenty after they'd pulled away.

"I don't blame you," she said to Mann at last. "I did, I think, at some point, but not anymore. Asking you to keep Pasha on the boat is one of my biggest regrets. It wasn't fair to you. It wasn't fair to him. I should have known how treating him that way would make him feel. I was so scared of losing him, I was blind to everything else. But whatever was between Pasha and I, it was beyond anyone's control. Ours, and certainly yours. If I'd just..." She stopped talking, still studying the table.

"It was you," Ves said. "Whatever happened to Eheene, you did it."

She shrugged, the gesture ambiguous under the tattoos, and took a breath like she might explain, but then she sighed and all she said was, "More or less. Yeah."

Ves rubbed his face with his hands. "Whatever went down

in that city of assholes, the world is probably better off now. Hell, and not just the Merchant's Syndicate—it's better off without naphtha too."

Syrina shrugged. "Maybe. It doesn't feel that way. And anyway, someone else is making naphtha now. I don't know who. Maybe even the Syndicate, or whatever's left of it." She glanced up at them.

Mann, who'd also been staring at the table in front of him, looked up. "For what it's worth, I'm still sorry."

Syrina gave another vague shrug. "The remaining High Merchants have gathered in Tyrsh. It turns out I didn't change anything, except..." She swallowed. "Well. It's done now. That's why I need to get to Tyrsh. I have a friend, I guess you could call her. I think she's trying to do something about all this."

"What about the war?" Mann asked.

"That, too."

Nobody said anything for a minute, each lost to their thoughts.

"Another thing," Syrina added with a sigh. "Be careful who you go after, if you keep up this pirating business. I hear some of the Kalis who didn't flock back to the High Merchants really have hired themselves out as ship guards. For the N'naradin, anyway. I don't think Ristro has any Kalis on their side except me. There's one other, but she's got better things to do than guard ships, too. Turns out the Church and the Syndicate have been cozy from the start, though, until this Grace went her own way."

Ves arched an eyebrow. "Where'd you hear that?"

"About the Church and the Syndicate? Long story, but it's reliable."

Mann nodded. "Nothing surprises me anymore. Where'd

you hear about the Kalis working for the Church? Just as reliable?"

Syrina shook her head. "Just rumors. Bars in Fom. It's the type of thing people love to talk about. Who knows if it's true, but enough people are talking about it that it could be."

"Thanks for the warning," Ves said. "But we only hit Ristro these days. Not a respectful look, if the wrong people think we're taking sides in the war."

Syrina nodded. "Smart. Still, be careful."

Ves studied Syrina, then Mann, before he nodded in the way he had, like in his mind everything had been settled. "Good. Let's have a drink." He pulled a crooked bottle of rum from a cabinet behind him, along with three glasses, and poured.

He held up his glass to the others. "To Pasha and Anna," he said.

Syrina looked at the glass in front of her a moment, then wiped her eyes and held it up. "To Pasha and Anna." Her voice was soft.

Mann grunted and gave a sideways look at Syrina before picking up his own glass. "To Pasha and Anna."

They drank and fell into a comfortable, sad silence.

4

ASKING QUESTIONS

KA'ID WISHED KIRIN WAS THERE. THIRD-HAND RUMORS were all she could dig up on her own without raising suspicions, and even then, she worried someone was getting close to figuring out who she was. Or rather, who she'd been.

Third-hand rumors they might be, but they still kept her up at night. Someone had found research notes pertaining to the Eheene disaster, or at least what had come before it. No details, other than it had to do with Kalis and the manipulation of old Artifacts. Nobody knew whose research it was, but even without seeing them herself, it had Ormo's stink. Kirin might dig up more, but no telling when she'd be back from Fom.

It wasn't all bad news, though. Her Kalis had sent word a week ago. She'd contacted Ormo's rogue Kalis at last. Kirin described her as "broken," without elaborating further in the coded hawk message, but she confirmed Syrina was on her way.

In the meantime, though, Ka'id was afraid she'd stirred up the hive with her own digging. More than once she'd spotted someone linger a little too long in front of her building or idle in the hallway in front of her flat. They looked innocent, but they would, wouldn't they?

It had gotten bad enough that she'd decided to move to the Flowers Ward a few days after getting Kirin's last message, where the gardens were nicer, but the view wasn't as good. Not that that bothered her as much as the fact that Syrina would have a hard time finding her once she dragged herself to Tyrsh. Kirin could track Ka'id down. They'd come up with enough contingency plans in their years on the Island that she wasn't worried about that, but she wasn't sure Syrina had even been to Tyrsh before, and it wasn't like she could leave a note on her flat door with her new address.

Well, she was a Kalis, so she'd figure it out, as long as she wasn't too "broken." Whatever that meant. And if she was that bad off, she wouldn't be much use to Ka'id anyway.

Ka'id chewed on her lower lip while she lit a naphtha lantern to push back the oncoming night. It was only a quarter full. There'd be no naphtha deliveries for at least a week with the new restrictions, and she wondered how much longer the people of Tyrsh would support the war effort now that it affected them. she went to the cupboard and took out a bottle of wine, then struggled with the cork. She didn't really miss being in the High Merchant's Syndicate, but she missed having infinite resources and more than one person she could trust. Then again, she reflected, beyond their own Kalis, the High Merchants couldn't trust anyone, least of all each other. Even their own Kalis were a stretch. Take Syrina for example. Whatever had happened between her and her Ma'is, it hadn't worked out for Ormo.

A knock at the door made her heart skip. Kirin wasn't due back, and Syrina was still on her way. Supposedly, no one else knew she was here. None of her clients had known where she lived even before she moved. She took a deep breath, filled her glass, and forced herself to saunter to the door, unhurried, wineglass in hand.

A man she'd never seen before, wearing plain brass armor, lacquered in gleaming black, stood on her stoop. Three other men stood behind him, likewise dressed, though they had the N'naradin sun and eye emblem set on their breasts in tin.

"Ehrina Ka'id, I presume."

Ka'id nodded and took a sip of wine to hide her shaking hand. "Yes? How may I help you?"

"I am Inquirist N'thoon, here on behalf of Cardinal N'nafal, to ask you a few questions about your previous business. In Eheene, if I am not mistaken."

"Yes, that's right. I reported everything when I—"

"Please, Miss Ka'id, may we come in?"

Ka'id nodded again, not trusting herself to speak. Her years away from her seat on the High Merchant's Syndicate had, she decided, softened her mental fortitude against unwelcome surprises. The wheels of her mind churned. She hadn't even registered her move from the flat on the square yet, which meant they'd been watching her this whole time. They hadn't even waited until she'd finished the paperwork, so they didn't care if she knew they'd been watching, either. That didn't bode well, but it begged the question, *why?*

She led them into her dining room and took four more glasses out to set around the table. "Wine?"

"No, thank you," N'thoon said, taking the seat at the head of the table. The other three men only responded with curt shakes of their heads.

Not a good sign, Ka'id thought, but she sat down to the left of the inquirist and refilled her own glass. "Now then. Could you be more specific as to what you want from me? As you no doubt know, I recently moved, and am not taking any new clients until I get settled. However, you lead me to think you're not here to hire me for my talents as an accountant."

"That is correct. You worked closely with some merchants in Fom during your time in Eheene. Is that correct?"

"Well, yes, but almost anyone who had any international business interests in Eheene could say the same. As I'm sure you are also aware, I was born in Pom, not Fom, and my loyalty to the Church—the Arch Bishop's Church—has never come into question."

"Nor does it now, Miss Ka'id. You misunderstand why I am here."

"Please enlighten me, then." She took another sip.

"One of your clients was a Mr. Xereks Lees. Is that correct?"

Ka'id's heart skipped another beat, but she didn't let it show. "There's a name I haven't heard in years. Yes, that's correct. He ended up involved in some kind of unsavory business, then disappeared, or so the rumors went. That was long after I terminated my dealings with him, as I'm sure you also know as long as your records are accurate."

"He died. A suspicious accident in Maresg. *Highly* suspicious. And yes, I assume our records are correct in that regard. We are not, however, interested in what happened to Lees after you ended your relationship with him. Rather, Cardinal N'nafal would like more information about what Lees was doing while he employed you as his accountant. He worked for a client in Fom, making various machine parts and the like, yes?"

Ka'id shifted and took another drink. "Among quite a lot of other things, yes."

"Yes, of course. That is precisely the answer we were looking for. If you'll please come with us, the Cardinal would very much like to discuss with you details about what sort of things Lees produced for this particular client."

"You realize I was just—"

"Yes, yes." N'thoon's tone was too smooth, too apologetic. "I realize you were just his accountant, but I believe you also acted as something as a go-between for your clients in Eheene and their importers in Fom. That is correct, yes? The Cardinal believes you might have some inside knowledge, as it were, of the items he shipped to the Crescent City. With the destruction of Eheene and the unfortunate...falling out between the Arch Bishop and the Grace, I'm afraid you are the True Church's best hope in shedding light on this, shall we say, gap of information. Information the Cardinal himself is desperate to acquire. I'm sure if you have no knowledge of such details, he will be understanding."

Ka'id drained her glass and took a deep breath. "Yes," she said, standing. "Yes, of course. Please lead the way."

"Thank you, Miss Ka'id. It shouldn't take long."

She followed N'thoon out her door, the silent guards flanking her.

5

ABSENT FRIENDS

THE FIVE-DAY JOURNEY TO POM WITH VES AND MANN wasn't as awkward as Syrina imagined it might be. The three of them fell into their old camaraderie, such that it was, but there was an empty space where Pasha should have been. They all felt it, and they avoided talking about it. Twice they saw Tyrsh ships on the horizon, heading east, but they ignored the Heaven's Compromise. Mann said he didn't know if he should be glad about that, and Ves told him to count his blessings without looking too closely at the details. Syrina said nothing, though she thought of what Kalis Kirin had told her.

Docking at Pom was out of the question. The Heaven's Compromise had been raiding Ristro ships for almost a year, and there was no telling how many of those had been bound for the Isle of N'narad with supplies. Instead, they dropped Syrina off along the coast about seventy spans to the south. Ves offered her a lifeboat, but Syrina declined. The weather was pleasant, the water warm, the waves calm. It was only two spans to the beach, and the tide was going in so it would carry her most of the way. Syrina advised Ves and his crew lay low in Maresg for a while and said she'd come and find them.

Ves was noncommittal, but their time of easy loot at sea was coming to an end. They had quite a bit of tin saved, and Maresg was where they'd end up whatever else they did, and they all knew it.

The rolling, wildflower-covered hills of the N'naradin coast stretched away to the south and north until it disappeared in a bright haze, while to the west they marched onward until they climbed into the granite cliffs of the Central Range. Syrina struck out north, and by dusk, the wildflowers had become rolling pastures for goats and berry orchards with a few scattered wheat fields between. She pilfered food and rum from cottages when she was hungry, but avoided contact with anyone.

On the fourth day, she skirted around the northern, grey edge of the mountains, mounted a grassy rise covered in scattered groves of pine, and saw Tyrsh spread out below her.

The city swept away to the east and west, the fields beyond almost lost in the warm, summer mist. Due north, it reached almost to the horizon. Tyrsh was second only to Fom in size, in every other way its opposite. Gleaming white domes, minarets, and church spires poked up here and there from the sweep of townhouses, shops, and squares. Straight lanes spoked out from the Plaza of Heaven, which long ago lay in the center of the city, but it now sat well to the southwest. Steam cars, camel wagons, and pedestrians flowed to and from the surrounding farms, and the wide, paved road leading to the Pom port stretched out of sight to the northeast.

Nice place to settle down, the voice said.

Syrina almost jumped. Even after she'd cut down on the rum, it had hardly spoken since she'd found Ves and Mann.

She'd wondered if it was angry at her, blamed her for Eheene and what happened to Pasha. Not that she could hold that against it. Eheene had been her fault.

"Well, no use just standing here," she said. "Let's go see if Ka'id's home."

———

Syrina took a week to find what she needed to make herself a proper face before getting settled in to a hotel named the Hierophant's Stand. She'd planned on showing up at Ka'id's as herself, but found the flat at the address Kirin had given her vacant and up for sale. A shame too, she thought. It looked like it had a pleasant view.

She decided on a whim to go with her old persona, Rina Saalesh. It had been years since she'd worn the eccentric low merchant's skin, so she reasoned that on the off chance anyone recognized the woman, they wouldn't be surprised by any subtle changes in her appearance. It also might be useful to be someone Ka'id had met before, even if the former High Merchant didn't know that Rina had been her. Anyway, old habits die hard, and it felt good to go back to some semblance of her former life. She added a few more wrinkles to Rina's face and a few streaks of grey to her black hair and tried not to think about Triglav.

I could have been talking to you, you know, the voice said without preamble as Syrina was putting the finishing touches on Rina's elaborate outfit.

She paused. "When? You mean this whole time? These years of silence after Eheene?"

When you were drunk out of your mind pretty much the entire time, yeah. I just wanted to clear that up. You think the copious amounts of rum kept me away, but that's not what happened. I'm telling you in case you decide to go back to the bottle. That's how it works, right? You start thinking about Triglav, then you think about—

Syrina's stomach churned, and she talked over the voice before it could say his name. "Why didn't you say anything sooner? You could have..." She trailed off, not sure what the voice could have done.

What? Kept you company? You didn't want my company. Force you into sobriety? You didn't want that either. Hell, I didn't want that. I knew—know—I remind you of him. Of both of them. You needed to get over it in your own time. I did too. You know what happened in Eheene happened to me too, right?

Syrina toyed with the lavender dress she'd been fitting for Rina, not really doing anything with it. Somehow, she'd never thought about how the voice in her head might have felt, or even that it felt anything, and she felt suddenly guilty for it.

But all she asked was, "What if I never got over it?" Her voice was soft and sad.

You did.

"Did I? I quit drinking all the time because Kirin found me. If it wasn't for her, I'd still be in Fom, drinking and picking fights, waiting to be drunk enough to let someone kill me. I don't know if that means I'm over anything. It doesn't feel like it."

The voice was quiet for a time. *That might have taken quite a while. You getting killed in a bar fight, I mean. Or maybe you'd be dead by now. We'll never know because that's not what happened.*

Syrina didn't answer, and she heard it sigh in the back of her mind. *I just wanted you to know. It's time I came back. I don't know what's going on, but you'll need my help.*

"You're right." She paused and began working again on the final seams of the dress. "I can't believe I'm about say this, but I'm glad you're back."

I know. Now let's go find Ka'id.

———

"I'm sorry. You said you were who?"

"Rina. Rina Saalesh. An old friend of Miss Ka'id's from Eheene. I'm sure she thinks I died with the rest of the city. She had no idea I'd moved my business to Valez'Mui months before all the unpleasantness. We'd fallen out of touch before then, but I've come up to Tyrsh on business, and I'd like to correct that while I'm here. This is her office, is it not? Her name is written above the door, anyway, unless there's more than one Ka'id in Tyrsh, and they both happen to be accountants."

The gaunt, callow man with thinning hair who sat at reception thumbed through a stack of papers before looking up at Rina again. "Yes, you have the right place. But Miss Ka'id hasn't been in for the past, well, it's been almost two weeks, and nobody here knows where she is."

Rina's brow furrowed. "Oh, that's distressing. She moved not long ago, did she not? I ran into an old mutual acquaintance who gave me her address, but I was quite dismayed to find the place vacant and up for sale when I popped by."

"That's right. She moved to the Ward of Flowers shortly before she stopped coming in."

"I see. I wonder if her absence relates to her move. Have any of you been by her new place to see her? A simple visit might clear this whole mystery up."

The man sighed. "Yes, I myself went by last week, but nobody answered the door. Not even her maid."

"But you haven't been back since?"

"No. Miss Ka'id is a private person, as I'm sure you are aware, being her dear, close friend." His tone was dry. "She is the sole shareholder of this firm, and it is well within her right to not come in. Without knowing something is wrong—terribly wrong—I am disinclined to repeatedly show up at her house and bother her."

"How could you be bothering her if she's not there?"

The receptionist sighed and rolled his eyes, as if answering that question was beneath him.

Rina let the matter drop. "I see. She's not come in for extended periods before?"

The man hesitated. "Yes. Well, yes, but not for such a long time. A few days here and there, perhaps. Maybe a week."

"I see. Well...since I have come all the way from Valez'Mui, and I am desperate to find my old friend now that she seems to be missing, I don't suppose you could give me her current address so I could have a look for myself? After talking to you, I've become overwhelmed with concern."

The man studied the woman in front of him. She wore a finely cut lavender dress, patterned in little green leaves and white flowers. Grey streaked her black hair, which was piled in loose curls on top of her head. Her green eyes were earnest. She wore fine leather black gloves that reached to her elbows, the small and ring fingers on the left tied in a neat bow. He wondered how a woman of such obvious stature could have lost part of her hand, but he was in no position to ask, so he kept his face locked on hers, with a few brief glances at her ample bosom pressed into her high-necked dress. Her clothes and demeanor declared her a woman of stature, wherever she was from.

"I suppose I could make an exception," he sighed at last,

and began shifting through the top drawer of his desk. "Just a moment, please."

He pulled out a small, leather-bound journal and flipped through the pages before copying down Ka'id's address onto a slip of paper and handing it to Rina. "Here you are. If you find her, tell her she's missed at the office and we hope she's well."

"Of course." Rina smiled down at him. "I hope we will all see her soon."

———

Syrina crept around the abandoned townhouse. She wasn't concerned about getting caught, even if she was still wearing Rina, now dressed in brown leather leggings tucked into high black boots and a white linen blouse. Ka'id's house stood back from the tree-lined street, connected to the houses on either side but blocked from their view by trees and a high stone wall encircling the garden. Through the window in the locked kitchen door, she could see five glasses set out on the broad dining table—four clean and untouched, the fifth stained, with a trickle of red still in the bottom. Between the stones on the path to the gate, which she'd found unlocked, were the boot prints of four men, faded but still intact, thanks to the clear summer weather. A few traces of a fifth, smaller set of shoes led back out, too jumbled with the others to tell whether their owner had left with the men or sometime before or after.

Someone got to her.

"You'd think after three years of not talking to me you could come up with something useful to say," Syrina whispered, still peering into the window.

Kirin said the surviving High Merchants came to Tyrsh. Do you think they found out who Ka'id was?

Syrina thought about it and gave her head a little shake. "I don't think it was them. Or, if it was the Syndicate, they didn't know who she was. They wouldn't take her if they'd known she'd been the old Kavik—that sort of thing leads to people poking around, and the High Merchants have never been fans of that. They would have just killed her and made it look like a mugging or an accident or whatever."

The Church, then.

"It must be. I don't know what the Syndicate would want with Ka'id if they didn't know who she used to be. There aren't any organized crime families in Tyrsh or anywhere else on the Island that I know of, and I can't think of any reason any independent operators would risk something like this."

We should check out her house.

Syrina hesitated, looking around the garden. A steamcar rumbled by on the street. They were a rare sight with the naphtha shortage, and it seemed the people of Tyrsh weren't fans of tarfuel engines stinking up the city. "It might come to that, but not yet. I don't want to risk incriminating Rina. If we need to, we can come back."

She worked with Fom for years. Maybe they think she knows something that can help them with their war.

Syrina considered what Kirin had told her. "Maybe. Or they think she's a spy. Whatever the reason, we have to get her out. If she's even still alive."

Fine, I'm with you. But how do we find her?

"I'm working on it," Syrina whispered, leaving the garden and easing the gate closed behind her.

The voice was silent as Syrina sauntered back onto the main boulevard and began a causal stroll towards her hotel, but as they climbed the steps to her room sometime later, it asked, *Can we trust her?*

Syrina had been thinking about that. She'd saved the woman's life years ago, true, but Ka'id had been High Merchant Kavik once, and in Syrina's mind, she always would be.

"No," Syrina answered as she sat down on the end of her bed to pull off Rina's shoes. "But I need to talk to her anyway."

6

THE AMBUSH

"The Stone's Fall is Fom's. Don't know what it would want with us." Ves handed the lens back to Mann and shrugged. "Unless Syrina was right. Loot enough Corsair ships bound for either side of this idiot war long enough, and it'll piss someone off." He paused. "What does Ristro have that Fom wants anyway? Tyrsh, sure. Most of their navy was naphtha. A lot of work to convert everything to fuel they can actually get. But Fom?"

Mann looked at the approaching ship through the lens and grunted. "Tarfuel, with the naphtha shortage, though as you say, that hit Tyrsh a lot harder than Fom. Food, maybe. The Grace's hold on the Great Road is precarious. Who knows how many grain barges the Arch Bishop's navy scuttled between Great Spring and Valez'Mui? You were right about that captain's message you found, though. It seems like all the ships we've hit going north have been headed to Fom since then. Not sure why the Astrologers would start taking sides."

"We should've asked Syrina."

Mann coughed a laugh. "It wouldn't have done any good. If

she knows anything, she'd have told us if she felt like it, but she didn't say shit, so she either didn't know or she didn't think it was any of our business." He looked through the lens again. "Well, we've got this to deal with now, anyway. Run?"

Ves shook his head. "They're between us and Maresg. They'll chase us and even if we get away, we'll run out of tarfuel. We barely have enough to get there as it is. No, we can take them. They're about the same size as us. Their crew might be a little bigger, but if we stand our ground on the Compromise, we'll have the advantage."

Mann sighed, nodded with a last glance at the oncoming ship, and climbed below. "Stall the engine!" He shouted down to Saphi. "We're baiting one more time."

Ves stood alone, watching the encroaching vessel through the lens as he listened to the engines on his ship fall silent. He could make out a few figures on the deck. One—the captain, he presumed, wearing the red and white of his station—peered into his own brass lens, though Ves didn't think the man could make him out through the glare of the sun on the window of the wheelhouse. Soldiers milled along the rail, six or seven that Ves could see, wearing strange, black-plated armor. Something was off, something familiar, but he couldn't put his finger on it. *Too many years and too much rum, he thought.* Things were never as clear as they used to be. He wished Ash was there to sort him out. He'd always known how to keep Ves in line.

But the thought of his old first mate and lover made Ves' throat catch, and he forced it from his mind.

He stuck his head into the hatch, but didn't climb down the ladder. "New plan," he called.

Mann appeared below. Ves could hear Saphi mucking about with the stalled engine, getting it ready to jump back to life again in a hurry. That was good. His nasty feeling kept growing. "Edge? Chank? You down there?"

"Yeah, boss, we're here," Edge's whiny voice called from somewhere out of sight.

"Get over here you two. They'll come through the main hold when they board. I locked the bridge up, and they won't take time to dawdle with it as long as the engines are cut and there's people still on board who don't want them here. Everyone else, do what you always do. Fight door to door, and for fuck's sake, keep Saphi safe. She's our ticket out of here. Us three will pop out of the wheelhouse as soon as they're down, lock the hold behind them, and pay the Stone's Fall a visit of our own. Won't be more than a few people left on their ship."

Chank's curly mass of grey and blond hair appeared next to Mann's. "Why not just do what we always do and scare the shit out of them with the firepacks?"

"First, because we don't have enough naphtha left for a demonstration, and I don't trust anymore they'd fall for it without one. Only ones who's got naphtha these days are a few of the Arch Bishop's stoolies, along with whoever is giving it to them. The Grace knows it, and you can bet her people know it. And second, there's something off. I don't know what it is yet, and I don't trust it. So, like I said, change of plans."

At that moment, there was a twin *thunk* of the boarding lines hitting their deck.

"Right then," Ves growled. "Everyone knows what to do. Mann's in charge until I get back. Nobody give the old man a heart attack but me, yeah?"

Footfalls pounded across the deck and the hold doors banged open. Ves counted to ten while he listened to the hatches close below as his people got into position.

At ten, he burst up and out of the wheelhouse, the steps of Edge and Chank behind him. He heard Edge slam and lock the door to the bridge. Good. The N'naradin were with his people, and his people knew his ship better than the intruders.

And now he would to get to know the N'naradin's.

———

Mann made it as far as the mid-deck passage hatch when the first N'naradin dropped from the open cargo door. Clad in black wood, he clutched a curved black cutlass in one hand, with another hilted at his belt. He saw Mann and started toward him. More N'naradin climbed down behind the first.

He recognized that black wood. They were in trouble. He made it to the door, slammed it closed, and jammed the crossbar into place. His hip complained and popped as he hurried back to the aft and Saphi, wondering if the barred hatches plated in brass would be enough.

"Change of plans!" he shouted as he limped to the engine room. "Lock the cabins! Fight in the doorways, one at a time, and only if you have to." Then he added under his breath as he yanked open the engine room door, "And pray we can come up with a better plan."

He heard the locks bolt behind him, where the rest of the crew had been waiting to ambush the invaders. He stumbled into the engine room and slammed the hatch closed. The metallic clang of the N'naradin as they hacked at the mid-door faded.

"Something wrong?" Saphi's tone was light, but when she saw Mann's expression her face fell. "What is it?"

There was a loud *clank* from beyond the hatch, and Mann winced. "Blackvine," he said. "The Grace has blackvine. I'd heard rumors, but..." He trailed off when he saw Saphi's blank look.

"Am I supposed to know what you're talking about?"

"There's not a lot of time to explain. It's a plant from the

Black Wall. You can make it harder than bronze or even steel. And these fuckers are clad in it from head to toe."

"Oh. What do we do?"

Mann thought. "They'll be coming to us. Still no use in them trying for the wheelhouse unless they can start the engine. They'll search all the cabins first, though, to make sure nobody sneaks up on them from behind once they get here. That means we have until then to come up with something. Not long."

"What do they want with us?" Saphi's voice was frightened now, and Mann regretted scaring her but only for a moment. She was in it with them, and it was better to be scared than stupid.

"I don't know. Maybe Ves can get something from their ship that will tell us what's going on. They might think we're working for the Arch Bishop or something, in which case they'll want to know what we know."

"But we don't know anything."

"Nope. But it will be too late for us by the time they figure that out."

Saphi looked thoughtful and turned to the stalled engine. "I could rig something. Vent the tarfuel exhaust into the hallway if we can trap them in there. Nobody could live through that." She paused again. "Don't know how we'd live through it, either."

Mann's voice softened. "If you can do it fast, we won't have to. But won't you need to keep the engine room door open for the smoke to get out?"

She nodded. "Yeah, but I can lock the engine. They won't be able to turn it off before the fumes get them. I think. What about everyone else?"

Mann swallowed. "They should be alright, as long as they can keep their doors closed. Once they figure out what's happening, they can break out the portals to get some fresh air. We don't have time to come up with anything better. You do what you have to, then come up topside. Lock the hatch behind you." He started up the ladder. "I'll go lock the mid-deck hatch. That will keep them stuck down here long enough. I hope."

"Okay." She looked up at Mann as he climbed. "I'm scared."

"Me too. You're young. You'll get used to it," he lied, and clambered into the bridge.

Mann ran at a limping jog out of the wheelhouse and down the short ladder to the deck. He thought he could hear fighting coming through the thin bronze plates beneath his feet, but he couldn't be sure it wasn't his imagination.

No, as he reached the opened hatch to the hold, he was sure he could hear sounds of battle. Damn. That meant they'd already gotten through to at least one of the crew compartments, but a second later the engine roared to life, drowning everything else. Black smoke began billowing from the wheelhouse as he slammed the central hatch closed and dropped the crossbar across it. A moment later, Saphi emerged coughing from the bridge. The smoke cleared, save a few tendrils reaching out from the closed hatch behind the navigation table.

"I disconnected the propeller mechanism so they can't make us move before we pick up Ves and the others." Her face was black with soot and streaked with tears.

"Good thinking." Mann didn't know what else to say.

"Edge," she whispered, almost inaudible over the rhythmic banging of the engine. "I heard him shout. They were fighting in the gangway. I saw them when I opened the door. They saw me, tried to get around, but Edge wouldn't let them. He...I just left. I left him down there and ran away."

Mann put his arms around her. "You did what you were supposed to. You did what Edge wanted you to do."

She didn't answer. A couple feeble clanks against the cargo hatch made them both jump, but after that no more sounds came from below, save the banging of the engine.

———

Ves returned not long after, alone, his face grim, bleeding from a gash on his forearm. He climbed down the boarding line to stand with Mann and Saphi on the deck of the Heaven's Compromise.

"They ambushed us," he spat. "Our own goddamn tactics. Hit us from in front and behind, cut us off. Only three of them, but in that fucking armor it was enough. They could move easy as us, almost, but nothing we swung at them got through. Needed to get close, and close was messy. What's worse, I found a message on the captain's desk when it was over. They were heading to Maresg. They know Tyrsh is getting naphtha from someone in Skalkaad, and the Grace wants the canal. I think that's why they attacked us—they thought we were going there to warn them. Ironic, since now that's what we'll do."

He glanced between Mann and Saphi. "Things went about as good over here, didn't they?"

"Worse," Mann said and told him. Ves nodded when he finished, and returned to the Stone's Fall without a word. He came back a few minutes later, clutching a mask with a long, filtered tube from its mouth. "Guess they've been up the Great Road, or at least through the wastes."

Saphi reached for the mask, but Ves pulled it away and put it on. "My ship. My problem."

He disappeared through the wheelhouse. Black smoke billowed, and a moment later the engines cut. Mann stepped over to the hold door and flung it open. More smoke rolled out.

When enough of the fumes had cleared, they went below

together. Edge, Blotter, Gesh, and Farrid were dead—Edge killed in his fight with the N'naradin, the others from the tarfuel smoke. Mal, Bini, Jag, and Flitter were alive, but pale and hacking, so weak none of them could speak more than a word or two at a time. The whole ship stank.

They worked in silence, and by the time the sun set, they were again plugging towards Maresg. The Eye glared in the east.

———

A week later, they arrived in a tense city. News that one of the Grace's fleets was on the way around the Upper Peninsula to lay siege from the north had arrived a day before, and rumors were that a second fleet was preparing to leave Fom to strike from the south at the same time.

Ves and his crew weren't the only ones who'd seen see the strange, black armor the Grace's soldiers wore. Some said it was some new material developed by the Artisans of Valez'Mui in secret for the Grace. Others, that they were tearing up the vineyards to the south of Fom to plant the gnarled, thorny black brambles that produced the stuff, so she wouldn't need to transport it up the Great Road anymore.

"Will the tribes help?" Ves asked Mann as he pulled the Compromise into her berth under the broad, overhanging branches of the looming mangroves. The city of Maresg wound its way through the trees above them. Every house, bridge, and rail were painted in a riot of clashing colors like some permanent, mad carnival tangled though the giant trees, but they could feel the tension in the air around the city, and nobody was laughing.

"The karakh tribes?" Mann thought about it as they swaggered together onto the dock and began tying the ropes. The engine burbled beneath their feet, then fell silent. "I don't know. They've never had a great relationship with Maresg. It's a foreign city in the middle of their territories. Still, I can't imagine they'd be happier if the Grace took over. They won their independence from N'narad a long time ago. They won't give it up again without a fight, and they know that's what would come next if either side of the Church took Maresg."

Ves helped Mann tie the last of the ropes, and they both turned and waited in silence for the rest of the crew to join them. Saphi came first, then the others, still coughing and pale from the poison of the tarfuel. None of them blamed Mann or Saphi for their decision to gas the N'naradin. Ves knew even the dead wouldn't have blamed them. If they hadn't done what needed to be done, they'd all be dead. The survivors lived, and had eight sets of blackvine armor and twice as many cutlasses thanks to them. Ves was too big for the armor, and Saphi too small, but still, it was something. Both Mann and Saphi blamed themselves though, despite his crew's unspoken forgiveness, and he knew nothing anyone could say would change that.

As they trudged together up the plank to the awaiting lift, Ves spoke. "You should talk to them."

Mann blinked. "To who? The tribes? Me? Why do you think that would do any good?"

"You stopped a rebellion. Peacefully, and in their favor. They're not the sort to forget about that."

"That was thirty years ago."

"They're not the sort to forget about that," Ves said again.

Mann still looked doubtful. "I'm responsible for the deaths of almost twenty karakh and shepherds too—chieftains' husbands, every one. And that was more recent. A lot more recent. That's what they will remember. More than some negotiations I did on their behalf a generation ago, before most of them were even born."

Ves shrugged. "I doubt many of them blame you for what happened in the desert. They're not stupid. They know you had no choice when you took their people to the Black Wall. No more choice than they had. Anyway," he sighed. "This city is fucked without someone's help and you know it. There's no one else we've got time to ask, and no one better. Worst that will happen is some karakh chieftain will kill you for the death of her husband, rather than some fucking N'naradin fop killing you for betraying the Grace a week later." He paused. "Or worse, nab you and throw you back in the Pit. I don't think I could get you out a second time, and hell if I'd go back to Fom to try."

Mann didn't respond, but when they reached the top of the lift and shuffled into the nervous throngs teeming on the docks, he nodded. "Alright," he said. "I don't know how a pirate who's drunk half the time can be right so often, but I'll go. And no sense in waiting, I guess, so I'll go now."

Ves clasped his hand. "I'm right because I *am* drunk. Clears the head of all the bullshit. If you don't make it back, die knowing you probably went out better than we will."

Mann frowned, but he nodded his goodbyes to the others, gave Saphi a hug, and disappeared into the crowds.

"What do we do now?" asked Saphi. Her girlish face was tired, her eyes lost.

Ves forced a laugh and nodded to the other crew. "We find a place to rest up, then do what we always end up doing in Maresg. Drink blovey wine and wait."

7

SUSPICIONS

"Yes. Yes, fine." A few wisps of hair the color of steel had drifted loose from the Grace's severe bun and wafted in the air currents swirling through Wise Hall.

General Rohm frowned, but he knew better than to say anything. The Grace had changed the past few weeks. That much was obvious even to the casual parishioners that came to her nightly lectures. He knew some of her other advisers whispered to each other about how the war had gone on too long; that it was fraying her nerves. That weasel Heine had started half of them. Rohm had wondered at first if he'd been the one somehow responsible for the Grace's current state, but Heine was an idiot, too stupid by far to come up with a scheme so subtle; barely smart enough to take advantage of it, though he appeared to be trying. The Grace elevating him to Hierophant didn't suddenly fill the void between Hein's ears. No, this was something else. Something or someone. Since long before Mann's mission to the Black Wall, the Grace of Fom had been solid as the steel doors of Wise Hall. She was the foundation on which they could build the new Church. More stalwart even than her predecessor who'd taken in Albertus Mann all those years ago, and that Grace had had a will of stone. This Grace, like him, had the hawk's eyes to see the corruption in Tyrsh, but she also had the steel spine to do something about it.

As Rohm's mind drifted to Mann, once his friend, now his predecessor, the Grace's voice pierced through his reverie. "Will that be all?"

He bowed. "Your Grace. As I said, the blackvine we retrieved from the Wall is flourishing in the soil of the old vineyards, as are the more recent cuttings from the first local batch. Our problem now is security there, outside the city. While I thank you for releasing funds for more guards, my concern now is with the *quality* of the guards who are available—"

The Grace blinked at him, as if trying to remember what he was talking about. Or maybe trying to remember who he was. "I'm sure there are thousands of mercenaries within the city willing to take the Church's tin and the promise of a Higher Heaven in exchange for their services."

Rohm stifled a sigh. "As am I, Your Grace. Like I said, my concern is with their quality, not quantity. I would be much more comfortable with a few faithful—perhaps even as high as those in the Book of Feasts—to at least oversee the project, which will no doubt be the most important of the war effort."

"And I would be more comfortable lying in a bed of rose petals, sponged by pubescent virgins, General. If our world was comfortable, we'd be in Heaven already." She made an uncharacteristic rub at her eyes and blinked at him, face rigid and angry.

"Yes, Your Grace." Rohm gave up, spun on his heel, and strode from the Hall. A susurration of voices filled the air—hangers-on and sycophants, waiting for their turn to take advantage of whatever demon had possessed the iron soul of their leader.

He thought about Mann again as he stepped into the twilight drizzle of Fom. The city buzzed, but he drifted through it, oblivious, on the way to the Grace's Walk and his waiting steam car. Mann had been a good general. Right up until he wasn't. He'd loved both his men and the Grace—the former to the fault that became his undoing. Rohm hadn't grieved over Vimr's death. That wretched little Cardinal had been responsible for the deaths of hundreds aboard the ill-fated Salamander. Rohm wished—still wished—that Vimr had met his end any other way than with a dagger in the back by the hand of General Mann. Rohm had never been ambitious enough to want to be General to the Grace, but he was loyal enough to fulfill his duties now that he was.

What would Mann do if he were still here now, in Rohm's stead? He wouldn't believe something as ephemeral as stress would reduce the Grace to her current state. She'd showed the first cracks after they'd returned from the Wall with the black-vine. It didn't make sense. Already the coils they'd brought back had turned the war in Fom's favor. With the Arch Bishop's not-so-secret allies in Skalkaad reduced to vapor in whatever disaster had befallen Eheene, the end might at long last be in sight. If she hadn't cracked during the siege of Fom or any time in the stalemate after Eheene, why would she crumble now?

However fatal Mann's flaws turned out to be, the old man wouldn't have just given up.

Rohm wheeled and marched back up the hill.

He passed the immense steel doors engraved with the Sun and Eye and circled around the narrow, tree-lined flagstone path leading behind the Cathedral and the quarters of the Grace's personal servants. A few soldiers stood chatting by the plain, polished wooden door, but they stood straight and saluted him as he approached. "Korbat, isn't it? And you're Torala N'gal."

The pair nodded. "That's right, sir," Korbat, a middle-aged, stout, balding man said, looking pleased.

Torala N'gal was young and pretty, if a bit skinny, Rohm thought.

"What brings us this honor, General?" she asked.

Rohm returned their salute. "Any new staff around, lately?"

Korbat thought about it. "You mean servants to the Grace? None come to mind, sir, though to be honest I pay little attention to them. They're all screened before they get here, if I'm not mistaken."

"No, you're not mistaken."

Torala N'gal pressed her lips together. "How long ago is lately, sir?"

Rohm frowned. "Good question. I'm not sure. Six months?"

She nodded. "I've only been stationed here three, Korbat two. But I bet that's something we could find out, General."

Korbat nodded.

"Alright. But keep it low key. If I check the employment records, someone will notice. If you look into it, it's just some guards doing their due diligence during a time of strife. Do you understand what I'm saying?"

"We understand. Something up we should know about, General?" Torala N'gal's concern looked genuine.

Rohm gave her a little shrug. "I doubt it. Call it a personal project to put my mind at ease."

"How should we let you know what we find, sir?" Korbat asked.

"Don't worry about tracking me down. The fewer ears, the better. I'll pop by every few weeks. Something I've been meaning to do anyway. Whatever you think of my predecessor

—no, don't tell me, I don't need to know—he taught me the value in getting to know the soldiers."

"Thank you, General. We're just House Guards. Means a lot to us." Rohm thought Korbat might blush if he stuck around any longer.

"You're not 'just' anything, soldier. We're all bound for Heaven. It doesn't matter what level you're headed to—we're down here together, now. We'll be in the Books together too. See you in a few weeks."

8

KA'ID'S PREDICAMENT

"Miss Ka'id, you have a visitor."

Ehrina Ka'id turned her gaze from the window overlooking the flowery courtyard of the Bower House—a prison in everything but name. Even if the beds were more comfortable.

"They didn't bring any wine, did they?" She asked the custodian, a stocky, bald, aging fellow with piercing blue eyes. A prison guard in all but name.

"I don't think so."

No humor this lot, she thought. "Fine. Send them in anyway. Thank you."

It took a moment to place the short, voluptuous woman with large, slightly slanted green eyes and black hair, now streaked with grey. "Rina?" She guessed as the other woman crossed the room and sat down across from her at the small, round table next to the window. "Rina Saalesh. Am I right?"

The other woman smiled. "You are, old friend." Rina gave a meaningful glance at the door. "How are you? It's been a long time."

Ka'id blinked. "Yes. I...well, yes. Forgive me. I never

expected to see you here. Or anywhere, for that matter. I assumed you'd perished in Eheene."

"I was fortunate that I was away on business in Valez'-Mui." Rina looked around the sparse, comfortable little room before turning her own gaze out the window to the walled courtyard. "Whatever are you doing here? It was hell finding you."

Ka'id sighed. "Not by choice, I'm afraid. Someone seems to think I know something about the Tidal Works, and I cannot seem to convince them otherwise, no matter how many times I tell them."

"Oh dear. You're a prisoner? I suppose it's pleasant enough, as far as that goes."

Ka'id turned to look around her room, eyes lingering on the heavy door. "In so many words, yes, I'm a prisoner, though the Church doesn't like to call it that. Since I've done nothing wrong and I am, fortunately, a citizen of status, bound to the Heaven of Plains, I am 'a guest of the Bower House.' But that is something of a misnomer. They allow guests to leave, don't they?"

"Usually." Rina studied Ka'id through her black lashes. "Do you remember the last time we spoke?"

Ka'id pursed her lips. "Yes. Vaguely. You were looking to go to Fom, were you not? To sell some salvaged items away from the eyes of the Merchant's Syndicate, if I recall. You insisted on meeting my contact there in person. Of course, I suppose my association with Miss N'nareth is now the reason I find myself confined to the grounds of the Bower House. Though that's not your fault, of course," she added. "Or anyone else's, as far as that goes."

Rina continued to study Ka'id, eyes intense. "No. There was one last time we met after that, remember? In your office. Just after poor Storik met his end on the claws of the karakh that was supposed to be protecting him. That's what we discussed, in fact. I was only there for a few minutes."

"Hmm. Oh. Oh, yes." Ka'id nodded slowly, understanding blooming in her bright eyes. "Yes, how could I have forgotten? Just before I left Eheene, as it turns out."

Rina smiled. "That's right. You do remember. I was just thinking it would have been nice to have been able to talk longer that last time, all those years ago. Tell me, are you allowed out of your room?"

Ka'id's smile was sincere. "Anywhere on the grounds, pretty much, though there are some restrictions, obviously. I often enjoy walking through the garden."

"Excellent. Because I was thinking—I need to go now, some business in the city, you understand—but I'd like to return soon, if it's alright. For a longer chat. Maybe a walk around the wall or something?" Rina gave the briefest of winks.

Ka'id stood to shake the other woman's hand. "Yes, I think I would like that very much."

"Excellent," Rina said again as she crossed to the door. "I'm so glad you're not in a real prison. So much more difficult to chat. See you soon."

"Thank you for coming by." Ka'id, still smiling, gave a brief wave as Rina bowed and made her leave. "I am quite looking forward to seeing you again."

9

THE RESCUE

Syrina spent four days looking for a loophole in N'naradin law that would allow her to get Ka'id out of the Bower House without making a scene. It was no use. Nobody below the Hierophants could get someone released from the fortified mansion on the edge of Tyrsh, besides whoever put them there. Since there were only five Hierophants and Syrina had never met any of them, that idea was out. One person knowing she was an impostor was all it would take for them to up security to an untenable level, or worse, move Ka'id somewhere more secure.

As was so often the case, just when she was reaching the end of her wits, it was the voice that came up with the most practical solution.

Why not just break her out?

"You mean as myself? As a Kalis?"

Why not?

"Yeah, right." Syrina scoffed in a whisper and went back to paging through the ancient law tome she'd found in the basement of the Archibald Library, looking for some clue she'd missed the last three times.

I'm serious. Think about it. You've been drinking your guilt away for over three years. Meanwhile, everything's changed. There are Kalis' everywhere, and everyone knows it now. You were picking fights with anyone who didn't believe in Kalis, for fuck's sake. Who's going to know why one of them broke Ka'id out? You don't even know who put her there. If Ka'id is locked up because of the Church, they'll blame the Syndicate, or whatever's left of it. If the Syndicate had her thrown in there, they'll probably think it was some rogue Kalis working for the Church or even better, one of their own. You know however they're pretending to get along, they're trying to get one up on each other. Or ideally, both the Church and the Syndicate will blame some renegade working for Fom. The point is, nobody will know it was you, and nobody's going to know who Ka'id really was when you do it if they don't already know. They won't even know for sure she was in on the escape ahead of time.

Syrina stopped flipping through the crumbling pages and looked up, staring at nothing as she thought. "Shit, you're right," she whispered. "It might even be better if I make a scene. With a little luck, they'll all be pointing at each other while Ka'id and I figure out what's going on, and someone could tip their hand so we know who had her nabbed. The Heavens know every faction has enough interest in the Tidal Works to pester her about it."

That's what I'm saying.

"Thank god it won't involve any paperwork," Syrina hissed as she mounted the stairs to the main level of the library.

———

It was so easy to sneak into the Bower House after dark it made her nervous. Pairs of guards—or "custodians," which amounted to the same thing—patrolled outside, and more manned the front desk and at the desks at the ends of each hallway, but the "guests" could wander freely, so none of the doors of the main manse were locked save for those that led to the staff areas and the main gate itself. For all of Syrina's elaborate planning, she only had to walk in the building, up to Ka'id's door, and slip inside.

Behind the gossamer curtains, the half-Eye glowed high in the clear summer sky, illuminating the little room in violet twilight. Ka'id lay on the bed, but as Syrina shut the door behind her with a gentle *click*, the former High Merchant stirred.

"Hello," she said from the shadows that blanketed the bed. "Do I know you?"

"More or less," Syrina said in Rina's voice.

Ka'id sat up. "I thought it might be you, but you can never be sure." She paused. "From our previous conversation, I thought maybe you'd be back during the day."

Syrina flitted through the shadows to sit at the table beneath the window again. "That was the plan, but there didn't seem to be any legitimate way to get you out of here, so we'll do it my way."

Ka'id let out a little laugh. "I don't know what that means, but it sounds exciting."

"You still don't know who put you in here?"

"You mean ultimately? No. Either the Church or some remnant of the Syndicate, I'd imagine."

Syrina stood. "That's my guess too. Okay. No problem. I have a feeling we might know more tomorrow, depending on how they react to what's about to happen."

Ka'id rose from her bed. She was wearing an under-blouse

and a loose night skirt, and she pulled some clothes from the dresser at the foot of the bed and tugged them on. "What's about to happen?"

"I told you. We're getting out of here. My way."

"Excellent," Ka'id said, tying the laces of her calf-high boots and rising to look at the shifting, indiscernible shape of Syrina. "Let's go."

Syrina led her into the long hallway. Neither the guard at the far end of the hall nor the one at the desk by the stairway leading down to the ground floor had noticed them yet.

"If they don't notice me, will they stop you from going outside?" Syrina whispered as they started towards the stairs, pace casual.

"I don't know. We have free rein of the house, but I don't know of anyone who's gone to the courtyard this late. I suppose we'll find out."

They were halfway down the hall when something struck Syrina from behind, knocking the wind from her lungs and sending her sprawling to the floor, face first. The custodians at both ends of the hallway shouted, and Ka'id let out a yelp of pain as something unseen tugged her over Syrina's prone body back towards her room.

Blood dripped from Syrina's nose as she clambered to her feet and saw an indistinct female form give Ka'id a shove against a closed door, then turning to face her.

Oh shit, the voice managed.

Syrina was on her feet, painfully aware of how out of practice she was in a proper fight. Nothing in all the drunken brawls she'd been in the past three years had kept her in any condition for a confrontation with another Kalis. She took a deep breath, eyes half-closed, trying to find the Papsukkal Door. Nothing.

"Help," she muttered to the voice the moment before the

other Kalis launched into her solar plexus, driving Syrina back into the ground.

She thought she could feel the voice scrabbling around in her mind, trying to calm her. Trying to help. It hadn't occurred to her until now that it was just as out of practice as she was.

The other Kalis kicked her heel towards Syrina's face, but she rolled out of the way fast enough that it only clipped her ear. Blood on Syrina's face was giving the other woman an easy target, and the voice seemed to be having a hard time finding the Door. The flood from her broken nose had slowed to a trickle, but it hadn't stopped.

Syrina sensed more than saw the other Kalis pause long enough to take a deep breath.

"Oh, shit," she said to anyone listening.

She somersaulted backwards as the blur of her attacker thinned to nothing, then became invisible with the speed of her Papsukkal Door. Syrina got to her feet in time for the Kalis to smash her in the face with an elbow, knocking her back down. Syrina felt one tooth launch down her throat and heard another clatter across the floor into the wall next to where Ka'id crouched. She gasped, trying to get air into her winded lungs.

The hallway spun. Darkness bled into the edges of Syrina's vision as she clambered to her feet, waiting for a killing blow she wouldn't see.

All at once, her mind grew still, and she felt her heart slow and stop. The world around her froze, but she didn't.

There, the voice said. *Finally.*

The other Kalis was easier to see, now that she appeared to the only other thing moving, and she was hesitating. Even after three years of trying to forget how to be a Kalis, Syrina moved faster. She closed in, happy to be on somewhat equal footing at last.

Somewhat equal. Despite her advantage in speed, blood

covered her face, and she could still only track the other Kalis with her peripheral vision. The woman circled while Syrina shuffled to follow her, wiping at the blood dribbling from her chin.

Grab Ka'id and run, the voice advised.

The other Kalis made her move, wheeling in with another elbow strike to Syrina's eyes she was barely able to dodge. The motion made her head swim and the darkness around the edge of her vision closed in.

You're still losing. Get Ka'id and run!

Syrina dodged a second strike at her face and rolled once, landing in front of Ka'id. The former High Merchant was frozen in place. For the first time, Syrina saw fear creased around the older woman's eyes, but she hesitated. "That could kill her."

Maybe. Staying here will kill you, though. And wherever Ka'id ends up, you can bet it won't be as nice as this mansion, and it won't be anywhere you'll find her if you somehow survive long enough to try. As long as you don't break her neck when you pick her up, she'll probably live.

Syrina ducked another blow to the back of her head and brought her foot up behind her, making contact. Her attacker staggered backwards with a satisfying cough.

Grab her and run! The voice commanded again. *Speed is the only thing you've got going for you. Use it to get out of here.*

Not sure if it was her action or the voice's, Syrina scooped up Ka'id and fled towards the stairs.

She felt Ka'id try to say something; a slow, indistinct noise from the other side of the Door, but the speed of their movement sucked the words from her lungs as Syrina vaulted over both the desk and the guard and down the stairs. She sensed the other Kalis pursuing, but she was falling behind, and Syrina was out the front door and halfway up the courtyard wall before she streaked into the night after them.

Syrina jumped across the alley to a rooftop, then down into a narrow street, winding blindly this way and that before stumbling into the farmland that backed the steep hill Bower House squatted under. She dropped into a muddy irrigation ditch choked with foxtails, falling out of the Papsukkal Door while the voice fought off waves of unconsciousness. She slathered the limp form of Ka'id with mud, hoping it would be enough to hide her from anyone passing above . The woman's breath was shallow and uneven, but she was alive.

They lay there for a long time, as still as the long grass growing on the banks beside them, but there was no sign of pursuit. She wasn't sure if the voice was losing its fight with sleep or it had just given up, but as the Eye set into the west, slumber took her.

Syrina opened her eyes to daylight. She blinked. The sun was high. Almost noon. Her face ached and itched, and she realized she was probing the gap of her two missing teeth with her tongue. Well, she could make new ones. They wouldn't help her eat, but they'd fill the hole so she wouldn't need to explain their loss every time she wore a different face. She sat up and looked around. They were still lying in the drainage ditch, covered in mud. Her heart lurched when she saw Ka'id's prone body, then relaxed when she noted the slow, steady rise and fall of her chest.

With a groan that might have done Mann proud, she crawled over to Ka'id. The woman opened her eyes and blinked up at her.

"That was..." Ka'id began, swallowed, and started again.

Her voice sounded like dry rocks. "Well, I don't want to do that again, if that's alright with you."

Syrina turned her head to spit a blob of old blood into the foxtails. "Yeah," she said, noting her own voice was worse off than Ka'id's. "Let's not."

"Thanks are in order, I suppose," Ka'id said. She already sounded better. "Not that I don't feel worse now than I did in the Bower House, but that was bound not to last, I think."

Syrina made her way a few steps to the stream's edge and started washing the mud and dried blood from her body, starting with her face. "I wasn't expecting a Kalis. I suppose that means it was the Syndicate that's so interested in you and the Tidal Works, and not the Church. Not that they aren't working together though, so maybe I'm reading too much into it."

Ka'id followed suit, splashing her face with cool water, then scrubbing at her bare arms. She plucked at her blouse and skirt. "I suppose these are done for."

She looked over Syrina, still dabbing at her clothes. "No, you're right. As you say, it could have been a Kalis working for the Church, but I can't help but imagine at least one High Merchant was involved with her presence. I don't think they've lost so much control here that they didn't at least allow it to happen. So. What now? I rather think I shouldn't go home."

Syrina finished her scrubbing and rinsed out her mouth with stream water. Then she rested back on her haunches, once again almost unnoticeable under her tattoos. "The city will be an unpleasant place for you to be for a while."

Somewhere nearby, the rattle and clatter of a camel cart blundered by. Syrina risked climbing up the bank to get a look around. Tyrsh began in an abrupt line less than a span away to the north, with the rocky hill blocking their view of the Bower House just beyond. Opposite, the northern most cliffs of the Central Range loomed, pine forests blanketing their feet. To either side stretched hilly farmland and orchards that disappeared in a bright haze. A road to the city lay a half-span to the west. The camel cart they'd heard, burdened with baskets overflowing with oranges, trundled towards Tyrsh, but other than that the southern road was abandoned.

"I might know of somewhere," Ka'id said, coming up to stand beside Syrina. She gestured. "In the mountains. A cave. I've never been there, but Kirin told me about it once. She said that if they ever found out who I was—who I had been—we could hide there. She drew a map and made me memorize it. We always planned on going there at some point so I'd know the way, but we never got around to it. I never took it very seriously to be honest. I suppose that shows how lax I've become since, well, since my old life. I'm sure I remember the landmarks she mentioned well enough to find it, though."

"Nobody else knows about it?"

Ka'id shrugged. "I have no idea. This must have been three years ago or more. She thought it was safe enough back then. I don't see what might have changed. Unless we're just unlucky."

Syrina frowned, but she was new to the Isle of N'narad and she didn't have a better idea. "Alright, then. Lead on."

———

They found the cave the next morning, the sun high above the cliffs. They'd slept in the forest the night before, their only meal water drunk from a little stream. When Ka'id woke just before dawn, Syrina caught an enormous snake for them to eat, but she was reluctant to build a fire where anyone on the road might see the smoke, so she gutted it and carried it with her. She wasn't opposed to eating raw snake when she was hungry enough, but she wasn't there yet, and she was pretty sure Ka'id would object.

The entrance to the cave was so small they missed it on their first pass, hidden behind a thicket of shrubs at the base of the looming mountains. They needed to crawl to get in, and the only reason Ka'id found it was a distinctive spear of rock jutting from the cliffs above that, just as Kirin had told her, from a span away looked like an arrow pointing vaguely down to the entrance. After twenty hands, the passage opened up into a round, flat chamber. A trickle of cold, clear water ran down the back wall in a stream that dribbled halfway across the floor before disappearing into the rocky ground.

Syrina gathered some kindling from outside and built a small fire at the center of the cavern where she cooked the snake. Neither talked much until they started eating.

"You wanted to see me?" Syrina's tone was dry.

Ka'id chuckled. "Yes, actually. Kirin took long enough to find you. I was thinking about giving up and calling her back."

Syrina shrugged, but the gesture was invisible to Ka'id and after a pause she continued.

"There's an awful lot going on, as I'm sure you know. On one hand we have the Arch Bishop, rumored to be planning some kind of sabotage to the Tidal Works. Given its nature, I don't even know if that's possible, but I don't want to find out. The remains of the Syndicate are desperate enough to back him because they need Tyrsh to win this war or else they lose control over the whole Church and with it pretty much everything they've got left. I have no evidence of their involvement, but I know them well enough we can assume that's the case. As far as I know, only Ormo and myself knew enough of the true nature of the Tidal Works to second guess that course of action, so why wouldn't they try to cripple the Grace in the most obvious way?

"Meanwhile, the Arch Bishop's naphtha supplies are getting restocked from an unknown source in Skalkaad. Slowly, but it's happening. I suspect the High Merchants are involved in that too, or at least one of their underlings, but I'm less sure of that than I am of their intentions regarding the Tidal Works. Right now, it's all going toward Tyrsh, keeping the people comfortable enough not to turn against the war outright, but if their supply keeps increasing...well, this conflict might never end.

"And then we have stories of the Grace gaining control of some kind of black wood from the Yellow Desert, sculpted like clay yet stronger than steel. Despite this advancement, the Astrologers in Ristro, hitherto reluctant to take sides, have taken it upon themselves to support the Grace in a clandestine sort of way, more fearful of the Arch Bishop succeeding in his plans than of the Grace's newfound technology. If that's what you want to call it."

Syrina looked up from where she'd been staring into the fire. "Couldn't we just tell the Syndicate the nature of the Works and what would happen if the Arch Bishop succeeded? Anyway, if they're in control of the Church, why would the Arch Bishop want to break something his keepers have been so interested in for millennia? Even if they don't know many of the details, they must still think it's too important to destroy. If they even suspect what it might really be, why wouldn't they want to keep it intact? They've been obsessed with the old relics since they crawled out of the Age of Ashes."

Ka'id sighed. "You'd think that would be the case, wouldn't you? I told my...handlers, I suppose you could call them, at the Bower House, a little of what I know. Not everything, of course. Just what an accountant like Ka'id would end up knowing after years of working with those who'd been studying it first hand. That there was something ancient at the heart of the Tidal

Works that could be the key to everything else. Something left over from before the Age."

"And?"

Ka'id shrugged and jabbed the fire with a branch. Sparks swirled into the shadows clinging to the ceiling. "They were ambivalent. They kept asking me whether something within the Tidal Works would be able to interact with ancient technology."

Syrina froze. "What kind of ancient technology?"

"I don't know. It was rather frustrating, the way they kept asking me all these vague questions. They asked if I'd seen the Tidal Works myself. When I said I hadn't, they asked if any of the parts Lees had imported through me had any triangular apertures." She looked at the indistinct shape of Syrina. "I thought it oddly specific, but by your reaction, you know something."

Syrina swallowed. Drowned memories flooded back. "Eheene. It was me. Or rather, it was someone else, but I convinced them to do it. I lost someone when it happened, and I forgot about everything else..."

She sighed and started again. "Ormo built some machine, based on ancient designs, that helped him read what Albertus Mann brought back from the Black Wall. I'm sure you heard something about that."

Ka'id nodded. "A little. He retrieved something for the Arch Bishop. Is that what this is about?"

Syrina grunted. "The Arch Bishop never even saw them as far as I know. These...prisms. Long, with a blue thread of light through the center. Ormo got his hands on them before they even made it as far as Fom. He called them 'Libraries' and converted the room under his dais to read them. Only, he couldn't read them. Not without me. Or...someone else. Anyway, right before the end of Eheene, I was running away with them. With Mann's treasure. I knew something was coming, but I didn't know what. The explosion knocked me out, and when I woke up, all I could think about was...Pasha. The person I lost. It...I forgot about those stupid prisms. I left them on the ground in the ruins of the District."

Ka'id was quiet for a long time. "It seems someone found them," she said at last. "But they don't know what to do with them."

Syrina stood. "We need to get them back."

"And find Ormo's machine," Ka'id added.

Syrina shook her head. "It's gone. It was right under the daystar when it hit Eheene. The Syndicate Palace disintegrated."

"You said it was in Ormo's room under his dais, yes?"

"Yeah."

Ka'id chewed her lip, staring into the fire. "The substance that the High Merchant's laboratories are made from—the nonmetal of Maresg—it might have survived," she said at last. "If it was deep enough. Whatever was in it was likely smashed, but if we could recover the pieces..." She trailed off.

This is insane, the voice complained.

Syrina ignored it, even though she agreed. "You think you could put something like that back together again?"

"Maybe. I won't know until I try."

"First, we need to get Mann's treasure away from whoever has it. Any ideas about who that might be?"

Ka'id smiled. "I can't be sure, but I think I can narrow it down."

10

THE BATTLE OF MARESG, PART 1

Ves was almost glad the morning the Grace's navy hit Maresg. The tension had been killing him. Anyway, the tin they'd made from selling the blackvine armor was almost gone.

They struck just before dawn in a simultaneous strike from north and south, just as the rumors had predicted. The first cannon blasts came as distant, rolling thunder, followed by a shudder that rocked the hanging walkways and caused a slow, wafting rain of broad, oval mangrove leaves. Ves, more hungover than usual, half awake, staggered naked to his balcony in time to see the first billows of black smoke drift up from the north side of the city, illuminated by the first streaks of sunlight through the highest branches of the giant trees. Another peal from the south came a few seconds later, tumbling over him in time with the pounding of his head.

He stumbled back inside and started pulling on dirty clothes. He wished his crew had stuck around, but he couldn't blame them for finding work on new ships as soon as it became obvious Ves had no intention of leaving. Everyone but Saphi, and he knew she only stayed because she didn't want to leave Grandpa Mann. Not that she ever called him that, but Ves knew that was how she saw him.

"Saphi!" he shouted. "You'd better be awake. Things are about to get ugly!"

Saphi appeared from the next room, fully clothed, brown hair bunched on the top of her head and held there with a sliver of wood painted bright red. She'd let it grow. Ves thought it looked good, but it wouldn't be practical once he got her back into an engine room.

"You don't say?" she said, smirking. "I've been up for an hour. Even made you breakfast. Not that you've got time to eat, now."

"Never mind breakfast," Ves grumbled. "Where's the rum?"

She tossed him a jug, almost empty. "That's all of it. Shall we run to the bar?"

Ves drained the last few swallows and scowled at the empty bottle before tossing it out the door where it hit the balcony with a satisfying smash. "Yeah, shall we?"

More explosions rumbled, already getting closer. The Grace's forces weren't messing around. "We've got to get out of here," he said, face serious. "They're heading through the canal, and they'll blow the shit out of everything on either side of it. Including us."

"Poor Mann is missing all the fun," Saphi said, stuffing some spare clothes and tools into her pack before heading to the door. She tried to keep her tone light, but her expression was scared.

Ves didn't have a response to that. Mann had been gone nearly two months now. He'd been fretting about the old man for weeks, but he'd kept it to himself for Saphi's sake.

The girl was already out the door, and Ves needed to hurry to keep up with her. They jogged west across garish walkways and wooden bridges speckled with morning sunlight. After a quarter span, up and west as fast as Ves could stagger, a tremendous blast ripped through the trees, sending them sprawling onto the walkway, here painted in faded triangles of red and yellow. Saphi got to her feet first and stumbled over to tug on Ves' arm as he clambered upright. Behind them, black smoke billowed. Screams and crying drifted up from the lower levels. Through breaks in the rolling smoke, they could make out two massive warships of gleaming copper and brass making their way up the canal towards the enormous wooden chain a few spans to the north. Soldiers teemed on their decks, wearing black, smooth armor. They were pulling tarps off long ladders tied to the hulls. As the pair watched, the rear ship dropped anchor; the other continued on.

"Shit," Ves said. "They're coming."

Saphi stared at the soldiers as they erected the ladders against the overhanging mangrove branches and began swarming up into the city. "We should go."

By way of agreement, Ves took her hand and led her away from the canal through the panicked crowds.

They'd made it about half way to the west edge of the city when screams and the sound of fighting ahead forced them to a halt. Twin towers of the dingy white nonmetal ruins spiked up on either side of the tilted, purple bridge they stood on. Wooden shanties, shops, and houses cluttered their surfaces in every available space. A maze of ladders and steep, crooked ramps led to entrances black with shadows in the growing morning light.

"They're attacking from the west too?" Saphi's voice was plaintive, bordering on panic. Ves worried about her. Even in the most sideways moments of their time together, the young woman had kept her head better than most of his crew. He wondered if Mann's absence was getting to her even more than he'd thought.

"Yeah, I guess it makes sense they think they have to," Ves answered, gently guiding her by the shoulder to one ladder leading up to a leaning, two-story house slathered in orange and blue paint. "Not much point in taking the canal if they need to man it in the middle of a city full of people trying to kill them."

"So what? They're just going to kill everyone?" she climbed, her voice growing shrill.

"Not everyone. Just enough that the survivors have an easier time finding their faith in the Heavens."

They reached the unlocked door and climbed in.

"Please!" a man's voice called out from the gloom. "Please, just leave us alone!"

Ves' eyes adjusted enough to take in the room. A smattering of worn furniture upholstered in once-bright colors cluttered one side, while the other held an enormous water barrel above a drain in the floor that he suspected just emptied onto the levels of the city below them. The pale figure of a gaunt, middle aged man wearing the flamboyant clothes common with the well-off merchants in Maresg stood in front of a stairway leading to the second floor. A rotund, black-haired woman crouched behind him. The sight of her girth quivering behind such a frail-looking man was so comical that Ves burst out laughing, even though he'd probably be dead by the end of the day. Saphi glared at him.

"Stop your whining," he said, turning his back to the couple to peer out the door. "If you live through the day, it'll be because of me, so shut up and go upstairs. If we're lucky, these assholes will be too lazy to climb up here."

The simpering pair disappeared into the darkness of the second floor.

Ves turned to Saphi. He was thankful she looked more composed, now that the fighting was almost on them. "And if not," he said to her, "A doorway at the top of a fucking ladder is a lot easier to defend than anywhere else we've been today."

She nodded and drew her knives, stepping a few paces back from the doorway. "I'm ready."

"I know."

The blackvine-clad N'naradin came into view at a twist in the walkway a little way to the west. There was no sign of who they'd been fighting. Ves spat as the first pair started climbing up a ladder nine down from their own. Too close to the edge of the city, he thought. They've still got enough energy to take their time.

Still, the brutality of killing civilians in their homes surprised him. For its plethora of faults, he'd never known the Church to commit wanton murder. He wondered if the Grace had sanctioned such an attack or if he and Saphi were just unlucky enough to come across a rogue band hellbent on destruction. But as he watched the following group take the next ladder up, he decided it was the former. They were too organized to be miscreant soldiers. The Grace, no doubt, didn't want any surprise rebellions stabbing her in the back after she'd taken the city. And take it she would. He needed to get his own ass and Saphi's out. Someone was bound to recognize him if they got caught, and he held no illusions about how that would go for him and anyone he was with. Hell, the poor couple hiding upstairs might end up regretting his presence after all.

The first soldier's head appeared in the doorway. Ves booted the man in the face hard enough that his nose caved in with a crunch audible over the screams welling from the neighboring houses. He plunged down, knocking the soldier behind him off the ladder as he fell. They landed in a heap on the ramp below. Four men at the base swung bronze crossbows from their backs, already loaded, and Ves slammed the door shut in time to hear four heavy *thunks* against the thin wood. Bronze, barbed bolt heads blossomed in the door amid splinters, and a few flakes of yellow paint drifted onto the floor.

He looked back at Saphi, who still stood poised with her knives, frozen in place. "Here's where it gets interesting," he said to her.

After quiet stretched on from the street, Ves edged to the warped, filthy window next to the door and peered out. Six blurry, black shapes clustered at the base of the ladder around the unmoving forms of the two he'd kicked down. More soldiers swarmed around them, some up neighboring ladders, others continuing down the bridge toward the canal at a trot. Then he saw the glint of fire from the group below.

"Oh, shit," he had time to say, before the window exploded inward and the floor erupted in flames.

"Ves!" Saphi screamed behind him. He felt a burning on his abdomen and legs. He sprang back, dropped, and rolled on the wooden floor, the bile of panic eating at his throat. *Yellow fire,* his mind told him. *Not naphtha.*

Tarfuel smoke, black and reeking, filled the living room. There was a clatter of footsteps on the stairs, but Ves barely heard it over the pounding of blood in his ears and the raging pain coiling around the lower half of his body. Cool liquid splashed over him and around him across the floor, and the black smoke mixed with steam and the stench of ash. Fire still smoldered around the broken window, and the spindly man who lived there flung a clay jug against the wall beneath it. It shattered, drenching the flames in some kind of viscous fluid. The fat woman flung her own bucket across Ves' still-smoking pants as he clambered to his feet, just as another blackvine-clad N'naradin burst through the door, another vaulting up the ladder behind him.

Before Ves' mind could react through the cloud of pain, Saphi charged toward the first soldier with a primal scream that surprised the N'naradin almost as much as it surprised Ves. She ducked under his sword and jabbed one of her bronze knives into his side between the blackvine plates.

He grunted and pulled away. The blade hadn't hit deep. The hilt had caught on the edge of the breastplate, and the point had only sunk in the width of two fingers. The man swung again. Saphi jumped back, catching her heel on a plank on the uneven floor. She fell, and the soldier's blade caught the top of her shoulder. She cried out as he shook blood from his blade and attacked again.

Before he could follow through, Ves launched himself into him. He felt his elbow crunch against the plate, scaled with brass under the breast. The soldier, focused on Saphi, hadn't noticed Ves, and he fell onto his back, dropping his sword.

The second invader turned from the doorway. Saphi lay on the floor, clutching her shoulder, blood cascading through her fingers. He stabbed the point of his sword into Ves, who'd jumped over the first soldier he'd knocked down to charge the second. Ves twisted. The sword pierced his left side, just above the hip, but his momentum carried him into the N'naradin, and that man stumbled backward and out the open door. He fell, clipping the third man who was climbing up the ladder, but didn't knock him off.

The first soldier was halfway to his feet when the fat woman skewered him in the face with the sword he'd dropped. She let go with a look of angry shock as he fell back, thrashed a moment, and lay still.

Another barrage of crossbow bolts hailed through the open door and broken window, but none found their mark.

As they scurried at the bottom of the ladder, organizing another assault, a horn sounded, long and deep from the west.

The N'naradin began shouting in confusion, and Ves stumbled to the window, crouching low, and risked another peek outside. Soldiers were climbing down from the surrounding houses, gathering on the main bridge and peering west, though the massive mangrove trunks and dense foliage blocked their view.

And then he heard a cacophony of whistling and clicking from higher in the trees all around, and the commanders' calls for order turned to panic.

———

Mann dangled from his harness on the back of Gre'pa, again seated behind the gnarled form of Dakar, as if nothing had changed for either of them.

Except instead of careening through a valley in the Black Wall, gnawed by shame and regret over a people his army had massacred in the name of the Church he'd served all his life, they were careening through the high branches of the mangroves of the Upper Peninsula, charging towards Maresg to slaughter the soldiers of that same Church. And this time, he regretted nothing. But the karakh were the same. The karakh and the blackvine.

It had been harder than he'd expected to find the tribes, and as difficult as he'd feared to convince any of them to ride to the aid of Maresg. Well, almost as difficult. He'd convinced himself from the beginning that his mission would end in failure, and likely execution, so he saw it as a miracle when he'd found Dakar and convinced his wife and a dozen other chieftains to aid the city. He didn't believe in the Heavens anymore, so he wasn't sure what was actually responsible for that miracle, but he wasn't complaining.

The karakh swept down from the highest branches. The sudden drop jarred him and made his stomach rise to his throat.

He'd forgotten how much he hated riding. Black-clad N'naradin swarmed below as the outermost platforms and bridges rose to meet him. A few crossbow bolts whistled by. The soldiers were panicky, and none found their mark, but he knew that wouldn't last.

Dakar and the other shepherds waded into the mass of soldiers atop their karakh like angry children kicking at an anthill. Even the creature's claws and tusks couldn't penetrate the blackvine armor, but that didn't matter high in enormous trees the karakh called home. They swept soldiers off the bridge like brushing crumbs from a table. Gre'pa tried to rend the commander with his tusks and caught the man on the breastplate to launch him into the incoming tide four hundred hands below.

Mann smelled smoke. Gre'pa lurched, angling upwards, and the General leaned to look over Dakar's shoulder. He saw flames spitting from a few of the houses on either side of the walkway ahead of them. His stomach lurched again, and this time it wasn't from the motion. The Grace's forces were putting civilian houses to the torch. He wondered how desperate she must have become. She'd always been a hard woman, practical over emotional in every situation, but this was something new. Something bordering on panic.

They evened out and hurdled through the trees over the fires. A karakh to their right screamed, an almost human sound, and missed its branch as it plummeted sideways, great claws grasping at the passing limbs, smashing through them, a dozen long crossbow bolts buried to their fletching in its belly. Gre'pa twisted, tossing Dakar and catching him again so the shepherd wouldn't fall, as a chorus of ten more bolts whistled by. One caught the karakh in the forearm and it hissed and clicked in anger and pain, but flung itself further up into the trees, until the buildings of Maresg and the invading N'naradin were lost below the foliage. Ahead, the ruined nonmetal spires of the inner city thrust above the treetops. More smoke welled between them, and the sound of cannon fire from the ships drummed from the canal.

Through gaps in the trees, he saw periodic fighting, but most of the invaders were still confined to the edges of the city and the central canal. Maresg had no official army, but half of its citizens were pirates or mercenaries, neither of which would be happy living under the Church, and they would fight to the end. Hence, he supposed, the Grace's desperate actions. She needed the city and the canal, if for no other reason than to deprive the Arch Bishop of the same. If the rumors were true, and Tyrsh was getting naphtha from sympathizers in Skalkaad, the Grace's battered armada would be spread too thin to watch for shipments both coming through Maresg and from around the Upper Peninsula. If she could hold this city, she could afford to send forces north and maybe even seize the naphtha factories herself, or at least put them to the torch. The more he thought about it, the more he decided taking Maresg was what he would do too, if he was still General Mann of Fom.

But he wasn't General Mann anymore. And he had friends in Maresg.

Friends. Strange. Since his indoctrination into the Church when he was twelve, he'd lived his life without friends, and even before then he'd been a solitary child, happier to explore the tunnels beneath Fom alone rather than with other children, who he'd thought would just slow him down or complain about getting lost. He'd had companions, but he could never bring himself to think of them as more than that. Then, later, subordinates, even occasional colleagues. But no friends. Not until he was seventy-one years old.

He looked down at the chaos whisking below Gre'pa and hoped they were alright.

Another nauseating drop broke his reverie. Beneath them, smoke coiled from the densest part of the city, the area surrounding the canal. More cannons roared, and trees exploded as he and Dakar plummeted toward the massive steamships below.

11

MANN'S TREASURE

The same two men had interviewed Ka'id every day, asking the same questions while drinking tea in her room at the Bower house. Syrina was surprised the whole thing had been so cordial, but as Ka'id said, she was a well-connected woman who'd committed no crime, and it wouldn't have done for the Church's public image to imprison and torture her for information they weren't even sure she had.

Ka'id didn't know who they were, but she could describe them in detail, which was good enough for Syrina. One was a tall, thin man with wispy red hair and a bushy mustache. The other was equally thin, but shorter than red, and had a shaved head and bushy black beard. Both had cold, grey-blue eyes. Ka'id saw them at the Bower House most days, even on the few they didn't meet with her, and she knew she wasn't the only person they questioned. They were always together.

After making sure Ka'id was settled the next morning, Syrina headed back to Tyrsh, naked and unnoticeable. She skirted the main road to the edge of the city and perched at the top of the high wall around Bower House, watching people come and go all afternoon. There'd be an Eyenight soon, and she hoped she'd have enough information to act then. There'd be lots of people in the streets, and none of them would be paying attention to anything she'd be doing.

That evening, the sun low but still warm where it squatted on the western estates, she saw the two men exit the gate beneath her and set out together toward the central markets. Syrina tagged behind them.

They walked thirty minutes, wending northward, before disappearing into a blocky, unmarked office building a span from the pavilion at the city center. The sun had set, the Eye wasn't up, and the sky above flared pink and blue, settling into purple in the east where a few bright stars twinkled. A daystar strobed a few times with reflected sunlight before disappearing again. Syrina thought of Anna and the enormous cold and internal pressure above, and she shuddered.

Through the windows, she could see enough to know the building, whatever they did in there, was still busy. She was reluctant to go inside, not confident that her tattoos would keep her concealed in crowded hallways. Instead, she left the two men to their business and went back to her hotel to don Rina and wait until morning, when the city archives would open and she could find out who owned that building. Syrina was glad Rina had paid for the room through the month, but she was almost out of tin. She hoped she could finish before her persona became destitute.

A fellow named Cardinal Naris N'nafal, who in turn was employed by something called the Gallant Corporation, ran the offices, though it appeared his status as a cardinal came only from his voluntary, exorbitant Salvation Taxes rather than any actual service to the Church. After a full day of research, she still had no idea who might be at the top of Gallant. It was stereotypically Syndicate. That the Church allowed them to operate in Tyrsh the same way they had in Eheene surprised her, and she needed to remind herself that, according to Ka'id, the Church and the High Merchant's Syndicate were effectively the same thing outside Fom.

After two days spent in the archives as Rina, she concluded no more information was forthcoming, so she spent an afternoon back in her room to consider her next step. One of the Gallant Corporation's stated goals was salvage. They didn't list specifics, but she was willing to bet their salvage was, or at least had been, focused on the ruins of Eheene. There was too much value left in that smoking ruin for them to look anywhere else.

The best next course of action was to check out the records at Gallant. As bad as the Syndicate liked to be with recording names of people in charge, they were meticulous about almost everything else, and Syrina guessed there'd be extensive records of what they'd found, where they'd salvaged it from, and where they'd stashed what they brought back. All she'd need to do was get in and have a look.

———

It wasn't too hard for Syrina to get the files she needed after hours a few nights later, even with the added security because of Ka'id's escape. Gallant had sprung into existence three years ago, just a few months after the annihilation of Eheene. As she'd suspected, their first point of business had been sending well-equipped scavenging parties to the ruins to retrieve tin, equipment, and anything else of value. For over a year, they'd confined their operations to the Foreigner's District and the surrounding area because of the burning naphtha reservoirs, but as the flames died, Gallant's profits—and their influence in Tyrsh—soared.

There was a lot to unpack, but one of their early finds

caught Syrina's attention. Gallant had purchased seven crates of material from local scavengers, shipped them back to Eheene, and sorted them. Parts for various naphtha machines, tin (both raw and coins), ship equipment, and so on, all sold or sent off to storage in various places around the theocracy. One note though, listed "prisms," kept as private curios by none other than the good Cardinal Naris N'nafal himself.

————

"He has a private vault," Ka'id said. She reclined by the fire pit at the center of their cave. Syrina had brought her a few bottles of wine and a pair of glasses, and Ka'id sipped a glass now, calm and once again in charge. Syrina marveled at how relaxed the woman could look lounging in a cave, nibbling wild, roasted mushrooms she'd picked from the forest while Syrina had been in Tyrsh, as if she were in her mansion surrounded by servants in Eheene.

"It's in the basement of his estate," Ka'id went on. "And, as I hear it, he's the only one with the combination."

Syrina hunkered on her haunches by the fire, her form vague and translucent under the tattoos, green eyes sparkling in the yellow light. "That makes things complicated."

"There is someone who might help," Ka'id murmured, eying Syrina from under heavy lids.

"There is at that," a voice called in from the tiny entrance, the words sounding hollow and flat in the round chamber of the cavern. Syrina leaped up, even as she recognized the voice.

"Kalis Kirin. You're back." She turned to Ka'id. "You didn't think that was worth mentioning?"

Ka'id shrugged. "Apparently not. I rather enjoy her company and was hoping you'd be able to manage this on your own. Sadly, from what I know of Naris N'nafal, you'll need help. He won't be forthcoming about the combination to get into his vault, whatever skin you wear. 'Overwhelmingly paranoid,' you might even say."

Syrina watched the shape of Kirin clamber down the short tunnel and saunter to the fire. She had three small game birds with her, and she dropped them onto a rock and crouched to clean them with an obsidian knife, giving Syrina a little nod of greeting she almost didn't notice. "Do you think this N'nafal is one of the surviving High Merchants?"

Ka'id considered, staring into the fire. Then she sighed. "Anything is possible, but I don't think so. Born and raised in the Church of N'narad, I think. As far as I know, he's only left Tyrsh a handful of times his entire life, though I'd be the first to admit I don't know the man very well. I met him a few times at various social functions and asked a few questions. I've tried to gather at least a little information on all the high-ups in Tyrsh. Subtly, of course. Old habits, I suppose, but it still comes in useful now and then.

"No, I don't think he's a High Merchant. But he's close to one. My guess is he's an old contact that got elevated to something more after the Syndicate relocated. Anyway, he's high enough that whoever is pulling his strings trusts him with Mann's treasure. I would bet this Gallant Corporation's sole focus now is getting technology out of Eheene to read these prisms, whatever their original goals were. Lucky for us, Ormo was a secretive bastard. None of the other High Merchants had a clue what he was up to or how he was up to it. If they did, someone would have dealt with him before you came along." She waved her hand towards Syrina. "Or at least, they would have tried."

"Maybe they did."

Ka'id didn't have an answer for that.

Syrina downed her glass, poured herself another, and

joined the former High Merchant in staring into the flames. "If he's holding these things for the Syndicate, a Kalis will be monitoring them too."

Ka'id nodded. "I suppose that's a safe bet."

Kirin finished cleaning and plucking the birds and spit them over the fire. The only sound for a while was the sizzle of their fat. "We have two Kalis now," she said.

Syrina nodded. "That's true. They might expect trouble though, what with our scene at the Bower House."

Kirin stood and stepped over to sit by Ka'id. "Yes, thanks for that," she said.

The affection in her voice surprised Syrina, but then, there was a time she would have felt the same way about Ormo. But no, she thought, looking at the pair glancing at each other. There was more than that between these two. Her mind wandered to Pasha, but she pushed the image away.

Instead, she turned her mind to the voice, forcing herself not to whisper in front of an audience. *"Can you help me impersonate a Kalis?"* she thought.

Who? Kirin? Why?

Syrina grunted. Ka'id raised an eyebrow. *"No, not Kirin. If we're betting there's a Kalis monitoring the goods, then maybe Kirin can help me convince N'nafal to move Mann's treasure somewhere 'safer.' But he needs to think I'm the Kalis working for him, if that's even possible."*

She could hear the voice scoff at the question before it answered. *How should I know? How does anyone recognize you people anyway? Voice? Mannerisms? Then yeah, I might be able to help. I'd need to get to know the one you're trying to impersonate first, or at least you need to have a chat with her. And unless she has green eyes, you'll need to deal with that. Otherwise, in a dark room, already hard to see...I might help pull it off if you do most of the work.* It sounded skeptical.

"*Good.*" Syrina ignored its tone and looked up from the fire. "I think I have an idea. Kirin, sorry, you won't be able to keep Ka'id company for this one. It'll be Eyenight the day after tomorrow, so we have until then to hash this out."

———

So, I guess we've decided to trust Ka'id.

Syrina nodded to herself where she sat with her back against the cliff wall outside the narrow cave entrance, waiting for Kirin. "Might as well," she whispered.

She's a High Merchant, the voice reminded her.

"*Former* High Merchant. And that's why I think we can trust her. If the Syndicate, or whatever is left of it, ever finds out about her, she's as good as dead. Same goes for the Church, right?"

Sure, I suppose that seems likely.

"And it's not like anyone in Fom is going to trust her, right? Not when the Grace rebelled to get away from the influence of the Syndicate. Anyway, if she thought Fom was safer than surrounded by her enemies on N'narad, that's where she'd be. She's got nobody else, except maybe Ristro, and, well, I don't trust them either, but here we are, acting on their behalf.

In other words, she needs allies.

"And so do we, so here we are."

The voice fell silent as Kirin emerged from the cave. Syrina stood with a nod and they clambered together through the dry evergreens towards the road, naked and unnoticed by the trickle of traffic heading into the city for the Eyenight celebrations.

Syrina had never missed Ormo's infinite resources until now. She'd never cared about the luxury his wealth could give her when she was working and only took advantage of it when it fit the role she was playing. To her, sleeping in a sewer and in a high-class hotel were more or less the same—whatever came with the job. But now she wished she had more seals, documents, and disguises than what she could improvise. As it was, there was no way she could talk her way into seeing Naris N'nafal, or even gain formal access to his estate to case the place. Ka'id might have once been able to help her, even exiled in Tyrsh, but now she was exiled again, this time in a cave outside the city, and her resources had been reduced to whatever dead animals Kirin could bring her from the forest.

So naked it was. At least Syrina had Kirin this time, even if they were both out of practice.

The estate was a sprawling five story rectangle with a wide tower jutting from each corner, crafted from enormous white marble blocks. Well secured, but not heavily guarded. The Eyenight festival teemed through the city by the time they got there, but the N'nafal estate was quiet. No parties for Naris, Syrina thought.

A pair of gatemen watched the front door, and two more groups wandered the inside of the walls, but other than that, the house guard seemed light for a man of his status. It made Syrina suspicious, and she said so.

"If he's got a Kalis on staff, maybe he doesn't think he needs more than a few guards he's got to pay," Kirin said, but her voice was doubtful. "These Tyrsh nobles are too secure in their own importance. At least High Merchants show the proper amount of paranoia."

"Maybe," Syrina whispered, unconvinced. "Seems like if he's holding on to something as important as Mann's treasure, he'd be more worried about it. Or at least his boss in the Syndicate should be. Especially after my little display at the Bower House. They know there's a Kalis involved, even if they don't know details. They must have guessed what I'm after."

For all its solid appearance, the walls of the house itself were fashionably rough, and the two Kalis had no trouble climbing up to an open second story window. She felt Kirin shrug her response where she hunched next to her in the dark hallway they found themselves in. The sounds of revelry filtered in from the city. "A trap, then?"

"Might as well assume so."

They crept on. Syrina let Kirin lead. The other Kalis seemed to think she knew the layout of the place, and after a minute of skulking through dim passages, they came to a broad, curved stair leading down to the first floor. Beneath that lay a plain door with a brass knob molded in the shape of a sun, which led to a much drabber stairway going down. The sound of voices speaking softly welled up to them.

Syrina cast a glance in Kirin's direction that said, *see?* But she whispered, "I'll check things out. Stay out of sight unless it looks like there's no choice. If someone figures out there's two of us, this entire plan is out the window."

She expected some argument or snide comment, but Kirin's vague shape only nodded.

"Been working with you too long," she muttered under her breath to the voice. "I expect an argument every time I make a suggestion."

It didn't respond.

Syrina crept down to the first landing, bent down, and tried to peer into the basement, but the ceiling hung low, the beams even lower, and all she could make out was dim lantern light and three pairs of boots standing at the base of the stairs. The floor was rough, grey stone. She crept down a few steps more to get a better look.

A *bang* to her left startled her, and a mass of something sticky splattered the side of her face and body. The left half of her torso, arm, neck, and face dripped with something white and greasy. A dozen faces turned toward her. The guards down here were armed with short swords and clad in brass armor.

Watch your step, the voice advised from the back of her head.

The basement was two hundred hands to a side, with square wooden support beams jutting from the floor every thirty. There was a scattering of plain furniture, a dozen crates stacked along one wall, and an immense vault door set into the back.

The two closest guards charged her. The others hung back, edging toward the vault.

Syrina stepped around one as he swung down, grasping his wrist and twisting it to impale his sword through his companion's side, giving it a quick twist at the end of the motion to break his arm in two places. They both fell behind her as she stepped off the stairs into the basement and the swarm of waiting guards.

So, this is where they all are.

"I guess N'nafal put everything he cares about in that vault, rather than hire more guards for the whole house," Syrina hissed under her breath as she dodged around two swinging short swords, twisting one out of an attacker's hand but missing the other. She shifted so a pillar stood between them.

Very thrifty of him.

Four more soldiers surrounded her, and she cursed the paint drying on her body. The secret of the Kalis was out. "It was a lot easier when nobody thought we existed."

Try the Door. It should be easy this time.

Syrina doubted everything about that statement, but as two more soldiers circled, pinning her in, she realized she didn't have much of a choice. As good a fighter as she was, most of it depended on keeping her opponents off-guard, which was impossible when everyone knew where and what she was.

Her heart stopped, and she plunged into the Papsukkal Door.

She danced between the guards, taking down four in less than a heartbeat, if her heart had been beating. Something struck her on the side of the head just as she was beginning to feel like her old self again, sending her sprawling into a beam. She slumped to the floor.

The hazy figure of another Kalis streaked toward her.

Syrina jumped up and to the side, but the other Kalis followed her movement and hit her again, this time square in the face. Through the white light of pain, she again cursed the greasy pigment splattered over her body.

That gave her an idea.

She dodged to the right, scraping as much of the drying paint from her side as she could with her right hand and reached out to slap the shadowy form of the other Kalis, who ducked back, but not fast enough. A white hand-print appeared on the Kalis' neck, just below her left ear.

That's a start.

A start, but not good enough. Not yet. She baited another attack, then moved into the strike against her chest. The blow pushed the air from her lungs. Pain shot through her body and her head swam, but she ignored it and embraced her attacker, smearing a thin coating of paint across the back of her head, neck, and shoulders.

The other Kalis twisted away, spun, and struck again, her fingers rigid as a blade, cracking through the right side of Syrina's ribs. Blood boiled into her mouth. She wanted to shout something to Kirin, but she couldn't through the Papsukkal Door, and blood clogged her throat.

But she didn't need to say anything. The other Kalis lurched forward, brown eyes wide with shock, as she tumbled paralyzed to the floor. The hazy form of Kirin stood behind her.

Syrina fell out of the Door and onto the floor. Guards sprawled around the room, unmoving. She wanted to lie down, but felt the voice busy itself with getting her to her feet. "Thanks," she said.

"Good idea, smearing that paint onto her," Kirin hefted the Kalis under her shoulder, and Syrina moved to the other side after spitting a wad of blood onto the grey flagstones. "I doubt I would have been able to hit that spot if I couldn't see it."

"I'm glad it worked." Syrina fought off another wave of dizziness. "Wait a minute? You hit her without being through the Door?"

Kirin flashed a smile. "Impeccable timing, along with the paint. It's not like she kept moving the whole time. Sloppy. I bet she regrets that now." She paused and glanced at their captive. "The paralysis won't last. Let's get this one out of here. What are we going to do when N'nafal figures out his Kalis is missing and most of his house guards are dead?"

Syrina spat another wad of blood onto the stairs as they lugged the limp form of the Kalis between them. "I'll think of something."

———

Kirin doubted Syrina's ability to go through the Papsukkal Door again so soon without resting. Syrina doubted it too, considering she hadn't done anything like that since Eheene and she'd spent the last three years in a drunken stupor, but she gave the other Kalis a knowing smile anyway, and they went through together. Syrina tried to ignore the pain in her side and the bubbling in her lungs. The voice assured her she'd had worse, as if that would make her feel better.

They sprinted through the house into the surrounding gardens with their captive dangling between them. The only guards they saw were far enough away that Syrina didn't think they'd notice anything but a trick of the light, even still covered in paint as she was, and a minute later they were over the wall and into the streets, where they flitted from shadow to shadow towards a half-constructed townhouse a few blocks away that they'd staked out beforehand. She cursed the paint again as they paused every few seconds in doorways or alleys to dodge around staggering revelers. Nobody gave more than a brief, bewildered glance in their direction, and the naphtha shortages meant only a quarter of the lamps were lit, forming small islands of light amid the sea of the darkened city, making it easy for them to slip back to their improvised safehouse unseen.

"Job done," she said to Kirin as they lay their captive onto the muddy floor and began tying her wrists and ankles with the crossbow strings they'd stashed there that afternoon.

The first part of the job, the voice reminded her.

"The hard part," she whispered back.

Hopefully.

Kirin grunted, but said nothing, and Syrina realized the woman was fighting off unconsciousness without the aid of a voice in her head to help.

Kirin passed out before she could finish tying the Kalis' ankles, so Syrina finished the job, fighting her own waves of nausea and exhaustion. The other Kalis was awake by the time she finished, watching her with groggy, brown eyes.

Syrina couldn't do much more than double check her bindings before sliding into sleep herself, hoping she'd wake up before their captive figured out a way to escape.

———

When Syrina woke, Kirin was sitting next to her, watching the tied Kalis, who stared back at them with wide, calculating eyes.

She didn't look groggy anymore. Brown eyes, Syrina noted with irritation, wondering how she could emulate them without Ormo's resources.

Kirin studied the other Kalis. "What now? I don't think we should stay here. Even with Eyenight going on, someone might show up."

"No," Syrina agreed. "We need to get her out of the city, back to the cave. If we can wash this paint off, it shouldn't be too hard."

It wasn't. Kirin left and came back thirty minutes later with some industrial grease remover she'd found at another construction site, and it did a commendable job cleaning Syrina and the other Kalis up enough to sneak out of the city. Syrina had wanted to question their captive while Kirin was out, but decided against it. Too many things to go wrong if she took off the gag with so many people outside.

They left together, carrying their captive between them, tied, blindfolded, and gagged. Three indistinct shadows amidst the darkness and crowds, which had thinned enough by now that they could go unnoticed. Once out of Tyrsh they cut across the hills, keeping away from the roads heavy with the traffic of country revelers on their way home. By the time they plunged into the thin forest the Eye was a black hump on the western horizon. The sun, free of its shadow, flared above it as it followed it into evening.

They found Ka'id where they'd left her, idling in the cave, drinking wine and looking pained with boredom.

"I see you've brought a friend," Ka'id said when she noticed the trio clambering down the narrow tunnel to the main chamber. The other Kalis eyed Ka'id in what might have been surprise, but didn't struggle as they plopped her down without ceremony next to the cold remnants of the fire.

Syrina squatted next to her, while Kirin moved over to

Ka'id's side to watch. Syrina turned to her companions. "You want to ask anything?"

"No," Ka'id said, a brief smile on her lips. "You seem to have everything well under control. Please proceed."

Syrina glanced at Kirin, but the Kalis sitting by her master didn't say anything, and Syrina couldn't read her expression under the tattoos, so she turned her attention back to their prisoner. "I'm going to take off your gag, and we're going to talk, right?"

The Kalis nodded.

Don't trust her, the voice offered.

"Obviously." Syrina pulled off the gag.

"You'll kill me anyway," the Kalis said as soon as she could speak. Her voice was calm. "It doesn't matter what I say to you. Or don't say."

Syrina sat back on her haunches. "I've been thinking about that actually. There was a time that would have been true, but things are different now. Kalis are free of the Syndicate, or some of them are, doing all sorts of things to make their own lives. It's terrifying, isn't it? Unless you're a Kalis, that is, in which case it's a world of opportunity. What's your name?"

The Kalis scoffed. "So what? You'll just ask me questions and then let me go to do...whatever? Become some faithless mercenary like you two?" her brown eyes darted between Syrina and Kirin, who still sat next to Ka'id, watching.

"Maybe. Maybe something like that. I take it from your reaction you're on assignment by the Syndicate and not some hired guard of N'nafal's. That's commendable. Expected, but commendable. If my Ma'is was still alive, I might feel the same way. It was hard at first, but to be honest, I don't miss him. Not anymore. It was Ormo, by the way. No reason not to tell you that."

The Kalis grunted what might have been a humorless

laugh. "Ormo? He was an asshole. He spied on my Ma'is using some old tech. Blackmailed him and the others. Rumor is, he was the one that destroyed Eheene by dabbling in shit he didn't understand."

Syrina nodded, exaggerating the gesture to make sure the other Kalis could see it. "More than a rumor, I can tell you. And you're right. He was an asshole. Such an asshole he thought he could take control of the Syndicate and rule the world. Only, like I said, you're right. He fucked with things he didn't understand and got himself and a million or so other people killed. It took me a while to see all that for what it was. But I do, and I'm better for it. Which is why I don't know if we'll kill you or not."

The other Kalis was quiet for a minute, staring at the remains of the fire. Then she looked back at Syrina. "Jaya. Kalis Jaya. So. What do you want?"

"Nothing, actually," Syrina said with a glance over at Ka'id and Kirin. "At least, nothing you haven't already given me."

She checked Jaya's bonds again, then went over to where the others crouched against the wall, whispering. "I think I can do it," Syrina said, voice low enough Jaya wouldn't overhear. "More or less. As long as it doesn't take too long and I can make my eyes brown."

Kirin nodded. "We should kill her."

We should, the voice agreed at the same time Syrina said, "No."

Kirin's eyes widened in surprise? "No? Why not? She'll go running back to the Syndicate if we don't."

What the hell else are you going to do with her? The voice demanded. *She's still loyal to her Ma'is or whoever is in that role now, N'nafal or his boss. You let her go and everything goes to shit.*

"Not if we do what we need to do first," Syrina said to both the voice and Kirin, realizing how stupid it was now that she was saying it out loud. But she hated the idea of killing Jaya even more than she hated sounding stupid, so she pressed on. "We knock her out, drag her back to the city, let her go. Her boss will find out we have Mann's treasure, but there's nothing he'll be able to do about it."

"I'm sorry, but that's insane," Ka'id whispered. "She's seen me, knows who I am, even if she doesn't know who I used to be. She knows I'm the one that escaped from the Bower House. That's enough. She's seen our cave. They'll send an army into the mountains looking for us."

"We won't be here," Syrina protested. "None of us. After we get the prisms, we'll need power to get anything out of them. We can't lug fuel and a generator up here, and it wouldn't be enough even if we could. So, we leave, and not soon enough if you ask me, which you didn't, but I'm telling you. You can go to Ristro. You'll be safe there, and the Syndicate is too fragile at the moment to go after you, even if they figure out where you've gone.

"I'll get Mann's treasure, give the prisms to you, and you go to Ristro. I head up to Eheene to see if I can't dig up something there that will help us read them. Unless you want to wait years while the Astrologers try to figure it out themselves."

"That's fine," Ka'id said. "It's a solid plan. But why must we keep this other Kalis alive?"

Yeah. The voice sounded angry. *Do tell.*

"A few reasons," Syrina said with an exhausted sigh. "First, because there's a chance, however small, she'll remember this and realize the Syndicate has gone to shit. She might help us out someday."

"And your second reason?" Ka'id seemed less angry and more genuinely curious, but Kirin gave a snort.

"I'm goddamn tired of killing people who aren't trying to

kill me. 'Because it might be inconvenient later' doesn't seem like a good enough reason anymore."

Ka'id stared into Syrina's eyes for a long while. Syrina could feel Jaya watching from her place on the floor.

"Fine," Ka'id said at last. "We'll try it your way. But if she causes any problems while you're gone, Kirin will kill her."

Syrina looked at Kirin. "Fine," she said. "Good. I wouldn't expect you to do anything else."

"I'm glad that's settled," Ka'id announced in her normal speaking voice, standing and stretching as if she'd just sat through a dull council meeting that had dragged an hour over-schedule. "Now, let's see what we can do about your eyes."

———

The eyes, in fact, ended up being easy. Ka'id had brought a trunk full of old Kalis equipment to Tyrsh, and though her resources weren't close to what they'd been in Eheene, it proved to be more than enough for what Syrina had in mind. She didn't wait, but left as soon as she finished talking to Jaya, and found the old trunk in Ka'id's abandoned townhouse hidden under the basement floorboards just after morning. Then she rested until dark and made her way back to N'nafal's estate.

She found him brooding in his dining hall, sitting alone, sipping a glass of twenty-year-old Fommish wine, no doubt imported in better days. Syrina stopped in the shadows around the door, blinking her eyes, which were stinging from the thin, colored glass lenses. "You're here," she said, keeping her voice soft, not trusting her skills at mimicking Jaya's enough to talk louder.

N'nafal jumped, spilling a few drops of wine across the back of his hand, and scowled into the shadows. "And you left," he growled. "The fiasco in the basement was an unbridled disaster, you know. And that's before giving consideration to the guards I'd been rather fond of."

Syrina took a step forward and forced herself to speak louder, conveying a confidence she didn't feel. "It was another Kalis. You probably gathered that much. When she realized she couldn't get into the vault, she tried coming after you. I stopped her, but it was a close thing, even with the paint trap. She got hurt enough that she fled, and I followed her as far as an abandoned townhouse in the Flower District. I lost her after that, and I needed to rest."

"You suspect I was—perhaps likely still am—a target? Yet you failed to warn me before this very moment." He was still frowning, but his voice was less combative.

"I know, looking back. I wanted to find out who she worked for."

"The District of Flowers? Hmm. Almost undoubtedly one of Ka'id handlers sent her, whoever *they* are, considering how that insufferable accountant escaped from the Bower House a mere few days ago."

Syrina risked a sigh of resignation. She didn't know how well something like that fit the other Kalis' personality, but it seemed to put N'nafal a little more at ease. "I figured. It makes sense that whoever owns Ka'id would want their Kalis to come here next."

N'nafal drained his glass and poured another. "Whoever Ka'id and that Kalis work for has made it as clear as the Eye above that they know something about Mann's treasure. That much, at least, is incandescent in its obviousness."

Syrina didn't risk an answer, but she was growing to hate N'nafal.

After a minute of drinking in silence, he said, "She killed half my house guard."

"I know. You said. She'll be back, you know."

N'nafal nodded, looking bleak.

Syrina decided now was the time to push. "Mann's treasure isn't safe here. Or to be more accurate, you're not safe as long as it's here."

N'nafal thought a moment. "We'll set a trap. Not just paint on the stairs—crude, that, but I suppose it proved an effective enough strategy. No, we need something that will pull her limbs from her very torso. Next time, we'll be ready."

"Fuck." Syrina almost said the word out-loud. *"He's not going for it."*

Calm down. Listen to his voice. He's scared. Desperate. Use that.

"That's an excellent idea, but we should still move Mann's treasure. If the trap doesn't work, we can let her get in, see it's not there, maybe give her a false lead on where we've taken it, and try it again. We could even use your vault to trap her some-how. But if what she's after is still here, she'll get the combina-tion out of you, then kill you.

"She would fail to get the combination from me, even if she managed to orchestrate herself into a position where she could try. I'm the only one who knows how to open that door. My life will remain secure as long as I don't give the combination up. In your hypothetical situation, that is a fact we would both be aware of, and she would get nowhere." N'nafal's voice was strained.

"You must realize a Kalis has more things than death she could threaten you with. Give Mann's treasure to me. Tell me somewhere I can take it outside the city. Maybe to one of your other estates." It was a risk, but the odds were good he had another mansion somewhere beyond the city limits. Not that it mattered too much where it was, but the further he sent her, the longer it would be before he'd catch on. Ka'id and Kirin would need time to get off the island.

"If you go, you won't be here to protect me if she comes back. And then, couldn't she just find out from me where I told you to take it?" His voice was plaintive now.

"You know protecting you isn't why I'm here." It was an even bigger risk, but this man must know why the Syndicate had sent a Kalis to hang around his house, and if he'd been a High Merchant himself, he'd keep Mann's treasure somewhere else and have more than one Kalis on the proverbial payroll. "Anyway," she continued, noting his cringe with satisfaction. "This other Kalis doesn't give a shit about you. If what she's after isn't here, she'll leave, as long as she thinks she knows where to go. Tell her, and by the time she gets there, the trap will be ready."

"She might still kill me." His voice was soft.

"No," Syrina said, feeling more confident. "Killing a cardinal would cause a scene. The Church, the Syndicate; everyone would get involved. A Kalis wouldn't risk such a shit-show unless either a shit-show or your death were what she were after. And they're not, because she could have had both by now. She wants Mann's treasure. Let's use that against her."

N'nafal drained another glass, frowning at the lacquered table. "Fine," he said. "I suppose you're right. I have a boathouse in Pom. It's not as secure as my manse here, not by far, but few people know about it. I haven't been there in years."

"Does Ka'id know about it?"

He shrugged, then shook his head. "I don't know. I doubt it. I don't think I've ever mentioned it to her. I've only met Ka'id a handful of times. I don't know the last time I've mentioned that boat to anyone, in fact, much less a pretentious accountant I avoid at parties. It was my father's. There are servants in Pom to maintain it of course, but..." He trailed off.

"Good," Syrina said, hiding her swell of relief. "Then nobody will show up before I'm ready. A boat is good. I can trap her there." She paused. "But I should go tonight. I don't know when she'll come back—I hurt her, but I couldn't tell how bad, and she won't wait around for you to hire more guards."

N'nafal sighed and stood. "Fine. Yes, you're right. Shall I send word to you if she returns? How would I even be able to do that? But it would be safer if you could be warned ahead of her arrival, would it not?"

"Don't bother," Syrina said, following him out the dining room to the basement door under the stairs. "You don't even need to talk to her. Head out of the house for a few days. Just leave a clue as to where Mann's treasure went. Subtle enough to not be suspicious, like a forgotten letter in the trash or something. If she finds it, and she will, she'll come after it. I'll be waiting."

She stifled a smile as she followed him down the stairs.

12

THE BATTLE OF MARESG, PART 2

Mann's stomach churned as they plunged through branches and broad leaves towards the N'naradin steamships. Maresg burned on either side of the canal where the Grace's navy had been pummeling the city with cannon fire. Most of the platforms and crooked warehouses that served as the port dangled in ruins like dead leaves from smoking, shattered mangroves. He could see bodies floating in the water between twisting arches of roots.

Gre'pa hit the deck head down, long arms outstretched like a pouncing cat, with such force that Mann could feel the big ship rock beneath them. Just behind, three other karakh flung themselves from the cover of the branches. There was an explosion of cannon fire, and one of them—Mann never learned its name—tore in half at the waist. Its back legs twisted as they hit the edge of the deck and tumbled into the canal, leaving a broad streak of blood down the side of the steamship. Its front half landed sideways on the deck, entrails splattering behind it, followed a second later by the body of its shepherd, his arm missing and spine shattered.

Then Gre'pa was around the aft castle, tearing at the rear cannons, and the terrible scene was hidden from view. N'naradin swarmed from surrounding bridges, sliding down loading ropes still dangling from the remains of the platforms in their panicked attempt to repel the karakh.

At the very least, Mann reflected, they'd given the survivors an opening to organize some kind of counterattack. He hoped they would take advantage of it.

To his right, a karakh screamed. Mann twisted in his harness to see a mass of black and brown writhing on the deck, face and eyes bristling with a dozen bolts. It swiped at everything, one great arm sending three N'naradin archers sixty hands into the trunk of a mangrove. With its other, it lashed out at a karakh, catching it on its hind leg. That one let out an angry, whistling click, whirled around, and swiped the face of the first, shattering a tusk, before leaping over to a mangrove and scuttling up out of range. The first animal bleated and spun, and Mann saw its shepherd—a man named Ghatt— hanging limp, one arm tangled in the chain connected to his mount's cheek. It seemed to sense Gre'pa, and charged in their direction, but Dakar made a few soothing whistles in his mount's ear. Gre'pa scuttled to the top of the aft castle and dived over the other side into another knot of N'naradin.

Gre'pa tore through them with casual ease before leaping back up to do it again on the other side. Mann turned to see the steamship behind them swiveling its guns to the front. Its deck swarmed with karakh. He had just enough time to think, *they wouldn't shoot at their own ship,* before he remembered the Salamander, and the twin muzzles flashed.

Gre'pa was in midair, descending on a group of fifteen blackvine-clad N'naradin sailors, when its head snapped to the side and Dakar's upper body disintegrated into red mist. Hot blood sprayed over Mann, peppered with sharp shards of bone.

Hands working on instinct, Mann undid his harness and pushed himself off with his good leg as Gre'pa's flaccid body plunged into the sailors. His hip flashed white with pain as it struck the deck rail on the way down, and then he was over the side, splashing into the warm, shallow water of the canal.

Shouts and confusion reigned around him, but all he could think was, *Dakar. My friend Dakar.*

He swam to the nearest cluster of mangrove roots, ignoring the thick spiderwebs and the miniature forest of slimy, brown blovey mushrooms clinging to the wet bark. A concussion behind him caused a heavy wave to roll over his head, washing the spiderwebs and most of the mushrooms away. Before he could get his bearings, another followed it.

Mann grasped another knot of arching roots and managed to grip the tattered, smooth bark enough to clamber out of the water. The N'naradin steamers were sinking. Both of them. Another explosion ripped through the rear ship as men swarmed from its deck into life rafts or back up the ladders to the surrounding ruins. The surviving karakh leaped away into the trees with high-pitched squeaks and clicks.

They were scuttling their own ships, Mann realized. Fire raged on the decks, but turned to hissing steam as the high tide waters splashed over them, then stopped as the hulls came to a rest on the muddy bed of the canal. The decks were still visible, ten hands below the surface, the fore and aft-castles jutting from the water like crooked, brass buildings. All around, the city burned.

More explosions ripped from the north. More N'naradin ships. The Grace had lost her gamble to take the Canal of Maresg for her own, but she'd made sure no one else could use it.

Mann clambered over the roots to an ancient, moldy rope ladder—one of thousands leading from the lowest level of the city to the salt marsh below. Hip lancing with pain, he climbed.

———

Mann tried three ladders from the marsh into Maresg before he found one that led to a place stable enough to stand on. Sounds of intermittent fighting echoed through the forest, but the explosions on the ships had signaled the N'naradin retreat. Where the surviving attackers could go, he wasn't sure, but it was a safe bet they wouldn't find sanctuary in the city they'd just destroyed.

He scrabbled up the rope ladder. It was missing five or six rungs but it was climbable, and he pulled himself onto the charred deck of a half-collapsed fishery, its roof still smoking. The damage around him was thorough, and he shook his head. What had the Grace thought she'd accomplish by burning down half the city she'd aimed to take into her fold?

Well, not much chance he'd ever ask her. He headed west, watching his footing along the shattered walkways.

A crossbow bolt whistled by his head, so close it nicked his ear. Instinct folded his legs before he was aware of what was happening. He dropped to the buckled wood of the bridge and peered through the slats of the guard rail, thankful that they were close enough together to make an almost solid wall of gaudy red and yellow wood.

Another bolt shattered through the plank by his head to stick in the rail on the opposite side. Maybe "solid" wasn't quite the word for it. He dropped lower to lie on his stomach and again looked through the narrow slats. There. On another crooked suspension bridge, not quite parallel and a little above the one he was on. A trio of N'naradin crouched, looking through their own rails, trying to target him through a drooping tangle of moss and branches hanging from the limb of a towering, scorched tree. There were still sounds of fighting echoing through Maresg, but he had the bridge to himself.

The N'naradin stirred and remained low as they hunched their way west with frequent glances in Mann's direction, trying to circle around. He peeked again and saw that a lone figure remained where the others had been, waiting for him to move.

He wondered if they recognized him. Not likely. He'd been away from Fom for over three years and was more grizzled than he had been when he'd served the Grace. More haggard by far. Still, anything was possible. Bagging him was bound to get someone elevated a few levels in the Books, if they figured out who he was before they dumped his body into the salt marsh. He hadn't talked to anyone from Fom since he'd left, but he doubted he'd grown more popular.

His hip complained as he crawled back the way he'd come, towards the canal and away from the freedom of the Upper Peninsula. But then he thought of Dakar—meeting his friend's wife, chieftain of two thousand united tribes' people, and decided that was a kind of freedom he had no desire to face. Not yet. And if these N'naradin got to him, not ever.

Just as he reached a walkway supported by ancient, white, nonmetal beams, wrapping around a mangrove trunk fifty hands thick, this one untouched by fire, the N'naradin came into view at the far end of the bridge. One of them shouted something, and they began running toward him.

The hanging foliage was thick here, obscuring the view from the crossbowman waiting on the other catwalk, and Mann stood and ran in his limping gait to put the tree between himself and the shooter. The boots echoing on the planks grew louder.

All at once there was another swarm of stomping feet,

coming from the other direction, and voices shouting in Skald. Eight men and women charged up from a stairway cut into the tree from the platform below, wearing copper and brass armor, holding ceramic short swords. They ignored Mann—he didn't even know if they saw him where he squatted in a giant wrinkle in the bole, coughing and gasping for breath—but they saw the N'naradin hesitating near the center of the bridge, and their faces twisted in anger. They charged.

Mercenaries and refugees from Skalkaad, Mann thought. He wagered they'd seen enough of burning cities.

He circled to the stairway they'd come up and went down to look for a different route heading west. Shouts and screams of fighting rolled like thunder from the bridge he'd been on.

He didn't meet anyone else until he reached the western core of Maresg. The areas away from the canal and the outer edge of the city had been untouched by fighting before the karakh had come and driven the N'naradin back, and here people teemed and jostled. Some cried and called for loved ones, while others sat hunched against walls or with feet dangling from bridges, staring at nothing. People, Mann thought, always found a way to be shocked about the predictable.

————

Ves saw Mann's hunched, limping form making his way through the crowd. His clothes were wet and clung to his wiry form, making him look even more skinny than he was. Either that, or he'd lost weight during his month looking for help from the tribes. Help the old man had delivered on.

Saphi saw him too, before Ves could point him out, and began picking her way down from the narrow, swinging bridge that spanned the broader, more stable platform below.

"There he is!" she called without turning around. Her voice was almost lost in the din of wailing, coughing, and muttering welling from the survivors. Ves wondered for the hundredth time how she of all people had taken such a liking to the stern, miserable old man, but he was happy to see him too.

It had been easy for Ves and Saphi to make their way to the Westbridge Thoroughfare with the other citizens caught in western Maresg, once the haunt of the most well-off merchants, fugitives, and retired pirates in the city—now, a mall of grief. From their elevated perch, Ves could see black smoke rolling from the canal. The percussions from that direction earlier hadn't been a surprise. As soon as the karakh arrived the Grace's defeat had become inevitable, but she wasn't the sort to just walk away. If her forces had scuttled their ships in the canal the way he suspected they had, it might spell doom for Maresg even in their victory. The tree city depended on tithes from merchants who paid to lift the chain across the canal. Hell, if she'd blocked it from both sides, ships wouldn't even be able to dock under the port. Maresg would be obsolete.

Well, no time to worry about that, he thought. Saphi was climbing back up the uneven spiral stairway that led to their perch above the Thoroughfare, plowing through citizens like a thug twice her size. Mann trailed behind her.

"You made it," Ves stated as the old general approached.

Mann nodded. "They scuttled in the canal. No way in or out now."

"I figured as much." Ves paused, looking down at the scene playing out beneath them. "It could be worse."

Mann followed his gaze. "Yes, it could. What now?"

Saphi, who'd been watching them stare down on the grief below, said, "As far as I can tell, there's not much choice. No canal, no port. Right? Unless you want to move in with Mann's pals on the Peninsula, we're stuck here. Unless," she added, "you want to walk to Fom, in which case, I think I'll stay here."

To Ves' surprise, at her off-hand mention of the tribes, Mann's face cringed with sadness. Saphi missed the look, but she seemed to catch the old man's tone when he said in a quiet voice, "No, I don't want to go back to the tribes."

Ves studied Mann again and for the first time noticed the new lines of grief etched around his mouth. "You didn't come back to Maresg on your own."

Mann only shook his head. Saphi blinked, then took a step closer and put her arms around him. A girl comforting her grieving grandfather, Ves thought. Maybe he understood her affection for the general, after all.

"Dakar of all people," he explained after a moment of holding Saphi back, looking simultaneously uncomfortable and relieved. "I told you about him. It almost resurrected my faith in Heaven again when I found him after a goddamn month of chiefs spitting on me while their husbands laughed. He found me and talked his wife Chaella into supporting me. He pointed out how they wouldn't want a Church city in the middle of their territories. Dakar asked her what she thought the Grace would do next, if Fom got a foothold here." He gave a humorless cough that might have been a laugh. "All the things I'd been saying to the others. Only she listened to Dakar, and the tribes listened to Chaella.

"We made it to the canal, but he..." Mann trailed off and wiped at his face.

"It doesn't matter how," Saphi said. "I mean," she added, "You don't need to tell us. We understand." She glanced at Ves. "I understand, anyway."

But Ves shook his head and took a step to wrap his enormous arms around both of them. "Don't think I don't know grief, girl."

She mumbled an apology, to which Ves just shook his head. They stood there like that for a time; an island of grief surrounded by an ocean of the same.

"What a fucking mess," Ves said, pulling away and wiping his eyes. He turned to the others. "Come on. Both of you. Someone down there must have a fucking drink."

13

FINDING FRIENDS

Syrina wasn't sure she could trust Ka'id and Kirin to let Kalis Jaya go, whatever they'd promised. She wasn't sure how much she cared, either, but she couldn't bring herself to have any hard feelings against another Kalis.

But she didn't want to spend more time thinking about it either, so she forced her mind to other things. Ka'id had spent their last afternoon together assuring her again something of Ormo's chamber would have survived the destruction of Eheene. The daystar's impact might have pulverized everything within, but Ka'id seemed confident in her ability to piece it back together. Or at least, as she'd put it, "the important bits." Syrina was in no position to question either the woman's knowledge or her skills, which obviously reached beyond creative accounting, so she took her at her word.

However, a power source to turn it on would be another matter. Ka'id had suggested again trying to rig something together in the cave, but Syrina described the setup in Ormo's lair, and Ka'id reluctantly agreed Ristro would be the safest place to try something like that. They weren't sure how much they could trust the Astrologers, except it was more than they could trust either the Arch Bishop or the Grace. Ka'id had then said she'd rather work in Maresg, but Syrina had argued against that too. They'd be hard pressed to scrounge up any more power there than the cave.

A few days later, Syrina departed to Pom to find a ship to Maresg, and from there to Skalkaad and the ruins of Eheene. She hoped it would be with Ves and Mann, two men she almost wanted to call friends. At least Ves. Mann she still wasn't sure about, and she was pretty sure he felt the same way about her.

Meanwhile, Ka'id and Kirin were off to Vormisæn in northern Ristro. It was closer than the capital in Chamælivishi, and Syrina had decided last time that she hated both the jungle and the swarming insects that called southern Ristro home. There were jungles around Vormisæn too, but they were nothing compared to the ones further south.

Once in Pom, she discovered getting passage to Maresg was impossible. The Grace's forces had besieged the tree city while Syrina had been living in the cave, and, though they'd failed to take it, they'd blocked the canal and the port with the wreckage of their own ships. She was surprised by the stab of concern she felt, but told herself Ves was more than capable of surviving a siege and occupied her mind with finding an alternate means of transportation. She wondered why nothing was ever easy.

After a few days, she decided it was hopeless trying to find transportation anywhere to the Upper Peninsula. Nobody had any commercial reason to go near the place, and she didn't have the resources to charter something. So, she did what any self-respecting Kalis would do—she stole a boat.

———

The port of Pom reminded her abstractly of the Lip, with the latticework of platforms and steep stairs that climbed from the grassy tops of the cliffs to the sea below, but the similarities stopped there. Where the Lip radiated the eternal feeling of being moments from collapsing, the Port of Pom gave the impression that it would be clinging to the cliffs when the entire Isle of N'narad slid under the waves a hundred thousand years from now. The Lip was pounded together with random beams of driftwood and held there by the collective despair of its inhabitants. The Port of Pom was crafted from great trunks of oak, held in place with spikes of stone, some longer than Syrina was tall, all of it coated in gleaming white enamel that protected the wood beneath from the ever-crashing waves. While the denizens of the Lip maintained the platforms once every few years and only enough to keep them from collapsing, maintenance crews in Pom worked full time scrubbing and repairing the maze of stairs and platforms that led from the town to the sea below. And where ships at the Lip needed to brave the nightmare of the churning tides bashing against the cliffs, in Pom, a long, white sea wall extended a quarter span out, curving gently around, leaving a gap at either end where steamships trundled throughout day and night, entering from the south and exiting from the north.

Syrina needed a boat small enough she could pilot by herself. She wasn't a skilled navigator, but she figured as long as she could keep it pointed north, she'd end up crashing into the Upper Peninsula. There, she hoped she wouldn't be too far off to follow the coast until she ran into Maresg. Steamships were out. She had no idea if it was even possible to pilot one by herself, and without Ves it definitely wouldn't be. He'd complain at anything less, she knew, but she didn't want to risk disaster just to make that fat pirate happy.

The half-Eye was high in the black night sky, peering down

and a little off to the west, when she made her way to the long, floating docks jutting from the bottom platforms and slunk onto a single-sailed catamaran called The Hound's Glory. There was hardly any hold to speak of, but the single cabin was opulent and connected to a full kitchen with a tiny table that seated four. Some wealthy Church-fop's pleasure craft. Syrina got an untoward amount of satisfaction thinking about how they'd feel coming down here for some fancy outing, only to find their boat missing, though odds were, they'd gotten little use out of it since the war broke out.

Even better, the voice observed. *No use causing a stir until we're long gone. Us and Ka'id, both.*

Ten N'naradin frigates had been on rotation for over a year now, guarding the Port of Pom from any of the Grace's shenanigans, but no one cared much who was leaving the Island, and nobody harassed Syrina as she steered the little boat north, the purple and red light of the Eye glaring behind her.

———

It took over a week for Syrina to find the southern coast of the Upper Peninsula. It seemed counterintuitive that she had such a hard time finding something so in the way that merchants had once paid literal boat-loads of tin so they wouldn't need to go around it. Someone who knew what they were doing could have gotten there a lot faster, but she only had a vague idea about how to position the sails when the wind wasn't conveniently blowing the exact direction she wanted to go, and she didn't want to risk drifting off course or capsizing by trying to experiment. She thought maybe she'd ask Ves for some tips if she ever found him.

Once the towering mangroves and occasional hill of the central Peninsula came into view, she turned east, or rather, she tried to limited effect. She couldn't angle the Hound's Glory into the wind, so she meandered ever closer to the line of cyclopean trees until her port pontoon grated against a submerged root, and she was forced to disembark with the nonmetal spires of the ruins of Maresg poking out of the canopy far to the east. Distant, but visible. *At least,* as the voice had put it, *on this side of the horizon.*

The going was slow without a road or even much solid ground, and it took her three more days of wending through the salt marsh, hopping from root to root and branch to branch, clambering up an occasional muddy hill, before she got to the edge of Maresg. There were no suburbs, and the line where the city began was abrupt—a vertical wall of once-brightly painted structures perched among the branches almost to the tide line, with rope ladders and lift lines dangling to brush the calm waters of the marsh. The buildings above her were scorched and abandoned.

She climbed up after she found a ladder that looked like it might hold her weight and began making her way through the ruins of the city. Suspension bridges dangled like moss, and more than once she was forced to find another route when the wooden walkway she was on ended in damp, black charcoal. She'd never been this far west in Maresg, so she didn't know where she was going except the higher walks were usually nicer than the ones brushing the briny roots, so she went up when she could until she found the wide, slanting bridge she recognized as the Westbridge Thoroughfare, untouched by the siege that had lain waste further west. People crowded along, civilians mostly, though Syrina saw a smattering of mercenaries and pirates who'd come to the defense of the last city on Eris they could call home.

There were also karakh. They lurched through the trees above the Thoroughfare, whistling and clicking, while some perched, motionless as statues in the crux of the giant branches or atop splintered spires of the ruins. As far as she knew, the tribes had never had much interest in the city or the canal it straddled or gave it much thought at all beyond vague contempt. She wondered who'd changed their minds.

The siege had been over for some time—a few weeks at least, maybe a month. A surprising amount had already been rebuilt. A lot of the city was still in shambles, in particular around the canal and where the N'naradin had pushed in, but along the Thoroughfare and other central areas life had returned to some semblance of normal. Shops and bars had sprung up in mansions and houses which now lacked owners. If Ves still lived, that's where she'd find him, but to ask around, she'd need a face.

———

Ves had just picked up his third bottle of blovey wine and started on his unsteady journey back to Mann and Saphi at their table when the short, filthy girl with clumpy hair and fierce green eyes plowed into his belly. She forced the jug out of his hand and took a long drink before his cloudy mind could react.

"You son of a bitch!" he slurred, grasping, but she twisted out of the way, smiling, the mouth of the bottle still to her lips.

She stopped drinking, still dodging around his angry flailing. Ves' face was growing red behind the dark skin. "Wouldn't I be a daughter of a bitch?"

The girl winked at him and finally passed it back, now half-empty, and for the first time he noticed the missing fingers on her left hand. His eyes found hers and widened. "Holy shit," he said. "Never thought I'd see you again."

"Likewise." She reached for the bottle again, but this time it was his turn to pull it away. She laughed with a shrug.

"Get your own," Ves growled as he again started toward their table. "This stuff is fucking awful, but it's not like there's anything else with the port blocked."

They made it through the crowd together and Ves chased off an adolescent in slapdash mercenary armor who was trying to take his chair. Syrina looked around for a seat of her own, found none, and settled for hovering next to Ves, a smirk on her face.

"Who's your friend?" Mann asked, glancing up at Ves.

Before the pirate could answer Syrina waved at Mann, wiggling her remaining fingers.

Mann coughed out his half-swallowed mouthful of blovey wine and blinked. "Holy shit."

"That's what I said," Ves stated, but now he was smiling.

"Anyone I should know?" Saphi looked annoyed at being left out.

Mann leaned toward her, his voice low. "Remember our Kalis friend?"

Saphi studied the woman hovering next to Ves. "Holy shit," she said.

Ves looked up at Syrina. "See? We all agree. Holy shit."

Syrina decided hunkering suited the moment and squatted down before reaching for the bottle and taking another long drink. This time nobody stopped her. "I'm glad I can still make an entrance." She put the bottle down in the center of the table.

Mann sighed. "I suppose you're not just here for a social call. We could have used you a few weeks ago."

"Been a month already," Ves said. "Or near enough."

"You guys been having that much fun?" Syrina reached for the bottle again, but this time Saphi snatched it and filled her cup before passing it back to the Kalis.

"More like every day is the fucking same," Ves complained. "But that's always how it is in this fucking city. Or town, more like it, since everyone is leaving."

"That bad?"

There was genuine concern in Syrina's voice, and Ves studied her a moment before answering with a shrug. "Canal is blocked, and so is the port. Nothing left to it. There's talk of building a new harbor, or even two, north and south, but without the canal nobody will want to come here except pirates and refugees."

It was Syrina's turn to shrug. "Seems like there's plenty of both these days."

Nobody said anything to that, and for a while they drank in a silence Syrina found comfortable.

They finished the bottle and Syrina got the next one. When she returned, she said, "I need your help again."

"Figures," Mann said.

But Ves asked, "Something profitable?"

"What do you think?" Syrina smiled. "Lots of loot still in the ruins up in Skalkaad. Or so I hear."

Ves grunted. "I hear it's a fucking deathtrap. Scavenger gangs, the Arch Bishop's fanatics, toxic fucking gas. Stories plenty say it's not worth it."

Her smile broadened. "I bet the people telling those stories didn't have a Kalis with them."

14

GOING HOME

Finding a ship proved more difficult than they'd hoped, but Syrina wasn't surprised. Scuttled steamships trapped every boat that had been in the Maresg harbor, and the tribes despised the ocean, despite—or maybe because—it surrounded them on three sides, and the only boats they had were little pole-driven rafts they used to navigate the salt marshes.

They left the city on foot and traveled east, toward the ambiguous N'naradin border, which was even more ambiguous now that Fom had claimed that territory but didn't have the manpower to do more than stop the Arch Bishop's navy from landing. And the Grace didn't even have that after her failed attempt at taking Maresg. For now, as long as the Arch Bishop kept the Grace busy elsewhere, the quiet fishing villages that dappled the easternmost part of the Upper Peninsula had their land to themselves.

The first town they came to on the north coast didn't seem to have a name. At least, no one who lived there was inclined to call it anything other than "the village." In quieter times, it had no doubt been a sleepy place, isolated from both roads and shipping lanes. They might not have had more than one or two visitors every generation beyond the last few migratory karakh tribes passing every year. The events in Maresg had changed that, and a shanty town had sprung up on the boggy, bamboo covered hills to the east, ten times bigger than the village itself. The lone, wide street teemed with people, and most of the residents had taken to staying out of sight in their sagging homes.

That made it easy for Ves to steal a fishing boat at high tide, when the Sea of Skalkaad flooded the little bay and lifted the leaning vessels out of the mud.

"Another fucking sailboat," he complained as he helped heave Mann onto the deck from where he spluttered in the calm, muddy water. The Eye loomed in the southeast, partly concealed behind the boggy hills that stretched for a hundred or more spans before they sank into the northern delta of the Upper Great Road.

"You think they could park a steamship in this muck, even if any of these people could afford one?" Syrina laughed.

Ves grunted at her, winked at Saphi, and began hauling up the anchor. "How far we going in this piece of shit?"

Syrina shrugged. She still wore the girl's skin she'd been wearing when she found them. Still filthy. She enjoyed the fact that her companions had someone to look at when they talked to her, and she knew they felt the same, but that would have to change once they got to Skalkaad. "I don't know where we are now. We need to get to Eheene or somewhere close to it, where we can dock without drawing attention. I think I know somewhere. Maybe six hours by foot west of the city. A village not much bigger than this place named Aado." She shrugged again. "It might have gone to shit after Eheene, but the harbor is probably still more or less there."

Ves finished hauling up the anchor with Mann's help. They

dropped it onto the sagging wooden deck, where it made an unhealthy *crunch*. "Better still be there. The Skalkaad coast is a bitch, if we can even get that far in this thing."

Syrina eyed the cracks in the deck planks under the anchor. She wondered if they'd been there before Ves and Mann had set the anchor down, and decided it didn't matter enough to mention. "We should make it. As long as the weather stays good."

Ves eyed her as if trying to decide how serious she was under her false face. Mann just shook his head.

Saphi was grinning. "I think I like you," she stated to Syrina before ducking into the gangway to investigate the tiny hold and even tinier crew quarters beneath the leaking wheelhouse.

Smiling, Syrina followed her. "Good," she said to the girl's back. "I could use an ally."

———

The storm hit the same day the south coast of Skalkaad came into view. It had blown them almost a hundred spans west of where Ves had intended to take them, and they saw no fishing villages or even isolated cabins along the treacherous, rocky coast in the time they could look before the grey overcast above them turned black. Driving rain blew up from the southeast, obscuring the endless forest along the coast and driving them aground in a rocky bay just after high tide.

It took five days of plodding along the tide line to reach Aado, and the first four were in the rain. Their mood was sour. Lighting a fire even in the protection of the woods was impossible, and the single, cramped tent they'd found on the fishing boat did nothing to keep out the damp. Nobody talked. On the fifth day the rain broke, but the clouds didn't, and neither did their mood. The terrain became hilly, the forest less dense, and that afternoon they crested a rise and looked down on the village of Aado, home of the Northern Resource Initiative.

Or at least, it used to be. When Syrina had been there serving Ormo two lifetimes ago, the fortress had teemed with private soldiers, scientists, and bureaucrats, shipping naphtha to the far reaches of Eris and researching the Tidal Works and other ancient machines for Ehrina Ka'id, back when she'd been the High Merchant Kavik. Now, even from the distant ridge, they could tell the walled compound squatting along the beach had been abandoned for years. The roof sagged and weeds choked the courtyard. The wide gate stood open, warped from the wind and rain. Scuffs from the karakh that had once prowled along the wall were still there, though Syrina doubted anyone could see them from that distance but her, and she didn't point them out. Memories flooded back, strangely bitter, considering how well it had worked out the last time she'd been there.

A few hunched figures still milled in the neighboring village. Syrina wondered if the citizens had been happy when NRI dissolved. No more strange comings and goings. No more karakh lurking over their heads. No more business selling fish and tubers to the compound, which in its heyday had sported three times the population of the town. Studying the ramshackle homes and the miserable, trudging posture of those who stayed behind, they didn't look better off.

"Well, we made it," she said, trying to lighten the mood, but nobody answered her. Ves' scowl edged downward.

"Should we bother looking around in there for anything useful?" Mann asked, studying the old fortress.

"I doubt it," Syrina replied, ignoring Ves' bitter grunt. "But we might as well have a peek. At worst, it'll be somewhere we can dry off for a day or two."

"How far to Eheene you say it was from here?" Ves didn't

take his eyes off Aado and the ruined compound looming next to it.

"Five, six hours." Syrina shrugged. "More now, since I imagine nobody's bothered to maintain the road. Still, it's not too far."

A few spatters of rain peppered the ridge, and Saphi squinted up at the darkening sky. "Well, let's stop talking about it and get down there. I don't know about you guys, but I'm tired of being fucking wet all the time."

Without waiting for a response, she started down the ridge at a sliding half-jog, using branches and scrub to slow her descent until it was something resembling controlled. Ves grunted a brief laugh, the first one Syrina had heard from the pirate since they'd washed ashore in Skalkaad, and followed her. Mann started down after them without looking at her.

She watched them for a few seconds, wondering at the inexplicable hurt she felt, before following. The voice stayed quiet.

———

NRI was more than just abandoned. Someone had tried to torch the main building, but they'd failed. The once Grand Skalkaad Spiral set into the floor of the enormous lobby was blackened with soot and obscured by debris from the scorched ceiling, but most of the building was built from marble and obsidian. Even the polished, dark lodgepole beams that supported the roof and upper levels had been treated with something that made them fireproof to anything short of naphtha, and whomever had tried to burn the place down, they didn't have any of that.

They searched the entrance and the adjacent rooms, but it was obvious the place had been looted a dozen times over.

They settled for making their miserable camp in one corner of the lobby, beneath the charred remains of a tapestry that had once hung from the crossbowmen's gantry running along the north side. Everything flammable had already burned, so again they had no fire, but at least it was dry.

They were silent as they crouched together in the near-darkness and listened to the wind and rain thrashing outside and the steady drip of the water dribbling onto the mosaic from innumerable holes in the ceiling.

Saphi woke them on her watch. Shouting echoed from the broken front doors, muffled to incoherence by the patter of driving rain and the moaning of the wind through the cracked roof. Shouts in Ristroan.

Syrina was up first, since she'd only been half asleep. Ves was behind her, creeping along the shadows under the burnt tapestry towards the doors. Saphi stayed back with Mann, her face uncertain, while Mann sat and rubbed his face as if trying to wake up.

She wondered if she should take off the face of the refugee girl, but thought she might talk to whoever they were. After all, she was pretty much on the Ristroan payroll.

Not that the Astrologers would have told anyone they'd send up here about you. Kind of liability for that sort of information to get out, or at least the loss of an advantage. I doubt even we'd be able to convince them a refugee from Maresg was working for Ristro.

There was that, though she was reluctant to give the voice the satisfaction of agreeing, so instead she turned her mind to the approaching voices.

Ves glanced at her but didn't comment as he moved to the edge of the door. Syrina stayed low and passed the opening in the shadows to stand at the other side. She was glad of the rain. Eyelight would have cast her shadow halfway across the lobby, whether or not the Ristroans could see her.

She risked a peek around the corner. A dozen Corsairs slipped through the courtyard, signaling each other with hand gestures. Two held tarfuel lanterns, now shuttered to block all but thin streams of light onto the uneven ground at the feet of the pair coming up to take point. In the illuminated bands, she saw the tracks her own party had made through the weed-choked mud.

No wonder they stopped talking.

She knew she could take them. They were cautious, but had no reason to suspect a Kalis. Then again, she didn't savor incapacitating or killing a dozen of her erstwhile allies just because of a misunderstanding. She motioned for Ves to stand down, took a deep breath, stood, and stepped out into the light of the lanterns, her hands raised to the sides of her head.

"I didn't expect to see you guys so far from the refineries," she said in accented Ristroan, squinting into the light because it's what they'd expect her to do. "At least, I assume that's why you're up here."

The group stopped short, but hid any surprise they must have felt by fanning out to either side. They all held crossbows, cocked, and now, half of them pointed at her. The other half kept them slung on their backs and pointed swords of white ceramic instead.

"Who are you? What are you doing here?" one of the lantern carriers asked. Syrina wondered if he was the one in charge.

"Honestly?" she began, mind racing. "Right now, we're looking for a place out of the rain. Ran aground down the coast almost a week ago and we've been drenched ever since."

The lantern bearer spoke in whispers to a woman standing next to him, quiet enough that Syrina couldn't hear anything over the sound of the downpour. He turned to Syrina again. "That was your boat we saw. Looters, are you?"

Look who's talking, the voice complained.

Syrina was forced to agree, even if she didn't risk muttering it aloud. She shrugged. "I guess if you want to call us that. All sorts of stuff up here for people willing to look for it. So they say." She hesitated. "The Astrologers commissioned us, same as you."

The woman barked a laugh and the others chuckled to themselves. Syrina's heart sank. "The Astrologers don't outsource, girl."

"Not usually," Syrina agreed. "They made an exception for me."

"Don't see why they'd do a thing like that." The woman wasn't smiling anymore, and at her change in tone the others fell silent. Syrina felt them tense.

She's the leader.

"Tell me," the woman went on. "Why you're here, really. Nobody's up here who isn't getting paid by someone else. Not unless they're real stupid, and you don't look stupid."

As she spoke, she made another subtle gesture and a pair of crossbow wielders—a man and a woman—along with the other lantern carrier, trotted around to the doorway. The lantern man opened the shutter, flooding the lobby in bright white-yellow light.

"Shit," Syrina said.

She was facing the wrong way, but the light cast by the lantern behind her flailed crazily for a second and went black. There was a twin twang of crossbows, followed by desperate shouting. Ves' voice bellowed something unintelligible. There was a thump and an odd choking sound. The lantern man, now empty handed, staggered out the door and back into Syrina's view. He clutched at the side of his face where blood poured over his hands and down his body. His ear was missing, and Syrina could see the gleam of bone at his temple.

At the same time, the lantern holder outside opened his shutter, set the light down, and drew his ceramic sword in one practiced motion. Four more crossbows twanged, and Syrina dropped and rolled backwards as the bolts pelted the stone wall behind her. She sprang to her feet as the swordsmen closed.

Ves shouted something again and burst from the door like a stampede of karakh.

"I'm on your fucking side!" Syrina screamed at no one in particular, but the declaration was hindered by Ves, who dodged around the five closing in on Syrina and carved through three of the four other crossbowmen with a pair of blackvine swords.

Fucking blackvine, the voice swore. *No chance of convincing these people you don't work for the Grace, now.*

"I think that camel left the barn when their guy staggered back outside without an ear," Syrina hissed out under her breath as she dodged under two sword swings, clipped the commanding woman's feet out from under her, and rolled through the opening.

She gave the woman a kick to the temple, hard enough she wouldn't be getting up for a few minutes, but, she hoped, not hard enough to do any permanent damage.

By that time, Ves had dispatched the last crossbowman—a woman who didn't look much older than Saphi and hadn't been able to draw her blade before Ves was on her. He was yelling something about finally being able to kill pirates again.

Syrina stepped around another attack, turning her body into it and grabbing the hand holding the sword, twisting until there was a *pop* she could hear even over the pelting rain. She relieved the Ristroan of his weapon as he dropped to the ground curled around his broken arm, the bone jutting from his jacket just above the wrist. The last man had turned to flee, and before she could stop him, Ves picked up one of the discarded crossbows and shot him in the back of the neck. He fell on his face and slid to a halt in the mud. The only sound again was the tapping of the rain.

From inside came a choking sob.

Syrina sprinted in through the darkness, Ves' heavy footfalls behind her.

Mann sat on the floor in the center of their little camp. Tears streamed down his face. Saphi lay with her head in his lap. Ves swore behind Syrina, ran back to the entrance to grab the fallen tarfuel lamp and sprinted back, fiddling with the shutter. It clicked open as he approached, flooding their corner with light. A bolt jutted from Saphi's neck, so deep the feathers of the fletching tickled her chin. Thin rivulets of blood dribbled from the corner of her mouth and one nostril, and her expression was one of surprise, her eyes open and unseeing as they stared up at Mann's sobbing face.

Mann stared down at the girl in the light and sobbed again.

Syrina could feel rage shaking off Ves as he stared at the scene before he turned and marched back to the entrance. She wondered where he was going, until she realized at the same time the voice said, *The woman, and the man with the broken arm.*

"Oh, right," she thought. "I wanted to ask them some questions."

But she didn't move from where she stood, and she didn't feel any regret when Ves returned, face hard.

"I liked her. I liked her a lot," she thought. The words seemed to echo in the dark of her mind.

After a minute, the voice said, *Yeah, me too.*

———

It took the whole of the following day to get to the ruins of
Eheene. The once well-used road between Aado and the
Skalkaad capital was clogged with saplings and potholes big
enough to be called craters. In some places, where it meandered along the high tide line, it had been washed out by winter
storms, and they needed to pick their way through the overgrown rain forest that stretched along the coast. No one said
anything.

They'd made a cairn for Saphi that morning, at the top of
the ridge where they'd first seen Aado. Watery rays of morning
light broke over the eastern horizon as they took turns placing
stones. The voice had complained about wasting time, but
without much conviction. Syrina kept telling herself Saphi was
just a lone innocent among hundreds that had fallen in her
wake, as if that would make it better. She hadn't even known
the girl, not really, but that somehow made it worse when she
looked at Ves and Mann and saw the grief chiseled on their
faces. She didn't know what to say, so she didn't say anything,
feeling guilty about her own sadness.

The sight of Eheene didn't make anyone feel better. A
shanty town had sprung up where the Foreigner's District once
sprawled, pounded together with charred planks and broken
bricks. The fallen daystar had reduced the stone and pine wall
once separating the District from the rest of Eheene to a jagged,
malformed line of charcoal and blasted rock stretching across
the back of a slum packed with scavengers, mercenaries, and
survivors who didn't have anywhere else to go.

What remained of the city proper loomed beyond the
shambles of the wall, reduced to crumbling black rubble, save
for a haphazard smattering of gutted structures somehow still
standing. The naphtha reservoirs once powering the city had
taken a year to burn themselves out. A few of the tarfuel wells
still burned, and more than a dozen black plumes of smoke

with feet of yellow and orange belched into the low, stinking overcast. Beyond everything, where the Syndicate Palace and its Fifteen towers once loomed, there was nothing.

In the hours before their arrival, they'd passed a few signs of fighting between Corsairs and the mercenaries who now ruled the north. The others had looked to Syrina for answers as to why Ristro seemed to have such a strong presence, but she could only guess they'd sent people there for the same reason as everyone else: naphtha and the salvaging of knowledge. Eventually they got tired of asking her for details she didn't have, and they lapsed back into the sullen silence that had consumed them since before NRI.

The trio was ignored as they descended the shallow ridge and entered New Eheene.

"Stupid name, if you ask me," Ves growled. His eyes scanned the shanties for a bar. Syrina joined him.

Mann shrugged. "I doubt anyone thought it up on purpose. The people who are coming here now, it's not like they give a shit what anyone calls the place. It's convenient. Nobody will forget it." He glanced at Ves. "No matter how drunk you get."

"Not a bad idea to try, though," Syrina muttered, mostly to herself, as she followed Ves into a leaning warehouse on what was once Exporter Row, patched with charred beams to keep out some of the rain, full of the sounds of drunks.

Mann sighed and followed them.

Their only tin was what they'd looted from the Ristroans in Aado, but it was enough for a jug of rum with plenty left over. A full jug too, not just a warped bottle.

"Guess there's a lot of people coming up to trade nowadays," Ves said. He took a swig, eyed the bottle and nodded before taking another one. "Didn't expect to find rum up here. Hell, I'd have been happy with fucking blovey wine."

Syrina plucked the jug out of his hand and took a long pull. "It's a start anyway."

Mann sighed again, but didn't refuse when she passed it to him. "What's our plan?" He took a sip and passed it into Ves' waiting hands.

"According to...a friend of mine," Syrina began. "Ormo's room...where he took Anna..." Her voice broke. She plucked the bottle from Ves' hands again and took another drink.

Her voice was steadier when she began again as she passed the jug to Mann. "His room under the Palace, it has what we need—the machine Ormo was using to control the daystars." She paused and swallowed despite her dry mouth. "And Anna."

Ves frowned, staring at the bottle still in Mann's hand. "The Palace is a fucking crater. Didn't you think of that when you brought us here?"

She ignored the jab. "My friend is pretty sure that room survived. It's made of that nonmetal Maresg is built around. She thinks it's the material the Ancients used in their ships that came to this world, and she's pretty sure it can withstand anything."

"Pretty sure?" Ves gave up waiting for Mann to pass the jug to him and snatched it out of the old man's hands.

Syrina's voice grew quiet. "As sure as she can be. Everything in it might have been destroyed, but the room should have survived. If we can dig it out."

Mann frowned. "If everything in it is destroyed, what's the point in digging it up?"

"She thinks she can put it back together again."

"And if she can't?"

Syrina shrugged. "Then I guess we move on to something else. No use worrying about that until we try."

Ves stopped drinking and looked at Syrina, who was staring

at the table, frowning as she spoke to Mann. "If the room survived, that means Anna..."

"Yeah." Syrina's voice was a whisper. "Maybe."

Mann shook his head. "We might have left her there? Buried alive?"

Syrina shrugged. "The impact probably killed her, and nobody could have gotten through that wall of fire even if we'd known. But...yeah." She looked up from the table, back and forth between their faces.

Then she shrugged again, feeling helpless. The knowledge of it had sat with her since Ka'id had told her as much, entombed under the needs of *now* and the voice that kept her despair at bay. Entombed like Anna. But saying it now, out loud where she had to face it, it threatened to consume her.

Ves broke the silence, clearing his throat and standing with the now half-empty jug. "We'll go in the morning and see what's what. Like you said, whatever happened, it's not like we could have waded through five spans of burning naphtha to get her." He cast a meaningful glance around the table. "We've all got enough to curse ourselves over without piling on not doing the impossible. Let's just find a quiet place to finish this off and get some sleep."

The others stood without comment and followed the big pirate out the door.

———

When they passed through the ruined wall into what was once Eheene proper the next morning, Syrina finally stripped off the skin of the refugee girl and glided parallel to the others out of the Foreigner's District.

No, it reminded her. *Not the Foreigner's District. New Eheene.*

Syrina pressed her lips together, but didn't respond. It was strange to think in a few decades most people wouldn't even know what the Foreigner's District had been. Just another story about the old city of Eheene and its wondrous wealth. She wondered if anyone would remember all the backstabbing, nepotism, and corruption. Probably not. As long as some vestige of the Syndicate was around to warp the narrative, Eheene would be a false memory of peace and prosperity to anyone who hadn't experienced it for themselves. Maybe it had been the same for Kamahush. Three hundred years later, everyone thought it had been the gem of Eris. A cornucopia of prosperity and wealth, and the only reason it hadn't been the envy of everyone was because they'd all been welcome to come and experience it themselves.

What bullshit.

"We don't know that," Syrina protested, but her whisper to the voice was half-hearted. She might not know it as fact, but from her experience, the voice was right; that was how it worked.

They weren't alone. She spotted clusters of vagabonds picking through collapsed buildings, and one group dredging the frigid, greasy waters of one of the few canals not chocked in rubble, but so far, halfway to the crater which had once been the Syndicate Palace, no one had bothered them.

Chunks of statuary and shattered marble facades cluttered the wide boulevard that ran to the Palace gates, but it had been cleared through the middle. A group of six mercenaries, filthy and grizzled in their mismatched armor, approached from ahead and hailed Ves. The pirate glanced at the shadow of Syrina off to his right and drew himself up.

"Problem, friends?" he asked in an amiable growl.

The mercenaries spread out, blocking the way. Their manor was casual, but they carried a tension in their shoulders and eyes obvious to Syrina where she watched like a gargoyle atop a collapsed wall fifty hands away. Judging by her companions' tension, it was obvious to them too.

"Just one." The woman who spoke was almost as broad as Ves, and none of it was fat. She had a scar under her right eye, and she was missing the tip of her nose. She glanced at Mann. "Maybe two. Ristroans aren't welcome in Eheene, you see."

Ves laughed. "The High Merchants are going to crawl out of that crater and enforce the old rules, are they?"

The woman shrugged. "It's our rule, so we'll enforce it ourselves. You can turn around and head back to New Eheene and any ship willing to take you, stink and all, you can die here, or you can come with us. Choice is yours, if you hurry up and decide." She made a show of looking Ves over. "Could probably get a good three, four days' work out of a monster like this, even if we don't feed it." She looked back at Mann again and spit. "You, not so much. Best be on your way, old man."

The crater is already getting excavated.

"Yeah, obviously," Syrina hissed. She should have guessed as much. The question was, who was in charge? Some scavenger group who made a lucky guess about something still salvageable at the bottom of a smoldering hole or a High Merchant who knew it?

Obvious answer.

She wished there was a way to tell Ves to take the last offer, threat though it was. It was the easiest way to get them into the crater to check it out, now that it was clear it would be under heavy guard. She saw Mann looking towards her, and she waggled her eyebrows at him in a desperate attempt to communicate her plan.

There was no way her intentions came across through her series of blinks and eye rolls, but she tried anyway, and the old man must have come to the same conclusion as her. With one last, intense look in her direction, which said, *you'd better come and get us,* Mann cleared his throat and announced, "It's not cost effective to starve your slaves. You know it. I know it. I don't know who your boss is, but I'm willing to wager that they know it too. If you want to take us to your camp, go ahead. Better than getting stabbed in the back on the way to the harbor."

Ves whipped around when Mann started talking, but the former general fluttered his eyes towards Syrina, and the pirate caught on. He turned back to face the mercenaries and shrugged as Mann finished talking. "What he said. Always listen to your elders."

Whatever the mercenaries' plan had been, they hadn't expected that, and the array of men and women shifted, now nervous. Their leader, though, turned to look at them with a bewildered smirk on her face before wheeling back to Ves and Mann.

"Fucking volunteers. Fine. Since you obviously think you're getting out of this somehow, let me show you what you're getting into."

She gestured, and four thugs circled to relieve them of their weapons before following. The woman smiled when she saw Ves' pair of blackvine swords and winked at him as she strapped them onto her belt. If his wink back disconcerted her, she didn't let it show.

The procession trudged toward the smoke rising a half-span ahead. Syrina flitted after them.

———

A professional ran the excavation.

Tarfuel machines like she'd never seen before lined the southern edge of the crater, blasting the pit with enormous, screaming fans clearing the grey smoke. Scaffolding ran along the near edge. They'd dug out the bottom of the hole to be more or less level, and slaves hauled up rocks and broken masonry in huge buckets attached to winches. Heaps of blackened stone and loose, charred soil heaped around the top, except along the southern edge where a handful of steam trucks waited to be loaded with anything worth keeping. Despite the fans, foul mist obscured everything.

It surprised her to see a few of the trucks half-loaded with machine scrap and unidentifiable devices. Most were twisted and ruined, but that anything had survived the explosion and more than a year of fire was astounding.

How many secret rooms like Ormo's did the Palace conceal? The voice wondered. *Anything in those might have made it.*

Syrina considered that. Ormo had made a few cryptic comments about other chambers such as the one he used, and he'd told her once that two-thirds of the High Merchants could tattoo their own Kalis. They would have had rooms similar to his, whether hidden within the palace or somewhere else. If Ka'id was right, anything in those rooms might be salvageable.

Whoever's in charge here knows there are rooms under all the trash, and they know where to look for them.

It was right. Another High Merchant ran this operation. And that meant there was at least one other Kalis around, either skulking and watching like Syrina was or posing as one of the foremen.

Maybe we can use that to our advantage.

Syrina wondered what the voice was talking about for a second and then figured it out. Maybe, indeed. She skirted the edge of the camp, to see what she could see.

The scaffolding went halfway around in a rough semi-circle, but there were signs they'd already completed excavating the far side. Traces of wheel ruts and cleared rock showed where they'd moved the fan machines around the perimeter to blast the smoke from wherever they worked. A little way to the west, rows of tents squatted, and a lone old woman stirred a huge, green copper pot of steaming gruel stinking of old fish. Mann was right. They wouldn't let their slaves starve, whatever threats the mercenaries spewed, but they weren't fed well either, and she wasn't surprised to see crooked rows of cairns running behind the slave tents. Far enough to be out of the way, close enough to remind them of their only way out.

There was a time the thought of people working to death in toxic air wouldn't have bothered her one way or another, but that was a long time ago.

Well, she hoped she'd be done here before they forced her companions to eat that soup. That stuff might smell worse than the smoke from the crater.

We'll need to go into the hole if we want to find anything worthwhile.

"I know. Can you keep the gas from killing me?"

Us. And I don't know. For a little while, probably. After that, I'm not sure, but there's only one way to find out, and meanwhile we're just wasting time.

"Great. I've got an idea of how to find the Kalis running things, but we should check out the pit first to see if it's worth doing."

Just what I was thinking.

"I know. Let's go."

She shimmied down one of the bamboo poles at the far western edge of the scaffolding, using the brass rivets as handholds. None of the slaves were close, and the smoke hid most of them. She wondered how Ves and Mann were doing. She'd lost track of them after they'd entered the compound, but she needed to assume they'd already been put to work. Ves would manage well enough, but Mann was another matter. He'd survived the Pit of Fom, but Syrina had the feeling this would be worse, even before considering he was older now. Three years could be a long time for an old man.

The bottom of the crater was flat where she came down, and she realized they must have started excavating as soon as it had cooled enough. She should have guessed the High Merchants would be on top of reclaiming what was theirs.

"How long do you think they've been at this?" she whispered to the voice as she whisked around the edge, away from the scaffolding. She could see rank smoke rising from another, deeper crater near the center of the one she was in.

However long it's not been on fire, the voice answered, repeating what she'd already been thinking. *What's that? A year and a half? Two years? Rumor had it this hole burned for a year or more, but you know how people talk.*

A year or two was a long time, Syrina reflected, if whoever was in charge had been working their people as hard as they were now. Long enough to get to Ormo's room. Ormo's and everyone else's.

Don't be stupid, the voice chided as Syrina, keeping her breath shallow, crept up to the first object she could make out in the gloom. It was black and scaly, vaguely oval, maybe fifty hands across. Like an enormous, scorched egg.

You don't know how awful things looked when they first got here, but you can bet it was bad. It probably took them almost this long to find anything worth digging out of this mess. Anyway, if they'd found Ormo's room, they wouldn't have been keeping the library rods in some fop's vault. They'd either be using them or keeping them under the guard of every Kalis they have left, if they knew what they are, and if they found Ormo's room, they would have figured it out. They knew Ormo was up to something, whatever details they had, the way he'd been screwing with everyone right up until the end.

Syrina sighed as she scanned the egg for an opening. "When you put it like that, sure." She thought of something. "If Ormo's room was right under the daystar, it might still be at the bottom of that smoking pit. We'll never get it."

The voice was quiet for a minute. *That's true, but I don't think that's the case. That crater is right in the middle, more or less where the central fountain used to be. Ormo's room was under his tower, off to the side along with the others.*

Syrina tried to remember where things would have been years ago. It was hard to get her bearings at the bottom of a smoke-clotted hole, but she thought the voice was probably right. And anyway, even if it wasn't, they'd come all this way. She might as well look around.

There was a door in the far end of the egg, pried open but still attached to the nonwhite metal hinges. *It must not have been locked,* the voice pointed out. *Not with the original locks anyway, or these scavengers wouldn't have been able to open it.*

The scorching on the outside had made the strange scaling effect, which up close was odd and uneven, but naphtha fire had otherwise not damaged it. She tried to imagine anything built since the Age of Ashes that could survive being coated in burning naphtha for a year and failed. Strong stuff, indeed.

I told you so.

"Ka'id told me, not you."

Inside was empty except for a dusting of ash and a few melted wires and solidified pools of copper. Scuff marks around the entrance told her something, or a few somethings, had been dragged out, but otherwise the contents of the egg had been roasted into puddles. The nonmetal might have survived, but it hadn't insulated whatever had been inside. She thought of Anna, and didn't know if it would have made the girl's fate better or worse.

Depends on how fast it got that hot. Either way, this wasn't

Ormo's room. Too small, and not deep enough. Remember that stairway down?

Syrina swallowed and shoved her mind back to what she was doing.

After another twenty minutes of creeping around the crater floor, she decided that they'd either already completely removed Ormo's room from the area or they hadn't found it yet. The place where she guessed his hall had been was closer to the central crater than anything they'd excavated so far. If she was right, it would have been further from the naphtha fires, but closer to the impact. She didn't know if that would be better or worse either.

She found five other capsules similar to the first. Two were the same size, and three were bigger—more like Ormo's, but in the wrong place. The explosion had shifted all of them to one degree or another, and they sat half-buried in ash and rock, one pushed so deep the only sign of it was a tunnel Syrina almost fell in as she rubbed her eyes against the stinging smoke. None held anything of value. Whatever they'd once contained had either been looted or vaporized in the cataclysm.

The slaves were all grouped to one side, digging and hauling buckets of rock up the scaffolds. She overheard enough to know they'd found another chamber, this one sunk deep, with the lone entrance pointing almost directly downward in what had been molten basalt after the explosion. They chipped away at it, but the going was slow. She looked for Ves and Mann, but couldn't make out any faces in the mist, and she had nothing to say to them yet anyway.

After she decided she couldn't learn anything she didn't already know, she scaled back up the same bamboo scaffold and moved into the ruins to catch her breath. The clouds hung low, but it wasn't raining, and she couldn't tell how much of the overcast was from the ever-rising smoke. It was afternoon. The late summer sun was still high somewhere above the grey, but a chilly wind had picked up, blowing from the north.

She gave herself a half-hour to rest, enjoying the air that seemed a lot fresher now than it had before her venture into the crater. Then she crept back to the camp to look for who was in charge.

———

Syrina found Mann and Ves as the sun sank over the ruins. The clouds had cleared enough to send rays of light stabbing through the camp a few minutes before it fell below the horizon. The pair sat together, a little apart from the others, playing with their small bowls of reeking stew without eating. They were both filthy. Ves looked even angrier than usual, while Mann leaned against a sagging tent wall, hunched, coughing, and pale. A pair of guards who'd been among those who'd intercepted them stood nearby, watching and laughing, talking together in indistinct voices. Ves and Mann didn't speak, and Ves scanned the mob of other slaves, eyes calculating.

There were about two hundred people crowded around the tents by the time the sun fell below the horizon and it became too dark to work, even with the array of naphtha lamps. Naphtha. Syrina wondered where it had come from. She wondered who the slaves had been before they ended up here.

The naphtha, well, we both know the answer to that. The people? Captured scavengers, the voice guessed. *Or, if the Merchant's Syndicate is pulling the Arch Bishop's strings, maybe prisoners of war from Fom. Listen to their accents.*

Syrina paused at the edge of the circle of light where the workers huddled with their foul-smelling gruel. Most weren't talking, but she could hear the hiss of a few whispered conversations. A lot of them indeed spoke with the clipped accent of Fom, though there was a fair amount of Skald too.

After watching the guards for an hour, she could pick out the command tent among the slave quarters, though she suspected that wouldn't be where the boss slept, given it was the same size and style as the others and offered little protection from the chill night or the reeking, ever-present gas. She wondered if it had been a tactical decision to make the command office the same as everything else, or if it was just all they had.

It was nice to have something to focus on again. Something to keep her mind off what happened last time she was in Eheene.

She monitored the command tent until it was dark. Guards ordered any slaves who hadn't gone to bed into their shelters. Then they changed shifts and posted themselves around the camp. They kept Ves and Mann together and ushered them into the tent just to the left of command. It was an amateur move, keeping two obvious trouble makers together like that, especially volunteers still fresh and unbroken. In fact, the entire guard operation was sloppy, the way they shuffled around, arguing about who would stand where and when. They even bickered over how long their shifts would be.

"How did they go this long without an incident?" she asked the voice. "If I was a prisoner here, I'd be out in a week. Even if I wasn't a Kalis."

I guess we don't know if there haven't been any incidents, it reflected. *But you're right. My guess is there's been quite a few, but that's not surprising. The food is awful. These fumes must taint it, and the air is worse. The turnover must be horrendous for everyone below management and above slave. I bet half or more of these mercenaries are fresh out of training, or whatever passes for training with this lot.*

Syrina nodded. "That's a good point. Hard to find good help when the place you're stationed at reduces your lifespan a year for every week you're there."

As she whispered to the voice, a woman emerged from the command tent, ducking out from under the flap without bothering to close it behind her. One man stationed there shut it for her, while two others fell in to follow a step behind and to either side. She seemed to ignore everyone and her surroundings, but Syrina watched her eyes take in every detail as she moved across the camp towards the ruins of the main palace gate.

There's our Kalis.

"Yup." Syrina followed the trio into the rubble of Eheene, twenty paces behind.

They didn't go far. She would have been surprised if they had. Just far enough that the air was a little cleaner, away from the stabbing light of the naphtha lamps.

Joana Baas had trained as a Seneschal as long as she could remember. She imagined that was at least as hard as training to be a Kalis. Sure, she didn't need to learn a dozen languages, mimicry, or endure the torture of the tattooing, but she and her kind needed to learn every whim, every hidden desire of the High Merchant they served, more often than not without the benefit of their master just telling them what they wanted. Not to mention learning the skills to see, identify, and, if necessary, combat a Kalis, should the need arise. That sort of thing seemed unfathomable, but she'd heard of it happening. Recently, even. Before the annihilation of Eheene.

Even so, she wasn't a fan of serving under Kalis Dari, here on the edge of this reeking pit, even if it was High Merchant

Kavik who'd sent them both to recover whatever it was they were supposed to recover, and she had a feeling not even Dari knew what that was.

She wondered for the hundredth time why Dari couldn't just dress up as a mercenary captain and run the operation herself. Joana had gotten frustrated enough to ask, once, but she hadn't gotten an answer. Not a satisfying one anyway. She'd asked Ma'is Kavik when he first sent them here too, but he'd just said Dari would be busy, and "her frequent absences would be noticed." Joana wondered what else the Kalis could occupy herself within this field of ruin, and hated the fact that she'd never know.

Dari was there tonight though, when Joana returned from another day of listing finds, slave logs, and doing mercenary payroll in her tent by the crater. She knew she should be happy she was at least permitted to stay in the ruins of a gutted estate, inexplicably spared from destruction a span from the old palace walls. "Keeping up the image," Dari had told her. Whatever the reason, it was better than trying to sleep next to that damn crater.

The hazy form of the Kalis sat at the splintered table they'd brought from New Eheene, looking over a ream of singed papers, which she put into a folder when Joana walked in. The Seneschal concealed her frown. So many damn secrets.

"Enjoyable day?" Dari asked.

Joana knew the Kalis was just doing her impression of being nice, but she wasn't in the mood. "Same as ever." She didn't bother hiding her irritation. "A few new slaves today. Slander and her crew grabbed them wandering around the ruins. A Ristroan and some old man with a Fom accent."

"Oh?" There was an extra level of interest in Dari's voice. Joana sensed her full attention bear down on her. "They were together? That's an interesting pair. I should meet them."

Joana could tell there was more to Dari's interest than just their age and nationalities, but she knew she wouldn't get an answer, so she didn't ask. "Go ahead. They're in tent seven."

"Together?"

Joana realized what a terrible idea that might be just as Dari asked. "Uh, yeah. Stupid, now that you mention it. Had a hard enough time sorting the new mercenaries—didn't even think about what they were doing with the slaves. I'll make sure they're split up tomorrow."

Joana, who watched Dari out of the corner of her eye, saw the Kalis nod. "It's probably fine for tonight. I'll meet them tomorrow, it's late now. By the time I put something on I'd just raise suspicion, showing up in the middle of the night. They're not going anywhere. Make sure—"

Kalis Dari stopped talking and faded from view further as she began using her tattoos. Instinct clicked in Joana's mind, and without thinking, she dove from her chair and rolled, drawing the pair of ceramic long knives she'd carried with her since returning to Eheene. A shadow flitted from the shattered doorway into the room. There was no sound from the guards stationed outside. No sound at all.

Another Kalis, Joana thought. *Traitor!*

Something flew past her head, narrowly missing her ear, and shattered on the blackened marble floor. She rolled again and thrust with her left hand, catching movement out of the corner of her eye, and felt the edge of her blade snag something and pull free. At the same moment, Dari smashed into the intruder and they both rolled to the floor in a blurred frenzy of motion.

Their attacker wasn't expecting Dari, Joana realized. *She probably thought I was running things.*

It only took Joana a couple of seconds to distinguish friend from foe, but it was still too slow. The traitor Kalis paused for a split second and vanished in a rush of air, moving too fast for even Joana's trained eyes to track. A mist of blood flecked the floor.

Dari spun to her feet, a graceful shadow with burning brown eyes, but was thrown back twenty hands against the far wall before she could enter her own Papsukkal Door. Joana heard a crunch and saw a splatter of blood on the wall as Dari slid down, limp.

Shit, she thought, lashing blind with both blades towards where Dari had been standing.

Something struck her neck and her body went numb. She felt herself falling in a distant way, but didn't feel anything as she hit the floor.

Shit, she thought again, before blackness descended.

15

THE PASSING OF KNOWLEDGE

Arch Bishop Daliius sat brooding behind the Alter of the Heavens, the enormous Tome of the Names of Light open and ignored on its rose marble stand in front of him. Eyelight from the arch of stained glass behind him flooded the cathedral with a riot of clashing colors, but the air seemed to reverberate with unforgiving emptiness. Strange, he thought, how vast rooms such as the Hall of Light could seem to echo when nobody made a sound.

Whatever else he contemplated, his mind always circled back to the same thing. The Grace's attempt to take Maresg had failed, but she'd blocked the canal, permanently. Most would consider that a draw, and a draw should have been good news, but something grated in his chest the more he thought about it. The Skald mercenaries he'd ordered there had done their part, but the true victory went to the karakh tribes that had ridden to the rescue like fairytale heroes. There was that old saying, older than time, about the enemy of your enemy. He'd adhered to it enough in these evil days, but those tribes were allies he'd rather do without, and he was under no illusions they considered themselves allies at all.

And then there were the High Merchants. They had raised him, trained him, used him for their own hidden agendas, pulling him this way and that, never letting on what they intended, though more often than not he could guess. The Syndicate and its corruption, as old as Eris. The Grace and her fanaticism that had come like a sudden storm—so easy to predict, yet they'd been utterly unprepared in their conceit.

Lurking across the Sea of N'narad, the ill-named Astrologers of Ristro schemed, sending their Corsairs to stir up trouble for everyone, everywhere in between. And now, worst of all, dozens, maybe hundreds, of ronin Kalis, working for whoever they pleased or no one at all, spread over the continent like stains ejaculated from the destruction of Eheene to impregnate the world in violence and mayhem.

"Ahem."

Daliius turned at the sound, which now truly did echo. He'd been so absorbed in his thoughts he hadn't heard the servant enter. Something he'd been doing a lot lately. Too much. So much going on, yet too much time to think in circles.

The servant stood at the base of the dais, head bowed, but looking up at the alter through her lashes; an absurd, elaborate slab of iron, gold, and marble. She was dressed in blue and black—one of the High Merchant Kavik's Seneschal. The new Kavik, he reminded himself, though since he'd never met the old one, the thought hardly seemed relevant.

"Yes? What is it? Don't just stand there." The acoustics of the hall made even his famously soft voice reverberate. He caught himself thinking about echoes again and pulled his mind back to the woman standing before him.

"We—they—the scavengers my master sent to Eheene, have found something, Your Holiness. Something important. Documents, records, notes written by High Merchant Ormo. Unsigned, of course, but in his writing, and from his estate." The Seneschal swallowed and paused, flustered.

"Ormo. The one rumored to have started this whole mess, yes?" And the one member of the Merchant's Syndicate Daliius had trusted, though he didn't add that out loud.

The Seneschal shrugged. "Yes. There are rumors."

Daliius sighed. This servant wouldn't know anything beyond what scant little Kavik had divulged to her. "I suppose Kavik wishes to meet with me, to speak of these notes in person."

"Yes, Your Holiness."

"Fine. When?"

She hesitated, glancing around the empty hall. "He waits in the narthex now, Your Holiness. If you are not busy."

"Do I look busy to you?"

The Seneschal flinched, and Daliius regretted his harsh tone. "My apologies, child. My irritation does not lie with you."

She blinked. No doubt an apology from the Arch Bishop was an unexpected blessing. "No need to apologize, Your Holiness. I—I will tell Ma'is Kavik that you will see him."

Daliius waived his hand. "Go in peace, child. Whatever peace you can find."

Kavik was small and thin, androgynous under his blue and white hood and the swirls of black and white on his painted face. The Arch Bishop had met him only once before, when he and the other surviving High Merchants had fled to Tyrsh. Even after more than three years of living in *his* city, they treated him, the Holy Ordained of the Church of N'narad, as just another one of their servants.

"Arch Bishop," Kavik droned. "It has been too long."

Daliius wondered if his tone had been as condescending as it had seemed or if it was just his imagination. "The information you found must be important enough for you to come here. Are you not concerned any longer with being seen by the public? You, whom they still see as their enemy?"

Kavik rustled under his robes in what might have been a shrug. "It is very late. From the car, I was unseen, Your Holiness. And in here—" he looked around for what Daliius imagined Kavik saw as dramatic effect. "Here, we are alone."

The Arch Bishop gave another dismissive wave of his hand. "What is it you think you need to tell me at such an hour, High Merchant Kavik?"

If the High Merchant felt any surprise at the insubordinate tone or the lack of the honorific "Ma'is," he didn't let it show under his hood. Instead, he produced a ream of crumpled pages from his robe, some half-burned. "Notes," he announced. "From the former High Merchant Ormo. Who was once a cause of much distress among the other fourteen."

Daliius gave another wave. "So your lacky said. Can you be more specific?"

This time he thought he could hear a hint of irritation in the High Merchant's response. *Good.*

"Plans," Kavik said. "Schematics. Blueprints of the Tidal Works. Not, we believe, directly connected to whatever caused the annihilation of Eheene, but perhaps still quite useful for the war effort."

At that, Daliius half-stood, leaning against the alter. "Yes, yes," he said. "This is not the first time I have heard the theory that Ormo was somehow responsible for the cataclysm in Eheene. What is this you say about the Tidal Works?"

He could hear Kavik's smile. "I see I have discovered a way to gain your attention. Look for yourself." Kavik shuffled forward to pass the mangled papers up to him.

Daliius thumbed through them with growing interest. Most were charred and torn, some almost illegible, but he could tell at once there was more here than Kavik let on. "And you are sure this is Ormo's work?" He recognized Ormo's spidery script at once, but he wanted to hear what Kavik had to say about it.

The High Merchant spoke as Daliius read. "They were found at his estate, far enough outside the city to be spared complete destruction." When the Arch Bishop didn't reply, Kavik continued. "My predecessor, as you may know, also had a keen interest in the Tidal Works. Spent years, some say decades, studying that wondrous machine beneath Fom." He paused. Daliius felt his intense eyes on him, but he didn't look up from the notes. "I say 'some say,' because the previous Kavik, whatever their reasons, did not leave their research where the High Merchant's Syndicate could find it before he died. Unusual. Unprecedented, even, since the supposed accidental nature of their demise would not have given them any time to hide such secrets ahead of time. It therefore stands to reason that they had been hiding the true nature of their work from the start."

Daliius looked up and frowned. "Why are you telling me this? What are you getting at?"

Kavik rustled again. "There is a secret within the Tidal Works. Something which that Kavik did not wish even the Syndicate he served with his life to find." He gestured to the papers clutched in the Arch Bishop's hand. "Ma'is Ormo gained information suggesting a substantial power source. His theories about it were insane, as you can see. However, the former Kavik's secrecy leads me to think there is some truth buried under Ormo's madness. Something we ourselves cannot guess at, but someone with your unique training might find." He paused. "Something useful to us."

The Arch Bishop raised his eyebrows. "'Unique training?' I have always been led to believe they raised me as a Kalis, sans the martial abilities and tattoos. Given the current state of the world, I would hardly call it 'unique.' Not anymore."

Kavik shifted, and Daliius thought he noted a glint of pleasure in the High Merchant's eyes, but it disappeared so fast it could have been a trick of the light, and Kavik answered before he could think about it further. "True. But you've had other education that most Kalis lack. Theology, of course, but also science. It may surprise you to know that the Kalis were never schooled about the Tidal Works, unless it pertained specifically to a job at hand. Even then, none now grasp that machine the way you do. Basic functioning, energy transfer, tidal theory. Theory which now seems to be outdated, to put it mildly, but theory nevertheless. There was a reason we sent you to the University of Fom beyond the obvious need for you to be 'from' the Theocracy of N'narad. While until recent times it is true the Graces of Fom have been more reliable than the current situation suggests, the Merchant's Syndicate has for many decades foreseen the potential necessity of having our most direct link with the Theocracy be schooled in the nature of the most powerful city on Eris. An education which even the High Merchants themselves lack. At least those of us who remain. There may be clues within these pages we have overlooked but will lay themselves clear to you."

Daliius nodded through Kavik's words, his frown now more thoughtful than irritated. He looked down at the papers with renewed interest. "Something for the war effort."

Kavik bowed. "Break the Tidal Works and we break Fom. Let us put an end to this conflict and reestablish the proper order of things."

Daliius didn't respond as he leaned on the alter, the charred pages spread before him over the Great Book of Light. After a moment, Kavik nodded and showed himself out.

16

THE FATE OF A FRIEND

Syrina stood at the entrance to Ormo's chamber, fighting with herself. Her own mind and the voice both told her she needed to push through, but she dreaded what she might find.

Or not find, the voice reminded her for the hundredth time. *Don't think you know something you don't know. Not until you've seen it for yourself.*

Her plan had worked, even after discovering her mark had been a Seneschal and not a Kalis, which had almost gotten her killed. There were only a handful of others—mercenary captains and a few of their lieutenants—who knew who'd really been running things, and the Seneschal had been the only person who might have been able to tell Syrina and the other one apart. With her out of the way, Syrina got the name the other Kalis had been using from the paperwork, and made up something vague about sending the Seneschal Joana Baas away on an errand; from now on the Kalis would deal with the commanders directly.

Syrina hated the idea of slaves, but she didn't have time to let them go and hire a brand-new crew with fair wages, so she set the worst off free and did her best to arrange more livable conditions for the rest. Mann, she reassigned to be her "personal assistant," an order that made sense. He was old and knowledgeable, and with the Seneschal away, she'd need someone to take her place. She gave Ves a promotion too, though she made him promise to be nice to his underlings. He'd laughed that she'd gone soft since Valez'Mui and made a crack about nepotism, but he didn't complain.

She redirected their efforts to the area around where Ormo's hall used to be, or at least as close as she could guess. Within a couple of weeks, they'd hit another chamber, and eight days after that they'd dug out the entrance. It was deeper than the others they'd found. Remnants of the stairway were still there, and the chamber was more or less level. That it was intact both pleased her and filled her with dread.

And now, here she was, at the moment of truth.

Syrina pushed open the door.

The naphtha light from the lanterns mounted outside cast sharp shadows around the room, making the place alien and at the same time familiar. Grey dust covered everything, thicker in some places than others, and Syrina realized they were the ashes of the two Kalis she'd killed here.

As far as she could tell, Ormo's machines were more or less intact, at least as much as they'd been when she'd fled. It looked like his chamber's greater depth had been enough to save most of his work. Copper and brass pipes lay twisted and ruined against one wall where she'd thrown one of the Kalis, and the bulky machine between the two reclining chairs slumped to one side with loose wires and piping jutting out of it, but its central mass was still in one piece. The pipes were slagged and would need to be replaced, but Ka'id could handle that.

The remains of Anna lay strapped in one of the chairs. Syrina's heart lurched.

The air was dry in her tomb, and her skin still clung to her bones like yellowed parchment, charred in a few places. Her short hair jutted from her crinkled scalp like fine wires.

Swallowing, Syrina approached her. She couldn't tell how Anna had died. The room was intact. Beyond burns there was no obvious trauma, and those hadn't been enough to kill her.

Means nothing, the voice's tone was soothing. *Neither of us can imagine what the impact was like when the daystar hit. She could have died the instant it struck.* The voice trailed off, aware that Syrina was thinking about the alternative.

"*Lying here in the pitch black, strapped to this chair. Buried alive. Waiting to run out of air.*"

The destruction of the daystar her consciousness was trapped in probably shattered her mind. Even if it didn't kill her, she probably wasn't aware... The voice faded, realizing it wasn't helping.

The thin tube still connected Anna's spine to the machine behind her, but it came out with a little tug. Syrina noticed a flat spot on the back of Anna's head. That was...good, she thought. It could have happened when the daystar hit, jolting the room so hard Anna smashed her head against the thin padding of the reclining chair, killing her, or at least knocking her unconscious so she could die without suffering.

Or it could have been there before, because she'd been strapped in the same position for months before Syrina had come to save her—

She cut herself off. She was obsessing over something she would never find the answer to. Something she didn't even want to find the answer to. Of the two or three possibilities, all of them would make her feel some degree of awful.

She forced her attention back to the machine. The gages

were cracked, the copper piping buckled, and in places torn to pieces. The screen mounted on the top was shattered, but the complex tangle of wires, tubes, and circuitry behind it seemed like it had held together. Could Ka'id do anything with this? She looked back over to the pile of pipes, gages, and teak levers on the other side of the room. Syrina didn't even know if that mess had been part of the same machine. This room had been filled with stuff like that long before Anna had come here. The other screens—she'd thought they were windows the first time she'd seen them—were all smashed in an array to the right of the door. She'd seen them when she first came down here to confront Ormo, but most of them hadn't been working then either.

Just take it all to Ristro and let Ka'id sort it out.

Syrina took one more long, lingering look at Anna, then called up the tunnel. "Get everything in this room onto a steam truck. I don't care how broken it looks. And get Mann down here!"

A few seconds later she heard someone scrabbling down the steep, narrow passage the slaves had cleared through the stairway a few days before. He'd been waiting.

She tried to ignore the constant tug she felt toward the body of Anna slumped behind her. Mann appeared in the doorway.

"She's here," Syrina said; she saw surprise in Mann's face at the emotion in her voice. "Make sure they get her out. Treat her well. She should go home, if she can. Or at least to the forest. She hated this place. Get Ves to help you. No one else."

She thought he would say something to that, but sarcasm had never been his forte the way it was for Ves. She saw a thousand thoughts and opinions brush across his face before he responded with a simple nod, turned, and headed back up the tunnel.

It felt weird, she reflected, to be issuing commands as herself. No one raised an eyebrow anymore at a Kalis being in charge. She didn't know what that meant for the future of the world, and she didn't savor finding out.

Syrina brushed pass the crews forming up at the mouth of the tunnel and headed toward the ruined townhouse now serving as her command center, thinking of Pasha.

———

Syrina wondered why the previous Kalis had been using steam trucks to transport their finds to New Eheene, when camels would have been both faster and more reliable.

Maybe they got sick of trying to drive camels into a cloud of poison gas every day. Those things are miserable enough in the fresh air.

Yeah, there was that.

It had taken the rest of the day and into the night to load the trucks with everything from Ormo's chamber. She could sense tension when she'd given the order to keep working after dark, but she assured them again this would be their last job, and they'd be free as soon as they finished. That eased things, though then she worried about the mercenaries, who weren't pleased to be out of work before morning.

Them, she paid upfront, and promised they could have whatever was left in the coffers if they stuck around until the work was finished. After that, they were more agreeable.

Ves and Mann had gone in first to wrap Anna's body in a few soft leather rain cloaks Syrina requisitioned from the officers. They made sure the girl had one of the three trucks to herself, even if that meant they'd need to take an extra trip to get everything to the harbor. The slaves were focused on their freedom and the mercenaries on their bonus, so Syrina didn't think anyone noticed. If they did, they didn't say anything. Not to her anyway, and if they complained behind her back, she didn't care.

Her last assignment to the mercenaries was to escort their caravan as it plodded through the ruined city and make sure none of the other scavengers got any ideas. Even with the road cleared it was tedious. They needed to stop a half-dozen times to let some disgruntled line of snapping camels cross from a side street. Every group they passed gave their caravan of trucks a hungry look before moving on. There must have been millions of Syndicate Bank Three-Sides buried around Eheene, Ves pointed out, heaped in depositories and private vaults. It was no wonder more people kept showing up.

Between Syrina and Ves, it only took them two days to scam a boat. A real tarfuel steamship, even if its hull was corroded and green, and it only had one stack. "Still better than a fucking sail boat," Ves had declared, and Syrina didn't bother arguing because she didn't care either way. She wanted to leave the bones of Eheene and never look back.

They took an extra day to go up the coast. They buried Anna on the ridge overlooking Aado, next to Saphi. Syrina and Mann had both wanted to take her back to the valley someday, but Ves reminded them that Anna had always said she never wanted to go back there. No one spoke as they stood together over her small cairn, but Syrina knew they all agreed the two girls would get along.

As they boarded Ves' nameless ship the pirate had taken to calling The Anna, Syrina felt more relieved and focused than she had since she'd fled the fires of Eheene almost four years ago.

Which, the voice pointed out, was good. She had a few things left to do.

She had first suggested they go directly to the Fom river

port along the Great Road, then wondered aloud why ships didn't always do that, rather than going around the Upper Peninsula or through Maresg, back when that was an option.

"A few ships *can* do that," Mann told her. "But none of the big steam ships can dock on the river—no space and not deep enough. The navy can sail up the middle of the Road fine enough, but docking there? That's another matter."

"More than that," Ves added. "Water from the Wastes eats away at hulls like you wouldn't believe. It was cheaper for most captains to pay Maresg or take the time to go around. Coating hulls of barges like the Flowered Calf probably cost twice the fee Maresg charged, and they'd need to reapply it after every few round trips. Hell, you saw how the Calf looked by the time we got to Fom. Worth it to get all the way to Great Spring or Valez'Mui. Just for the rare trip up from Skalkaad? Not so much."

"Fine, I get it. We'll go around," she muttered, and let the matter drop, feeling ganged up on.

———

"I'm not going to Ristro," Ves stated for the fiftieth time as they rounded the Upper Peninsula.

Syrina was beginning to think he meant it, but they'd run out of any other subject she felt like talking about since they'd left New Eheene ten days before, so she kept at it out of boredom. "It's been what? Thirty years? I'm sure the Astrologers have forgiven you by now." She swilled a mouthful of rum from the bottle. "For whatever it is you did to them."

Ves took the bait, though Syrina suspected it was only because he had nothing better to talk about either. "I'm not that old, witch. Twenty-three years. Or twenty-four. Twenty-five? Anyway, not thirty. And if you think those fucks are the forgiving sort, you haven't been around them long enough. Besides, *I'm* not the forgiving sort either, so fuck them and fuck their wretched, bug-infested peninsula."

She saw Mann roll his eyes and dropped it for now. They sat together at the little round table in the mess. Ves was due back in the wheelhouse any minute, to swing them east towards Fom, and she didn't want to keep him distracted.

"Fine," she sighed. "We can drop you off in Fom. Mann, too. I'll go by myself." Her vague sense of urgency had been growing since they left Skalkaad, but she kept it to herself. Taking them to Fom had been her plan all along, and she thought maybe after all this talk about Ristro they'd finally be ready to listen.

"Who's going to pilot my ship?" Ves asked at the same time Mann said, "I don't want to go to Fom."

Syrina looked at Ves. "I'll drive it. How hard could it be?"

Ves rolled his eyes and started to say something, but before he could get the words out, she turned to Mann. "And you *both* need to be in Fom. I doubt anyone will recognize you. Not if you're careful. If you want to stop this war, we need to stop it at both ends, or the other side will just escalate things. I need to bring all this junk to Ka'id, so she can figure out what the Arch Bishop and his handlers have been after, but the Grace started this war, and now that she has the blackvine, she won't end it if she thinks she's winning."

Mann frowned. "You want us to take care of the blackvine then."

Syrina shrugged, exaggerating the gesture enough so the others could see it. She'd grown used to her own skin, and she found herself reluctant to don another one. "I doubt you can get rid of it. Not completely. That baby is out of the crib, as they say, and there's no putting it back in. But you can at least stall production on this end of the Great Road. If the Grace needs to go back to the Black Wall to get more, it should slow things down enough that she might start considering other options."

Ves grunted. "You want the Arch Bishop to win?"

But Syrina was shaking her head before he'd even gotten the question out. "Have you been listening? I don't want anyone to win. Or lose. I just want both sides to give up. Even after her failure in Maresg, the Grace has the advantage because of the blackvine. We need to recreate the stalemate that was going on before—long enough that Ka'id can pull whatever she's been planning out of her ass. Then, well, we'll see."

"How are we supposed to halt Fom's blackvine production?" Mann asked.

"I don't know. You have more experience with that shit than I do. I'm sure you'll think of something."

Ves scowled. "Was this your idea all along? Why you asked us to go to Fom, even though your contact is in Ristro? You thought you'd get me all riled up about going to Ristro so I'd be lubed to do your dirty work somewhere else?"

She shrugged and tried to look innocent under the tattoos. Her two companions lapsed into an irritable silence.

We should take that as a win, I guess.

Syrina looked between the two sullen men, but nothing else seemed to be forthcoming, so she stood without comment and went back to the hold, which doubled as her quarters, and slumped down against Ormo's mangled machines. "Now that that's settled, what are we going to do until we get to Fom?"

I don't know. Brood?

17

RETURN TO FOM

VES AND MANN CLAMBERED FROM THE LIFEBOAT A DAY'S walk south from Fom. A span up from the beach ran the lone, southern road, abandoned and overgrown decades before the Grace had started her war. Once, villages had clung to the coast all the way to the Ristro border, but Corsairs had pushed the people north into the city before Mann had been born. Ves wondered if things would be different now, if anyone were to move back there. The Astrologers had become less aggressive these past decades, but he didn't know if that had made things better or worse. Maybe if the Grace had needed to worry more about pirates, she wouldn't have gotten it in her mind to go independent.

He'd complained and cursed at Syrina, who was taking his ship yet again. Her assurances that she could at least manage to keep it pointed south until she got close to Vormisæn didn't ease his mind. Well, fuck, he'd thought as he watched her sail away towards the clouds building on the horizon. There'd be plenty of boats in Fom he could steal. Again.

The two men walked up the coast together, not talking

much. They were cautious of patrols, but not overly so. Even after four years, this was a naval war, and most of the Grace's forces would be guarding the Bowl of Fom and the mouth of the Upper Great Road, driving off the Arch Bishop's next attempt at a blockade. Still, Mann said there'd be more security as they neared Fom, and he knew more about that sort of thing than Ves did, so they picked their way through the scrub and scraggly trees twenty hands to the side of the road, waiting to take cover at the first sign of anyone else.

They were watching the land ahead so intently they didn't see the dirigible until it was almost too late. It came over the line of hills from the east, no more than thirty hands above the tops of the gnarled pines that dusted the northern part of the Ristro Peninsula. Mann heard the faint thrumming of its propeller at the same time as Ves, and they only had a second or two to dive into the underbrush.

It passed over them. The bottom of its nose was glass, and Ves thought he could make out a pair of faces peering down, scanning the abandoned shoreline, though with the sun glinting off the brass frame, he couldn't be sure. As it reached the sea, it turned south and floated down the coast, following the old road until it vanished in the haze. The sky was growing ever blacker in that direction, and he found himself wondering how Syrina fared with his ship.

"Never seen one like that before," he said as they stood and brushed themselves off before continuing north. "You?"

Mann shook his head. "This Grace was always keen on developing more airships. She saw it as the future, difficult as the weather might make them to fly. I suppose it was foolish to assume she'd only been focused on blackvine."

Ves looked again at the storm clouds bubbling in the south. "Well, however good she makes them, I'd bet that one's going to be heading back this way sooner rather than later."

Mann looked up and down the road and scratched at his grey whiskers. He'd grown a full beard since they'd left Maresg. "We should be almost to the vineyards. I think they start just over that hill. No, not the next one—the higher one, a span or so ahead. From there, we can blend in with the indentured servants." He glanced at Ves, who loomed dark and surly even with the hood of his dirty grey cloak pulled over his head, hiding the diamonds in his skull. "At least as far as that airship is concerned. You're going to stand out where ever you go. I don't know why Syrina thought you wouldn't."

Ves scoffed. "She didn't, old man. She was just trying to get us to agree to what she wanted us to do, like goddamn always. And like goddamn always it worked, because here we are."

Mann nodded, slow and thoughtful. "I guess," he said after a moment. "But that doesn't mean she was wrong about it. Anyway, I'm looking forward to sticking it to the Grace. Even if it ends up being the last thing I do."

"Ha! Speak for yourself. You're old as bones, anyway. I don't want this shit to be the last thing *I* do. I've got the second half of my life to worry about." But Ves smiled to himself as he trudged through the bushes, keeping pace with Mann and the old general's newfound energy.

———

"Those aren't grapes." Ves' tone was dry.

They stood on the hill overlooking the gentle slope that rolled down to the valley where vineyards once spread. Fog shrouded the ridge three spans further on, beyond which lay the city of Fom. Where once quiet, neat rows of grapevines stretched to the distant hills ahead and the Sea of N'narad to their left, there were now tangles of black brambles set in hurried rows. The estates were gone, replaced with sunken stone buildings that belched so much smoke and steam they seemed to be competing with the Tidal Works spluttering beyond the far hills. Patrols of soldiers marched the perimeter, and smaller clusters of mercenaries and foremen wandered fields.

"Blackvine," Mann said, knowing it was pointless but feeling the need to say something.

"I guess we know the answer to the question, 'will blackvine grow around Fom?'"

It was Mann's turn to grunt. "What now?"

There was no humor in Ves' laugh. "You heard the Kalis. 'Destroy the blackvine.' Easy, right? You know how to do that?"

Mann sighed.

At that moment, the dirigible that had flown over them earlier—or a different one of the same design—came flying up from the south, higher than it had been. They scrambled to duck into the undergrowth before he answered. "Burning it will turn it hard as stone. Doesn't kill it, from what Pasha told me, but the bushes won't be usable again until next year."

Ves poked his head out and watched the seething activity of the plantation. "How do we do that?"

Mann looked with him, but didn't answer.

They crouched in silence for a few minutes, studying the activity, before Mann sighed again and gestured to a new, long wooden building on the very eastern edge of the shallow valley. "There. That building is one of the new barracks. It must be—there's nothing else a building like that is good for. My guess is, the servants stay there." He squinted into the fog and pointed again. "And there. Another one just like it. There are probably more too, closer to the city. There would need to be, what with all the people down there."

Ves followed his finger. "Fine. What about them?"

"They're guarded, but not overly so. They're watching the blackvine, not the servants' quarters."

"Servants. They paid well enough to be a problem for us?"

Mann hmphed a chuckle. "A pittance. They're indentured; probably the same families that used to work the vineyards. So no, they're not technically slaves, but most won't be freed from service for a few generations."

Ves frowned. "That sounds like a lot of words for 'slave.' But fine. Only, we're after blackvine, not fucking 'servants.'"

Mann nodded. "How many people do you think are working here at any given time? Five hundred?"

Ves studied the scene. "Sure, three, five hundred maybe. Hard to tell with the fog."

"The fog will help. You stand out—if anything gets us killed, it will be that."

"Fine, fine," Ves grumbled. "What's your plan?"

"As long as people come and go from those longhouses when they're supposed to be coming and going from them, and they're not doing anything untoward, they won't be noticed. Look at the guards milling around and the indentured scattered all over the place doing whatever jobs come up. They're not organized enough to notice two new faces down there. Not mine anyway."

"That's your guess."

"That's my guess."

"And what about me? Keep saying I'll stand out, and I won't disagree with that."

Mann studied Ves out of the corner of his eye. "I don't know. Just stay low, I suppose, and try to look like you belong. You wouldn't be the first captured Corsair working off his sentence."

Ves nodded. "Might as well try it, since I don't have a better plan. You're right. They look as organized as a discount whorehouse. They'll notice us in the barracks though. Probably packed full the way it is."

The old general studied the scene a moment more and frowned an agreement. "Good point. We'll lay low tonight and move off over the eastern ridge where we can wait until dawn or a little before. We'll be able to slip around the house and join the others when they come out for work in the morning. If we time it right."

"Probably. If we time it right. What do we do with our weapons?"

If Mann noticed the cynicism in Ves' voice, he ignored it. "Stash them in the scrub outside of camp, I suppose. Anyway, until you come up with something better, we're doing my plan. If you don't like it, don't ask me for ideas." He gave the pirate a crooked grin and headed off towards the eastern ridge, his ever-present limp barely noticeable as he navigated the scrubby trees and rocky outcroppings that ran to the tilled land some hundred hands below them.

Ves wondered as he started after the old general. There'd been a dozen times in the past three years he'd thought Mann was done for, but now that he had something to do, he seemed to be getting younger by the minute.

———

It rained all night. Ves doubted their ability to blend in with the indentured when they were more or less dry and he and Mann were dripping wet, but after sitting awake until dawn, trying and failing to shelter under the shallow overhang of a misshapen boulder, he didn't have the energy to argue. Anyway, Mann had that look on his face like he'd be a stubborn old shit about it if he brought it up. Ves hadn't slept, and he was sure Mann hadn't either.

It turned out the servants that streamed out of the long-houses into the drizzle that morning were too exhausted to notice, or at least if anything struck them as odd, they didn't bother looking like they cared. True to Mann's prediction, the lack of discipline among the guards kept them from paying attention to anyone who seemed to be doing what they were supposed to. Ves wondered how many times Mann had had other ideas since they'd been traveling together that he'd either not bothered mentioning or the pirate had ignored out of hand.

"Listen to your elders," he muttered to himself. "Better fucking late than never, I guess."

If Mann heard that from where he stumbled over the uneven ground two paces ahead, he didn't show it.

They had no idea how to go about torching the blackvine, and as long as the drizzle held, nothing they'd try would work, so what followed was three days of falling in with the hordes of other servants and clipping vines that had grown long enough to cart them over to the boiler rooms, there to be de-thorned and coiled. Within the first hour, they were both slashed and bleeding from the brambles—even through the leather aprons and gloves they'd grabbed from the bins flanking the entrance to the longhouse. However the valley people had worked with blackvine, Ves was willing to bet the next ship he stole they were better at not shredding themselves every time they touched it.

Housing proved to be complicated their first night, but not as bad as they'd feared. As Mann guessed, there weren't enough beds already, and due to the chaos they were first come first serve, except for a few closest to the stoves, which belonged to the unofficial bosses at each house, the determination of which, Ves assured Mann, was unimportant. He'd been in enough jails to know how things worked. It didn't matter what country it was in—it was always the same. He also knew he could have the best bed in the house uncontested within the week, but that sort of thing tended to get the wrong kind of attention. He stood out enough the way it was.

Mann was worried about the disorganization, even if it worked in their favor, and he whispered to Ves about it their first night in the house, huddled together on the floor in the shadows furthest from the stoves.

"This isn't like the Grace I knew." He glanced around at the others cramped around them, but they were all either sleeping or whispering their own conversations. "Not at all. The Grace I served would keep an operation like this running as smooth as the Tidal Works."

Ves shrugged under his thin blanket. "You saying there's a new Grace?

The old general scowled. "You know that's not what I'm saying."

Ves didn't open his eyes. "So, maybe she doesn't know how bad it is."

He heard the rustle of Mann's shaking head. "It's only a half-day trip from Wise Hall to these plantations, and this is the most important thing she's got this side of the Yellow Desert, unless there's some other secret operation we don't know about. Even if there is—and I don't know what it would be—this is the second most important thing. She wouldn't neglect it. Not like this."

Ves opened his eyes. Mann was lost in the shadows, but the old man's eyes glinted in the dim light from the central stoves. "You're ranting. Anyway, if it was organized as well as you think it should be, we'd either be still sleeping in the fucking rain under a rock or dead by now, so quit your bitching." He shut his eyes again.

Mann didn't respond, but Ves could feel him lying awake on the floor next to him until the pirate fell asleep.

———

Four days after the rain stopped, Mann declared that it was dry enough. The sun had blared down onto the vineyards since the weather broke, and by the second day, the steam belched from the kilns mingled with clouds of dust kicked up by slaves. Ves didn't know anything about blackvine, other than he liked swords made out of it, so he announced he'd go along with whatever Mann decided. They left from the longhouse like they always did, but this time they skirted around the edge of the plantation towards the boiling sheds—earthen bunkers that did their best to mimic what Mann had described of the kilns in the valley. Twenty miserable indentured crouched along the low stone wall of the nearest one, slicing long thorns from the coils with serrated bronze knives, their hands cut and bleeding through shredded leather gloves. A pair of guards stood nearby, watching and chatting together, looking bored.

"More mercenaries," Mann whispered, his voice concerned. "These guys don't give a shit about the Heavens. They're here to get paid."

Ves smirked. "Didn't think you gave a shit about Heaven anymore either."

"I don't," Mann said as they walked towards the boiler house. He tried to look like he didn't want to be there, which was easy enough, since he didn't. "But whatever you think of the Church of N'narad, at least it breeds loyalty."

Ves stopped and glanced at the old man, who hovered a pace behind him. The guards had stopped chatting and watched the pair as they approached, but they didn't seem motivated for a confrontation. "So that's a good thing, right?" He didn't bother keeping his voice down as he turned to face the guards. "People only in it for the money are easier to deal with."

"Get back to work," the shorter of the two ordered. "You'd better be here to—"

Ves lurched towards them with his impressive speed. They didn't have a chance to get their swords up from where they'd been drawn and hanging in their hands before he smashed their faces together. They fell to the ground, coughing and clutching at broken noses, swords dropped into the dry mud, blood gushing between their fingers. Without missing a beat, Ves picked up one of the blades and ran each man through the back of the neck.

The line of indentured crouched against the wall dropped their work and began to stir in panic. Mann wheeled on them. "Stay where you are," he hissed, glancing around. None of the meandering patrols were near, and it looked like it had happened fast enough that none noticed. "Nothing to see here. Not yet. If we get our way, you'll all be free by the end of the day, but if you make a scene, more guards will come. If that happens, we'll get killed and you'll go back to shredding your hands."

They muttered and stirred, but half of them crouched back down, convincing the others to do the same. One old woman looked up at Mann. "I recognize you. Even with the beard. I recognize you."

Ves started dragging bodies into the kiln house, and Mann moved to help him. "Maybe, maybe not," Ves said to her. "Either way, keep it to yourself." He handed Mann the second sword.

Heat and humidity rolled over them as they ducked through the low, open door. A massive stone cauldron boiled in the center, spewing steam through the hole in the ceiling. Coils of de-thorned vines lay jumbled along one side. Two men worked at a heavy wooden bench, long and curved to fit against the wall, hammering boiled vine into broad plates. Not armor or weapons. The hull of a ship maybe, or the frame for a dirigible.

An old woman in rags hunched at the stack of logs where she'd been gathering an arm-load to feed the fire, but she saw Ves and the corpses and let out a choked scream. The two men at the bench turned.

"Shit," Ves grunted and charged them. Mann stumbled behind. The sudden change in temperature made his bad hip grind in pain, but he needn't have worried. The two smiths were already exhausted, and they were unarmed beyond the heavy wood mallets they were using for their craft. Ves smashed their faces together like he'd done with the guards outside and lifted his sword, but Mann grabbed his arm.

"You don't need to kill them. They probably don't want to be here anymore than the thorn pickers outside. Let's just get this done and everyone can go home." He looked down at the two men crumpled on the floor, clutching their faces and raised his voice. "Right?"

When they didn't respond he poked one with his foot. "Right?"

They both nodded. He looked to the old woman. She clung to the forgotten brace of logs in her thin arms. She blinked, then nodded too.

"See?" Mann said. Ves still towered over the smiths, sword in hand. "You don't need to kill everyone we meet."

Ves eyed them a moment longer and lowered his blade. "Maybe it makes me feel better. Fine. Let's get out of here."

Mann gathered up four bulky tarfuel lanterns set about the room, and Ves picked up the half-full pony keg of spare fuel. Then they both selected a long, burning log from the kiln. The old woman sat down with a grunt on a stool by the stack of wood, while the two smiths watched through their fingers from where they squatted, clutching their faces.

Ves hefted the tank. "This going to be enough?"

Mann shrugged.

"Ha! That's what I thought. What about weapons?"

"You mean those swords? Leave them. If we need to fight, we've lost. Unless you think you can take every mercenary this side of Fom by yourself."

Ves sighed and tossed the swords into the raging fire. "Fine. Let's go."

Mann's plan was to get to the cliff, where the wind tore up from the Sea of N'narad, but they only made it two-thirds of the way there before Ves' bulk finally caught the attention of a patrol of mercenaries.

"You!" a woman leading the group called out.

Ves growled. "Fucking first day of clear goddamn weather. Go figure."

"Shit," Mann said. He pointed into the rows of blackvine. Ves took the signal and barreled through, the thorns tearing at his legs and arms. He ignored the blood that began dribbling down his limbs and started pouring a thin line of tarfuel along the ground.

Mann shambled behind him. Shouting and disarray welled from the edge of the plantation, but the mercenaries seemed reluctant to charge into the thorns, so they picked their way around on the crooked path, aiming to intercept Ves and Mann on the far side. Ahead, Ves cast the empty barrel into the bushes and unslung the pair of lanterns from where he'd looped them onto his shoulders, tearing the lids off and spraying their greasy, dark contents all around. After the last one was empty, he slowed. They'd sprinted half way across the vineyard. Mercenaries still trailed them, but a few had realized what they planned and began yelling at others to go back. More closed from the east along the rows, quicker than the ones behind them had been able to, ignoring the cries for retreat.

"What now?" Ves yelled at Mann.

Mann's lungs burned, and his hip shot spears down his thigh and up his side. He laughed. "We'd better keep running," he said, his calm voice belaying his heart pounding in his chest.

Ves laughed with him, and Mann dropped the torch.

18

WHAT AILS THE GRACE

GENERAL ROHM STOOD ON THE RIDGE BETWEEN FOM AND the plantations a day after fire had swept through the vineyards. Smoke still boiled from the blackvine. It had spread to what remained of the surrounding forest before Eyerise, but by morning the wind had died and with it the fiercest of the flames. Most of the area had already been cleared of trees to fuel the boilers, and now the fire had scorched the remaining groves away. The bareness of the hills around the vineyards saddened him, but at least the blaze had had no chance to spread to the estates on the edge of the city.

Behind him, though, a dozen fires still burned through Fom. The eternal fog hid most of them, but the occasional rumble of ruptured Tidal Works valves still rolled up to him, and the air was rancid with the smoke of burning buildings. The Arch Bishop's agents had struck hard, but by all reports the Grace's paranoia had paid off, at least this time. She'd increased the guard around Tidal Works access points fourfold, over the objections of both her Finance and Social Welfare Ministers, and the Arch Bishop's attack had sputtered and failed. Rohm shuddered to think what would happen if—when—they tried again. If the Grace's enemies could cripple the Tidal Works, they would win the war in an afternoon.

When he'd heard reports that the blackvine had been sabotaged just a few hours before the first explosions had rocked Fom, Rohm and everyone else had assumed it had been a coordinated attack on the city's two greatest resources. Now, though, he wasn't sure. The more details he heard about the attack on the blackvine, the more it sounded like the work of a pair of independent saboteurs—a Ristroan Corsair and a limping old man. Or rather, they'd sparked the rebellion among the rest of the indentured working the vines. They'd taken advantage of the disorganization that had bothered Rohm since he'd returned from the Black Wall, infiltrated the camp, and burned the area to the ground. The botanists assured the Grace that all the vines still lived and would grow again next spring, but despite the slow supply coming from the far end of the Great Road, the blackvine foundries had ground to a halt until then.

All this while the disastrous attack on Maresg still distracted him. She hadn't consulted him about the details, and it wasn't until it was long over that he'd heard about the slaughter of civilians by the Grace's command. There was a certain logic to it, he conceded, but the stories brought back dark memories of his first trip to the valley in the Black Wall. In the short term, had she succeeded, she would have gained some advantage by thinning a hostile population, but history had shown time after time that the people of the Upper Peninsula had very long memories, and the advantage to such slaughter would have turned to seething rage sooner rather than later. Likely, it already had. But what haunted him most about the whole affair was that it had been the Grace herself who'd taught him the lesson of mercy.

But what bothered Rohm most at the moment was the description of the two blackvine saboteurs. A huge Ristroan and an old man. Like the pair who'd escaped from the Pit of Fom four years ago. His mind circled. What were the odds the old man was General Mann? What were the odds he wasn't?

His thoughts grated to a stop at the sound of a steamcar trundling up the road from the city, stopping twenty hands from where he and his pair of silent retainers stood, staring at the burning blackvine below.

"General Rohm," a voice called. A young man he didn't recognize leaned out the window. "I know you've got your hands full, but I've got an urgent message for you."

"It's fine," Rohm said, walking to the car. "Who is it from?"

"Just a house guard, I'm afraid. Torala N'gal. I know we shouldn't bother you with the worries of someone only written in the Book of Water, but she swore on her life and her place in Heaven it was that important. She said she had a message that needed to be delivered to you, personally." He paused. "We know each other, Torala and I. Well enough that I trust her, and well enough she trusted me to give this to you." He passed a sealed envelope out the window to Rohm, who took it, frowning.

The driver misread his expression. "As I said, General, I'm sorry. I wouldn't have bothered you if—"

"No, no," Rohm said, breaking the plain wax seal and opening the envelope. "My irritation isn't with you. I encourage my soldiers to follow their instincts. But Torala was supposed to wait for me to..." His voice trailed off as he read.

He looked up. The driver was watching him, waiting. "Take me to Torala now, please. She's on duty at Wise Hall, yes?"

The driver got out of the car and opened the rear door. "That's right, General. She said you would want to meet right away. Told me I should wait for you so I could drive you back. Guess she's got good instincts too."

Rohm leaned out the window and called to his two retainers still standing at the top of the ridge, "Take over the investigation here. I think we've got all the details, but be sure. I'll take your reports tonight."

The pair nodded, but the steamcar was already turning around.

———

Rohm flipped through the jumbled ream of papers Torala N'gal handed him. They stood just inside the servants' entrance to Wise Hall on the damp marble flagstones of the foyer, sheltering from the drizzle of Fom pattering the path outside. Torala N'gal stood a few paces away, watching.

Rohm looked up at her. "This N'dora has worked in the kitchen for the better part of two years. I asked for someone recent."

Torala N'gal nodded, as if she'd expected him to say that. "Yes, but he's the second most recent addition to the Grace's staff. Not exactly what you'd call high turnover, here."

He looked through the papers again. "It says he's over seventy years old."

"Yes. Born and raised in Fom, or just outside."

Rohm frowned. He liked N'gal, but he was getting a growing feeling she was wasting his time. "You said second most recent. You checked the first?"

"Yes, General. Of course. A thirteen-year-old Temple boy arrived a year ago. He cleans the Cathedral after mass. I don't think he's ever met the Grace."

Rohm blinked. "A Temple boy brought in from the streets a year ago is the most recent addition to the staff?"

"Yes, General. Any others have mostly been pressed into military service since then. Like I said, not a high turnover."

"Ah. I hadn't thought of the draft touching the Grace's personal staff. So, this N'dora...what makes you suspect him?"

Torala N'gal's face fell. "I'm sorry General. I didn't mean to mislead you. No, I don't just suspect him. He's the man you're looking for. I'm sure of it."

Rohm raised his eyebrows and gestured for her to continue.

"We—Korbat and I—we followed the paperwork. This N'dora cleared all the checks, had all the documents. His previous job was at a restaurant just at the base of Wise Hill—Finnian's Bowl."

"Yes, I can read."

Torala N'gal cleared her throat. "So, Korbat and I went down there on our day off, you know, to talk to the owner. We asked him about N'dora. Yes, he used to work there. Yes, he's about seventy now. But while we're there, Korbat describes him to Finnian—that's the owner, obviously. Just to make sure it's the right guy. Korbat's hunch. So, he describes him, and some things seem off. Nothing definite, but off, you know? They start talking about whether or not N'dora has a big nose, the color of his eyes, cheekbones. That sort of thing. They can't quite agree on anything."

Rohm's frown was more thoughtful than agitated now, but he said, "A restaurateur's shaky memory of a cook that he last saw two years ago is not reason to pull me from the disaster at the vineyards."

Unconcerned, Torala N'gal pressed on. "I agree, General. And I told Korbat it wasn't much to go on, but he insisted something was off, and I agreed, so we decided we should talk to this N'dora ourselves. Before coming to you."

Rohm nodded. "You met with him? Maybe I'd like to meet him myself."

"I'm afraid that won't be possible, General."

"Oh?"

Torala N'gal took a deep breath. "We came back here and tracked him down in the kitchen, said we wanted a word. He seemed nervous, but the thing of it was, he didn't seem nervous enough, if you know what I mean. His voice was nervous, but something in his face...it just didn't strike us, Korbat and I, as someone who cared that he was being questioned by the House Guard. And no, that wasn't enough to call you, either, but it was one more thing that seemed a little wrong. It was building up, all of this, you know what I mean? So, while Korbat and N'dora are chatting, I went to N'dora's room—he somehow became one of the lieutenant chefs in just under a year, so he has—had—his own room. I tore the place apart. Was about to give up when I came across a loose floor stone under a bedpost. Just by chance—was about to go back and tell Korbat we had the wrong guy. And then there it was. I moved the bed to look underneath one more time and it made a funny sound. Still took me ten minutes to find what was causing it..." She realized by Rohm's face she was losing him again.

"So, anyway, I found this." She held out a leather purse.

Rohm took it and peered inside. It was half full of some dusty, sticky brown paste "What is it?"

"I tracked down another cook to ask just that. I thought maybe it could be some secret spice N'doral used or something, but no. It's an extract from the blovey fungus."

"You mean those big mushrooms that grow in the swamp around Maresg?"

"That's right."

"Don't they make wine out of that stuff up there?"

Torala N'gal nodded. "Yes. They call it wine, but really, it's a mild narcotic. Poisonous before it's fermented. Causes confusion, nervousness, lack of focus, eventually blood clots and death. In small doses it's flavorless, but it builds up in the body."

The papers hung limp and forgotten at Rohm's side now as he stared at her. "Another cook told you that?"

"Yes General. I asked how she knew. Turns out she grew up in a fishing village close to Maresg before joining the Church. It's not secret knowledge or anything, mind you. I'd wager everyone from Maresg knows those toadstools are bad news until you brew them right."

"Maybe he was making his own blovey wine. You said it was a narcotic."

"No. That's what I thought too. It was the next thing I asked about. It's a big setup to make blovey wine. Big enough people would notice it, and anyway, the cook said this wasn't enough to make much more than two or three bottles. Not worth the cost and hassle without access to a bunch of mushrooms. I'd wager that's why they make it around Maresg and nowhere else. And no reason to have this extract for that—they make blovey wine with the whole cap."

"And N'dora?"

"Yeah, so I went back to where Korbat and him were talking. The old man had Korbat thinking he was clean as anything, just like I thought before I found the bag. He was about to let him go when I asked about this pouch."

"And?"

"As soon as I pulled it out the old guy hit Korbat so hard he broke his nose and knocked out four teeth. Before I could blink, he was gone. Out of the room. I swear, no sign anywhere. A few hours later one of the servants found his clothes in the basement, but no sign of the old man."

Rohm had gone pale, but he regained his composure. "I see." His voice sounded flat to his own ears. "And Korbat is recovering, I take it?"

She nodded. "In the Grace's Hospice, General."

"Did this cook you spoke to mention how long the effects linger?"

Her expression grew grim. "Depends on how long they've been ingesting it. Weeks if they stop early enough. Sometimes months. Sometimes never."

"Thank you," Rohm said, still feeling far away. He needed to sit down and think. "And tell Korbat next time you see him I said thank you too. You've performed a great service to Fom. I will personally see to it you are both elevated into the Book of Flowers, with no increase to your Salvation Taxes."

She chewed her lip. "Just our job, General." She paused. "You think the Grace will be alright now?"

Rohm turned from where he was just stepping out the door into the rain, which was coming down fitfully now. "Better than she would be otherwise, yes. And keep this to yourselves, please."

He heard her say, "Yes, General," just before the door clicked behind him.

19

LAST TRIP TO VORMISÆN

Syrina was impressed with the setup the Vormisæn
Astrologer had provided Ka'id. They'd cleared a two-level
brownstone townhouse a few long blocks from the prefecture
building of every non-integral wall on the second floor, where
they'd set up five tarfuel generators connected to copper venti-
lation shafts. Ka'id used the bottom floor as her residence—a
modest set of three equal rooms with a heated bath in the back,
though she'd been spending so much time upstairs Kirin had set
up a cot for her in one corner. She'd proved herself as apt as she
claimed she'd be at sorting out Ormo's research; Ka'id had spent
her years as a High Merchant, not just financing the study of
the Tidal Works, but studying them herself.

Syrina almost hadn't made it to the northern-most Ristroan
city. The storm she'd sailed into after dropping off Mann and
Ves had turned out to be more than she could handle, as much
as she'd never admit it to Ves, and it had taken all her limited
skills as a navigator just to crash the little ship along the boul-
der-strewn shore. It was that or get washed out of view of land
and lost until the clouds cleared and she could navigate by sun.

She'd wrecked another one of Ves' ships, but the hold had held itself together, and she ended up only a few spans from an old road leading to one of the now-abandoned shipyards that dotted the coast. Her disguise had comprised of mud smeared over her tattoos and rags she'd found rotting in the shipyard, but it had been enough to hail help from a nearby plantation, and after a little chat with the Astrologer, the farmers she met were happy to go back with her on ramshackle steam trucks to help her salvage Ormo's equipment.

The Astrologer—the same one she'd met when she'd come to Vormisæn all those years ago—looked the same; an old man with a dusting of white hair and laugh lines creasing his face. He'd been expecting her. With a lack of words she found surprising given how much the Ristroan Astrologers liked to pontificate, he requested she change into something that would make her look "inoffensive to the people" and had a pair of his personal guard escort her to Ka'id. The truck with Ormo's machines had already been delivered.

"You've been busy," Syrina stated, looking at the tangle of pipes, cables, and generators scattered around the second floor.

Ka'id looked up from where she was lying under a four-legged device that looked like a kitchen cabinet covered in dials, quietly cursing. Tools were scattered on the floor next to her. Kirin, dressed again as a maid, held one edge of the device off the floor, and nodded to Syrina with a smile.

"Hello," Ka'id said, scooting out from under the machine to stand and wipe her hands on her dirty canvas pants. "Took you long enough. I was starting to think the Syndicate or someone got you a month ago."

Syrina looked around for a seat and retrieved a crooked stool sitting forgotten behind a pile of crates near the stairway. She set it next to Ka'id's machine and sat down before she spoke. "You don't have people in Eheene?"

Ka'id sighed. "What people I have anywhere are in this room now, I'm afraid, minus a few...well, 'friends' isn't the right word. Allies, shall we say, in Tyrsh. And the Astrologers, I suppose, though I'd hardly call them 'my people.'"

Syrina looked around again. "Not very organized," she quipped. "For all of Ormo's faults, at least he didn't run the risk of tripping over something and knocking his brains out onto the floor while he worked."

The former High Merchant laughed, but Syrina didn't think there was much humor in it. "Give it a week. If we can get some of this junk functioning, it should be by then. Then we can worry about cleaning the floor." She gestured to Ormo's notes resting in a neat stack on an overturned crate. "Ormo spent years figuring all this out so we could put it back together again. I sometimes enjoy thinking about how angry that would have made him."

Syrina rose, sauntered over to the papers, and began to thumb through them. "Where did you get these?"

Ka'id's voice grew serious, and she and Kirin came over to stand around the crate with her. "Now that you're here, that's something I'd like to discuss. After you left, Kirin and I went to the coast, but I sent her back to scrounge up support among those allies I mentioned, as well as put some things in place for what comes next."

"Which was more successful than I thought it would be," Kirin interjected. "Successful enough to know we have a problem."

"Who has a problem?" Syrina asked, dreading the answer.

Kirin shrugged. "All of us. Everyone. It turns out the Arch Bishop got his hands on some of Ormo's work too. All his research about the Tidal Works, or at least enough of it."

Syrina frowned. "What do you mean, 'enough.' I didn't

even know he'd been researching the Tidal Works on top of everything else he was up to."

"Not to the extent that I was," Ka'id answered. "Nor for as long, but it seems one of his Kalis had dug up some information on the machines under Fom, which piqued his interest."

"Oh."

"Apparently this Kalis of his came up with some theories about the Artifact at the center. The one storing all the tidal energy from the Eye." Ka'id gave Syrina a meaningful look she tried to ignore.

"I figured that's the Artifact you meant. Unless there's another one, in which case I don't think I want to know about it."

"No, that's the one. It seems the Arch Bishop has developed an... unhealthy interest in such a device."

"Oh. How unhealthy?"

Kirin made a face. "Rumor has it, he wants to disrupt it. Destroy it outright if he can, and apparently he thinks he has enough information to do just that."

"Oh, shit." Syrina lapsed into silence as she thought for a minute. "We could just let him know what that would do, at least according to every working theory. Wouldn't that scare him off?"

Ka'id shook her head. "He already knows."

Kirin was shaking her head too. "That's how I found out about this. People have been too loyal to him to talk until now." She glanced at her master, but Ka'id was staring in thought at the machine she'd been working on, and Kirin went on. "The Syndicate has a lot of people in Eheene, but I'm sure you already figured that out. They'd recovered some of Ormo's research from his estate just outside the city."

"Shit," Syrina said. "I should have thought of that. Searching his estate, I mean."

Ka'id gave a dismissive wave. "Even if it had occurred to you, you wouldn't have been able to find the facilities under his house if you hadn't already been there. Not in the time you had." She gestured at Kirin to continue.

"Someone in the know—we're guessing another one of his former Kalis—retrieved whatever notes he'd been keeping there and delivered them to the dregs of the Syndicate, thinking they could use the information to turn the tide, so to speak, and win this protracted war against the Grace. The Syndicate gave this information to the Arch Bishop."

"Why would they do that?"

Ka'id sighed. "Remember I told you the Arch Bishop has always worked for the Syndicate?"

"Of course."

"Well, that wasn't the entire story. The Arch Bishops i haven't just been working for them. They're *trained* by them. The same way they trained you and Kirin."

"You mean the Arch Bishop is a Kalis?" Syrina was incredulous.

"Not exactly, but, in a sense, yes. No tattoos, no Papsukkal Door, but all the manipulation, all the technical knowledge you possess. More, since that's all they focus on. And Ormo headed Arch Bishop Daliius's training. Others played a part too, of course, but Ormo was his primary handler and continued to be his Syndicate liaison after Daliius ascended to the head of the Church. The surviving High Merchants thought he could make sense of Ormo's notes faster than they could, and they were right. Daliius put it all together. Disrupting the Tidal Works would bring about a second Age of Ashes, or at least a disaster on par with what happened centuries ago in Kamahush."

Syrina's mind reeled. "Why the fuck would he want that?"

Kirin answered. "The Syndicate has lost control of him, the

same way they lost control of the Grace. Ormo was Daliius's handler. When Eheene went up and Ormo with it, I don't think the Arch Bishop took it well. Imagine losing your Ma'is like that, back when you were loyal. So, when the surviving High Merchants moved to his city, he resented it. When the Grace rebelled, he resented that even more. According to people close to him, he's lost faith—not in the Heavens, but in humanity. He sees this as a way to start over again."

Kirin put her hand on Ka'id's shoulder, who gestured for her to continue. "The Syndicate's plan was to figure out a way to disrupt the Tidal Works, but when Daliius told them what that might do, they backed off. They asked the Arch Bishop to do the same, but he didn't. Instead, he doubled down, had the advisers who disagreed with him executed, and sent out teams of loyal Kalis to, well, end the world as we know it. So far, they've failed, but someone is bound to get it right eventually. Or wrong, depending on your way of looking at it."

"Why would other Kalis help him? It either goes against the Syndicate, or will ruin their chances at a free life, depending on where their loyalties lie. What do they get out of it?"

Kirin shook her head. "You're right, but I don't know. It seems they don't see it that way. Somehow he convinced them."

"What about Kalis still working for the Syndicate? Why can't they do anything? If they can't handle a situation like this, what are they even there for?"

Kirin frowned. "I don't know what happened, but from what I hear, most of them have gone over to the Arch Bishop's side. He must be very persuasive."

Syrina slumped to the floor, annoyed with how much Kirin was understating the situation but too preoccupied to complain about it. Her head spun. She wished the voice would offer some advice. "The Arch Bishop is an insane Kalis with a hoard of other insane Kalis following him, and the Grace is a fanatic following a religion the Syndicate created thousands of years ago to control the very people who are now out of control."

Ka'id nodded. "In summary. I wouldn't call it a hoard, but yes. That is an apt enough way to describe the situation. Fuel a fire long enough and it will go wild, no matter how well you think it's contained."

"What do we do?"

Ka'id's face brightened, though Syrina thought it looked forced. "We have a few things on our side. For one, I know more about the Tidal Works than Ormo ever did. I believe there might be a way to stabilize them—the one under Fom and all the others too. *Permanently* stabilize them. With the way some Kalis—well, you—have shown you can interact with the Artifacts."

"Like the way Anna interacted with the daystar."

"Yes, just like that."

Syrina shuddered. "And?"

"The Arch Bishop is insane. So insane he's losing allies left and right. Everyone he doesn't speak directly to has abandoned him. He's used what inside knowledge he has on the Merchant's Syndicate to neutralize whatever they've tried so far and win over Kalis, but there are others—both High Merchants and Kalis still loyal to them—who would stop him, or at least be agreeable to a plan to stop him, if someone were to put a viable one forth.

"So, the plan is this. We finish this goddamn machine and get what we need from Mann's treasure. Then, I and Kirin go back to Tyrsh and usurp the Arch Bishop. Meanwhile, and this is something else that will work for us, I have it on good authority that the Astrologers are planning a push into Skalkaad while all the N'naradin are distracted with each other and whatever we do."

"For the naphtha?"

"Your deduction is flawless. If they can get their hands on even just a few of the refineries it will be another blow to both the Arch Bishop and the Syndicate. One, hopefully, neither will recover from for years. Even if they fail, their shenanigans should turn eyes to the north and away from what we're doing."

"And me?" Syrina asked, even though she knew the answer.

"You, my dear, head to Fom, armed with the knowledge you need to control the Tidal Works the same way your friend Anna controlled that daystar."

It's our time to shine.

Damnit, Syrina thought. *Now* the voice says something.

————

It took five days more for Ka'id and Kirin to set up Ormo's machines. Over half were ruined beyond Ka'id's ability to repair, and there were a few others she didn't understand and didn't have the time to figure out. But she thought it would be enough.

There were no recliners with straps this time, but there was no needle into her spine either. That was a win in Syrina's book. Nobody was certain whether she would lose consciousness the way she had with Ormo and Anna, so she forwent the stool—the only proper seat they had upstairs—and settled on the floor with her back to the wall. Ka'id said it should work with just her blood, so the needle went into her arm.

She didn't lose consciousness, there just a vague tingling in the back of her mind, and a sensation like the voice in her head was dividing its attention between her and something else—with most of it occupied with the something else. It was strange after it had been her constant companion for so long, even in those long months of drunken silence, and to Syrina's surprise, she immediately missed it.

Relax. I'm still here.

She wasn't sure she was happy or not.

After that came a long time of waiting. Images, like glimpses of memories not her own, flashed through her head. Some she understood. Most she didn't.

After an hour or two—she lost track of time—she felt the voice return to her.

"Welcome back," she whispered.

I got what we need. And a lot more besides.

More images projected into her mind, complete now. She swallowed. "So that's how it's going to be."

Yeah. I think so. It could be worse, but still. Sorry.

Syrina shrugged. "It's not your fault."

She turned to Kirin and Ka'id, who'd been sipping wine while they monitored a bank of gages. It only dawned on Syrina now how loud the jumble of generators had been, and she realized she could have shouted to the voice and they'd still be hard pressed to hear her from the other side of the room.

They stood when they saw her get up, their faces a mix of curiosity and concern.

"How did it go?" Ka'id asked.

"Uh, good, I guess. I know what I need to do. I just need to get there to do it."

"Excellent. I've already arranged transport. For you, a dirigible most of the way up the coast, then a fishing boat the rest of the way to Fom. For us, a smuggling ship to the Island."

"What about all this?" Syrina gestured around at the machinery, lingering on the bank of equipment that still held Mann's prisms.

"A donation to the Astrologers, for now, until we can make it back and decide what else to do with it. Though for some reason I don't think the Astrologers will be overly willing to return it to us. Well, win or lose, I don't think I'll need it after we've finished."

Syrina nodded. "Fair enough. I guess they've earned that much. Well, there's no point in sticking around. I've got work to do."

Ka'id smiled. "As do we. Thank you, Kalis Syrina. I'm glad we get to work together in a more formal capacity than the first time we met." She held out her hand. "When we meet again, I hope we can drink to our success."

Syrina hesitated, then took her hand and shook it. "Sure. Until we meet again."

Kirin flashed a grin and gave Syrina a nod. "Kalis Syrina."

"Kalis Kirin. Take care of this one, will you?"

She smiled. "Always have. Always will."

Syrina headed down the stairs without looking back, peeling off her false skin as she went.

20

A DIRIGIBLE UP THE COAST

THE CAPTAIN TOLD SYRINA IT WOULD BE JUST UNDER three days up the coast by dirigible, as long as the wind held. He was an old, scrawny pirate named Lechlasasalachin, with a heavy beard dyed dark blue and an enormous mop of white hair; Ves' opposite in every way but attitude. As soon as they broke away from the airship tower leering over eastern Vormisæn, he invited Syrina into his private cabin for "rum and conversation." It didn't seem to bother him at all that she was a Kalis—on the contrary, he openly leered at her body, despite the fact he couldn't focus on it, and insisted she call him Lech, either oblivious to the entendre or entertained by it.

She liked him immediately, though she made use of her tattoos when they drank together.

The dirigible was larger and more modern than the handful she'd been on before, and it didn't have a deck she could go outside on. The gondola was a sleek pod of dark hardwood from the southern jungles, with windows and floors of tempered glass framed with brass. Hatches ran along either side, where a half-dozen hound-head cannons stolen from the

Fom navy waited. Small crates of antipersonnel shot were stacked next to each one, though the fact the ammunition boxes were still sealed revealed how little action the new ship had seen. The engine was a tarfuel marvel—almost quiet as naphtha, with huge twin propellers in the stern and nine smaller ones running along both sides and the bottom, which helped the rudder that jutted from the oblong air bladder with steering.

The winds held. Syrina spent her time drinking with Lech and listening to him tell impossible-sounding tales of his exploits on the sea and in the air. She even told a few of her own once he was drunk enough that she was pretty sure he wouldn't remember most of the details. There was no passenger cabin to speak of, but she'd gotten plenty of rest in Vormisæn before they'd left, so she spent her time watching the Ristro Peninsula rolling by far below, trying to stay out of everyone's way.

She was focused on the scrubby hills and puffs of cloud rolling by in the bright morning light of the second day, so the window above her exploding inward took both her and the voice by surprise. She rolled at the sound of the sharp crack, but a shower of heavy shards rained on top of her, slicing into her back, cheek, and shoulder. The dirigible lurched and began to fall. Before she could get to her feet, there was another crack further down the fuselage, and more glass and splinters of black wood sprayed into the hold.

She twisted to her feet, ignoring the sharp pain, other than to note a few shards of glass were still embedded in her shoulder. She looked up through the jagged hole, but all she could see was the leather and copper of the bladder, ripped to shreds along the side, blasting air hot enough it made the air shimmer.

A third peel of cannon fire thundered, blowing three crewmen at the rear into red mist as they grappled with the engine. The gondola jerked down, then up, and the airship began to spin. The hills below came spiraling towards them. She lurched to her feet and saw Lech stagger from the bridge, clinging to the door. His eyes were glassy and blood streamed from a gash in his forehead, just over his left eye. He clutched a bulky backpack in his free hand. To her surprise, he called her name.

"Syrina! Syrina!" He shouted. "It's your last fucking chance to get off this thing! Where the hell are you?"

"I'm here!" she stumbled in an unsteady half-run towards him, falling, crawling, and getting up to run again. She wondered what he had in mind. The cannon fire from above had stopped.

His glazed eyes focused, and he shoved himself from the doorway towards her. "Put this on." He flung the backpack at her and pushed her towards one of the gaping holes in the hull. "You're stronger than me, so you'd goddamn better not let go. Remember, I could have left you here!"

Syrina threw the pack over her shoulders and let him lead her into the void, hugging the thin, surly pirate against her.

The ground rushed up. She hadn't realized how high they'd been, and was wondering about the wisdom of their plan when she saw the first dome of cloth bloom from a speck beneath and behind her like a white mushroom, followed by four others. A second later, Lech reached behind her and pulled something. There was a rustle of fabric and her shoulders lurched as the parachute caught the wind. Lech jerked down through her arms, but she caught him and pulled him up again as he cursed. It was awkward—he was over a head taller than her, but he wasn't heavy, and she locked her wrists around his waist. She doubted she would have been able to carry Ves like that, but knowing him, Vesmalimali would have taken the last parachute and left her to fend for herself.

The wind carried them north. Behind, their dirigible spiraled down in a plume of twisting black smoke, smashing itself on the side of a low, treeless hill. There was an anticlimactic pop of flame from the tarfuel engine as the airship slid down the embankment and came to rest in a shallow valley. Above and behind, a huge black shape loomed at the edge of the thin, high clouds. Syrina could make out the hound head cannons jutting from the side, silhouetted against the blue-white of the sky. It was twice as big still as the Corsair dirigible, and that had been the biggest one she'd ever seen. Twice as big and made of black wood. Even the air bladder was ribbed in blackvine, the leather beneath stained a coppery red.

The Grace has *been busy.*

Syrina didn't answer. She was afraid the gigantic ship would fire on the survivors as they floated to the ground, but it seemed content enough to have destroyed their ship and pulled away to the northwest towards Fom.

"Probably be reporting us," Lech said, watching her eyes track the airship and guessing her thoughts. "As soon as they get back. Send some people to come pick us up for 'questioning.'"

"Probably," Syrina replied. "We'll be ready for them."

Lech laughed.

––––––

They touched down on rocky slopes somewhere south of Fom. Lech helped Syrina pull two long splinters of glass out of her shoulder before they tracked down the rest of his surviving

crew scattered over the hills in a rough line a span long. None
of them were seriously hurt, and none knew exactly where they
were. They found cover in a shallow ravine three spans east of
the crash.

"Just because their goddamn dirigible went back to Fom
doesn't mean they're not sending someone else to look for us,"
Lech pointed out again. He turned to Syrina. "You go. Do what
you came to do. The least you could do is make all this camel
shit worth it." He grinned.

There was a time she would have left them without a
goodbye—something the voice still urged her to do—but she felt
a certain loyalty to the people who'd risked their lives to bring
her this far, so she insisted on going with them at least a little
further east, where they might find cover in the forest.

Lech seemed like he might argue, but finally nodded once
with a look like he was tired of talking about it, and led the way
northeast, covering their tracks as they went.

After the sun had disappeared over the hills, but before
full night, they found a shallow gulch overgrown with half-
dead willow trees. The creek bed was dry, but muddy
puddles suggested there'd been rain in the days before. The
rocks overhanging over the arroyo stuck out enough that they
wouldn't be seen from above, and the only easy approaches
were from the west and east, over the uneven bed of the
stream.

"And this shall be where you leave us," Lech announced to
Syrina. The rest of the crew watched the exchange, silent, but
none of them had spoken to her since they'd left Vormisæn, so
she didn't exactly expect them to say goodbye now.

She tried to think of a reason to stay and help them fight off
the search parties that might track them down but failed, and
she wondered why she'd grown to care so much for this dirty-
minded air pirate and his crew.

Maybe because you know they'll be the last people we'll see for a long time who we can pretend are friends.

She frowned, but didn't answer.

But we'll always have each other.

———

She picked her way over the scrubby hills through the night, stopping to rest a few hours after the Eye had set, more because she wanted to intercept any patrols from Fom than any need for sleep, though it did help the tattoos stitch together her sliced back. She got up before dawn, and before noon, she found the N'naradin, spread in a line across the hills like farmers looking for lost goats, trudging slow and steady to the southeast.

"They'll find them for sure," Syrina said to the voice, watching from the next rise a half-span away.

Not your concern. The voice sounded like it was pouting.

Syrina didn't bother to refute it, and the voice didn't sound like it expected her to.

It wouldn't work out to anyone's favor if she just killed them all, even if she thought it wouldn't be hard to do just that, now that she knew she could find the Papsukkal Door again. But a band of fifty soldiers getting wiped out or disappearing would raise all sorts of alarms in Fom. Then again, it wouldn't do to have the airship crew leak they'd brought a Kalis to the city either, even if the Grace wouldn't know why she'd come. Maybe, though, there was something else she could do that would at least give her Ristroan allies enough time hide, or better yet, make it to the Ristro border.

Distinctly aware of the voice's petulance, she scrambled down the southern slope, out of view of the oncoming soldiers, careful not to make any tracks.

Once she was two gulches ahead of them, she began

throwing together a few shelters out of stones and dry branches where people might have slept. She scurried around, making footprints in the dusty sand, before doing an intentionally poor job of covering them up again. Then she climbed up to the ridge to the southwest, backtracking a few times until it looked like a small group had moved through single file, trying and failing to cover their presence in a rush to the coast.

She did that for the rest of the day, moving southwest until she hit the Sea of N'narad, ignoring the voice's complaints about lost time and the task at hand. By her calculations, she ended up about thirty spans west of where she'd left Lech and his people. She hoped it would be enough; there was nothing else she could do for them. She followed her own footprints back again, far enough to confirm the search party had taken the bait. Then she looped far around them back to the coast, hoping she'd make it to the vineyards within a day or two. She wondered how Ves and Mann were doing and whether she'd ever see them again.

They did their job, the voice said. Syrina wondered where it got its confidence from, but she didn't argue.

21

SUCCESS

THE MANHOLE COVERS ALONG THE GRACE'S WALK THAT used to spew steam every morning vomited smoke. Alessi had been begging along the same stretch of road as long as she could remember. Her sister Narsa once told her she'd been doing it since she was four, and now she was fifteen. Eleven years was close enough to forever that there was no point in thinking about the difference, but even in that long span of forever, she'd never seen smoke come out of the manholes.

An explosion further down the street towards the harbor knocked her off her feet and into a rearing, panicked camel that had been clomping up behind her, hauling baskets of raisins. Something began thrumming deep underground. She felt it in the soles of her bare, muddy feet, and for the first time that she could remember, she was more afraid of what was happening below Fom than she was of Crane if she returned to the dive early—early and empty-handed.

She ran a block up the street to where Narsa stumbled from a doorway, dazed. "If the Tidal Works are going up, we don't want to be here!" she shouted and tugged on Narsa's arm, pulling her sister north, back toward the Lip.

Narsa wasn't a bright girl. She had been once, but not anymore. Not since she'd tried to run away and Crane caught her and hit her in the head with a copper pipe. Alessi was afraid her sister wouldn't understand the urgency, or worse, be too scared of Crane to follow her little sister home where she'd be safe. Well, safer. But she must have understood, or maybe that vibration shaking up into her feet pushed through whatever Crane had put in her brain with that pipe. She took Alessi's hand, and together, they fled toward the Lip.

———

The thought flitted through Mafat's head that he could just run over the beggar girl gawking in front of him, but he knew he'd feel bad about it. Besides, Bushes got other ideas the moment the plaza five blocks further down erupted in a gout of fire and steam. The camel reared, grunting in panic, toppling most of the baskets in the back of the wagon and sending raisins tumbling into the street like hail.

"Shit, Bushes!" Mafat yelled out of habit more than anything, since he'd learned years ago his camel would do whatever the hell she wanted, whatever he shouted at her.

A few of the beggars that plagued this stretch of the Grace's Walk materialized around his cart to scoop handfuls of raisins off the ground, but most were fleeing like the girl he'd almost run over, who'd darted by him and grabbed a hooker with blank, unnerving eyes by the hand before they both disappeared north into the milling throng.

He waved his arms at the looters, but he didn't put much heart into it, and they evaporated back into the shadows and smoke as fast as they'd come.

Goddamn raisins. He'd been a wine man once, and a successful one at that, before this Heaven-cursed war started and the Grace had the vineyards pulled up to make room for those vile, black brambles. Nobody wanted wine anymore anyway, except the fops in Tyrsh, and they wouldn't be buying it from Fom. But raisins were going for a Three-Side a basket, maybe even two on the piers where sailors were desperate for rations. The last vineyards in Fom were up beyond the Great Road docks, but that area was getting bad too, with the Arch Bishop's navy pushing up the delta a little closer every month. It was just a matter of time before he'd be forced to join these wretches on the Walk himself, only by then there wouldn't be any more raisins to steal. Raisins or anything else.

Bushes calmed. The camel stood in the middle of the street, waiting for instructions, shifting her weight from side to side like her feet hurt. Panic flowed around them as people ran away from the smoke roiling from the plaza, or toward it in a desperate, suicidal gambit to put out the fire. He glanced to either side, where the smoke coughing up from the Tidal Works had turned even blacker. He thought about the stories of Eheene. A fireball from the sky; the city engulfed in flames that burned for a year. Probably camelshit, those stories, like most of the others he'd heard about the Merchant's Syndicate, Kalis, and the machinations of Skalkaad. Anyway, Fom wasn't sitting on top of a giant reservoir of naphtha.

No, it was sitting on a cyclopean, ancient machine that powered the biggest city in the world with pressurized steam.

"Not going to make it to the docks today," he said to Bushes. "Let's go home."

He clucked his tongue and pulled the reins, and Bushes obeyed, pleased to be moving away from the mayhem. She made a skillfully tight turn in the street and trotted east, leaving a scattering of raisins behind them.

———

Orlin N'faitz frowned at the idiot merchant turning his camel wagon around, blocking the panicked citizens fleeing from the explosion just as much as he blocked those of more noble mien trying to get to the fire, presumably to put it out. Though, upon closer examination, the majority of them looked like looters.

He debated turning around himself and going back to Wise Hill, but the hypocrisy of that was clear, and he had a feeling Heaven would judge him for such actions, no matter how high his Salvation Taxes were. He smoothed his red robes of The Grace's Own Inquisitional Investigator, dodged around the spitting camel guided by the clucking raisin merchant, and marched with purpose towards the chaos blooming in the market plaza, less than a half-span from Customs Towers Square.

It was slow going at first, but after a block, the fleeing citizens had all but cleared, relieving the need to push against the herd like a fish forging its way upstream. A few small stones had been blown so high from the initial blast that they still pelted the surrounding roofs, and the smoke was so thick he couldn't see the source of it. But then, smoke had been thick everywhere that morning, belching out of the Tidal Works as if the whole undercity had been ablaze. He'd been coming to meet this section's overseer with a list of questions from the Grace, but as he neared, forced to cover his mouth with his sleeve to filter out smoke, he was starting to think the overseer hadn't survived, unless he'd been fortunate enough to be running an hour late.

Inquisitor N'faitz stopped when he got to the plaza. Or rather, what was left of it. Kiosks and stalls lay in splinters around a smoking hole in the center of the square, which N'faitz recalled had once been an elaborate fountain of sculpted flowers and fish, bubbling boiling-hot water up from the Works below. A few of the surrounding bars and inns spat fire from their roofs. Dead and pieces of the dead littered the area.

The bodies were sobering. He'd been a soldier in the Grace's army for years before his promotion to Inquisitor, a month after the Grace had declared Fom's independence, and he'd seen his share of death in the Yellow Desert under the traitor Mann. But here in the streets of the city—*his* city—the mangled bodies of simple citizens who'd just been living their lives twisted his heart. This was no accident. Thousands of years of stability, and only now, during a protracted war of independence against the corruption of Tyrsh, did the Tidal Works begin to fail? No. Coincidences like that didn't happen, and whoever was responsible would meet the justice of the Grace by his hand.

Keeping his left hand against his mouth and blinking against the acrid smoke, he drew the ceramic sword of his office with his right and started towards the center of the plaza with cautious steps. It would be hard to find any evidence in these conditions, but looters already darted here and there around the edge of the square, stealing what survived from the blasted market. If he waited, every clue worth finding would be gone.

He caught a shadow of motion out of the corner of his eye, just to his left where his sleeve mostly blocked his vision. The inquisitor wheeled in time for something hard and impossibly fast to smash into his nose. His face collapsed around the point of impact with a crunch he didn't hear.

———

Kalis Charisi smiled as the rain of stone, burning wood, and chunks of charred meat peppered the ground around her. She'd been skeptical, but the Arch Bishop had insisted a few powder bombs placed in just the right places would have a dramatic effect—an understatement she now found amusing. The maps he'd drawn for her were specific, and the explosion that followed her work had rinsed all remaining doubt from her mind.

For two months she'd been in charge of countless minor operations in Fom. She'd grown to know her way around the maze of the Tidal Works, at least this section of it, and she was glad it had at last turned time to put her knowledge to use. The first attacks had been suicide runs, but the men and women she'd sent below in workman's coveralls had gone knowing and willing, with visions of their promised Heavens in the forefront of their minds.

The true Tidal Works, the Arch Bishop had explained to her, had been built to last forever, and had bound itself to the machines built around it, granting them a portion of its longevity. Simple smashing would do little except leave sections of Fom without power or hot water, and Daliius sought a more permanent solution. Unbeknownst to almost everyone, including the Grace, certain sections were integral to relieving the constant, massive pressure building in the central device, eternally eating away at the tug of the Eye. Disrupt this release of power, give it nowhere to go, and it would be a simple matter of letting it build until it released like the cork in a shaken beer bottle.

And Fom was the cork.

She'd given specific instructions to her team. Exactly which pipes to rupture, which valves to turn. Where to place the bombs. Some had no obvious effect; others had been dramatic. Like the valves the team opened two days ago, filling the passage with super-heated steam and the choking, black smoke that now spewed from the Grace's Walk. She'd found her people early that morning, reduced to blanched, softened bones. She'd meant to use those three again now, in the ultimate act, but it was no matter, even if it meant Charisi's odds of survival had gone from good to dismal. She was a Kalis, and she lived and died to serve.

And serve she would. When she'd learned the Arch Bishop she'd attached herself to after the destruction of Eheene was a Kalis in all but name, she'd flung her loyalty at his feet. He was one of them. He alone knew the minds of the Kalis, because he'd been through all she'd been through. All but the tattooing, but she couldn't remember that anyway. He knew the Kalis more than the High Merchants, aloof on their thrones, could ever know them. When he told her his plan—his real plan, far beyond the whims of the Syndicate he supposedly served—she knew she would die for him as fast as she ever would have for her Ma'is Ormo. The Arch Bishop wanted to start over—build a better world where the Kalis would rule without the greed of the Syndicate or the deceptions of the Church. If she needed to die to build that world for whoever was left when it was over, she would die happy, whether or not she believed in the lie of Heaven.

She needed to squint against the smoke still flooding from the remains of the destroyed market, but as she neared the center, she confirmed that the last of her servants had been successful. The innocuous fountain of boiling water that had served as one of the major releases of the Tidal Works was gone, replaced by a sinkhole left by the sudden lack of machinery in the tunnels beneath it.

Almost there.

She saw the middle-aged Church bureaucrat approaching the crater, and she paused. He had one hand on his sword and the other over his mouth in a futile attempt to filter the smoke. Some official. She never had learned all the different ranks under the Grace, but it didn't matter who he was. He was too late. Still, she didn't want to risk his meddling now that she was so close to fulfilling the Arch Bishop's vision.

Charisi slid up beside him. She was pleased that he was so focused on the smoking pit that he didn't notice her, even with the smoke rolling around her body, which reduced the effect of the tattoos. Just as he turned, she made her hand rigid and struck at the center of his face, which imploded around her fingers and made a wet sucking sound when she pulled them out.

Without looking back at the falling body, she went to the edge of the ruined plaza, tossed up a smoking manhole lid, and climbed down.

The edges scalded her palms and knees, but she ignored the pain and the itching of the tattoos mending flesh that came after. When she climbed down to the third level of the Tidal Works—the first two were in ruins—she paused long enough to get her bearings. The maps the Arch Bishop had given her of this area would be as accurate as the others. Still, the destruction was shocking even for her, and in the ruin of broken pipes and shattered tunnel walls, it took her a few moments to figure out where she stood.

Ah, yes, she thought. That odd seventy-degree bend in the tunnel was just ahead and to her right. A span beyond lay the heart of the Tidal Works, which her sappers had left exposed and waiting.

22

DEFEAT

THAT'S NOT GOOD.

Black fingers of smoke streaked the mist over Fom, which flickered here and there with yellow flashes. Dull thumps rumbled through the ground even where Syrina stood on the south ridge overlooking the city.

On the bright side, it was obvious Mann and Ves had done their job, or someone else had done it for them. The blackvine plantations had been reduced to charcoal-black gnarls of thorny bushes harder than iron, and most of the structures built to house swarms of indentured weren't much more than a few blackened beams framed in scorched stones. The low mounds that had once served as the boiling pits and forges had all collapsed. It looked like it had happened days ago, and that more than a few people had taken part in their destruction. The indentured had apparently turned on their masters after the saboteurs had lit the spark. Wasn't that always the way?

She wondered with a pang of sadness if she would ever see them again. Ves and Mann had grown to be the closest things she'd ever had to friends, except for...but no, now wasn't the time to dwell on him.

We need to hurry, the voice reminded her. *Whatever the Arch Bishop had planned for Fom, he's going through with it now, and it's working.*

She wanted to say it didn't need to tell her, given the grim view, but she'd been dwelling on a past she couldn't change instead of getting to work, so she let it slide.

The fog reeked of charred stone and old steam. Foot traffic was light for the middle of the afternoon, and everyone was heading away from the city center. She'd never had much love for any of the cities of Eris, or really given them much thought beyond the places she ended up when she was working, but it was strange to think that first Eheene, then Maresg, and now maybe even Fom, would be reduced to sparsely populated ruins by the time this was all done.

The destruction grew worse as she went on. Some buildings lay in shambles or had been swallowed by the limestone ground. Three and four-story tenements had been transformed into smoking chasms, while other stretches remained untouched. It seemed random, but she knew it wasn't. The Arch Bishop had found the weak spots of the Tidal Works, and he was pushing on them until it all collapsed. The Tidal Works, and maybe everything else.

Just go down there—see, look, we're not too far from where N'talisan's lab was. That was close to the center of the Works, right? Whatever the Arch Bishop started will end there. That's where we need to be too.

She'd arrived at the mouth of the dead-end alley where she'd first met N'talisan. Where Triglav had died, and the voice in her head had been born. She swallowed to force the lump of grief down into her belly from where it caught in her throat.

Her sadness seemed every bit as overwhelming now as it had the moment the owl's body had fallen to the flagstones.

The room that once housed the lab was still there, but now it was full of boxes of dried fruit and unmarked barrels of something she didn't bother to examine. The low door to the Tidal Works was still there too, sealed with a thin layer of plaster behind a stack of crates filled with raisins, easy enough to get through. Forcing her mind on the present, she descended the hot, narrow stairs, wondering if she could find her way through the maze of tunnels from the memory of when she'd been there as Rina all those years ago.

———

It was dark. The glow lamps that once hung along the corridors had either been destroyed or left without power. It was hot, too. A lot hotter than she remembered, and it had been hot enough back then.

"Now what?" she whispered. Thrumming and thumping pounded somewhere beneath her, and pipes hissed and ticked all around, but no sounds of life reached her at the bottom of the steep spiral stairway.

The voice didn't answer right away, but she got the sense it was thinking, and she began making her way at a snail's pace in the direction she remembered N'talisan taking her, running her hand along one wall, probing each step with her foot in the blackness. By the feel, the machinery and pipes along this stretch were intact, at least on the side where she ran her hand.

After a few minutes the voice said, *You can't go on like this —it'll take days to get where we're going. We need to find light.*

Irritation burst like stars behind Syrina's eyes. "You don't say?" she hissed. "What do I pay you for anyway?"

I don't know why you're so mad at me. I wasn't even with you last time you were here.

Syrina stopped walking. Somehow, she'd forgotten there'd been a time before she had a voice in her head saying things behind her. Even when Triglav had been with her, it seemed like the voice had been around too, watching and silent.

"Fine," she whispered, mollified. "Well, is there was something you could do to help me see down here? I could go back upstairs and make a torch—it would probably only take a few minutes. But it'll also tell everyone within a span I'm down here, and I think we agree that anyone still alive in this hole will cause problems for us if they see us coming. If we can get closer to wherever they are without a light, or at least wherever they're going, we can use the light they're using without telling them we're here. Unless they're not using any lights either, in which case at least they won't see us coming.

"So, if you can't do anything, just tell me now and I'll go back up and notify the whole goddamn undercity I'm here."

Alright, you're rambling. Settle down. There's something I can try with the tattoos.

"You can either be more specific or just try it."

The voice sighed in her mind. *It's something I thought about a while ago. A long while. When we were with Anna. The same way you can use your muscles to increase your tattoos' effect so people don't notice you, I might be able to do something similar, but opposite. Increase your sensitivity through them so you can feel what's around you. Like an insect's antennae.*

"You've been thinking about it for that long and never said anything?"

There was a mental shrug. *It's never been necessary. Not enough to warrant the risk, and I knew you'd want to try it if I mentioned it.*

"Risk?"

It might hurt like hell or trigger the tattoo's reaction to your death.

"What? And burn me to ash?"

Maybe. Probably not though.

"That's reassuring."

If it was that likely, I'd just tell you to get a torch. Just a risk I thought you should be aware of. Like I said, it might hurt though.

"In which case you can stop it if it gets too bad. Turn it off or whatever."

Yeah. Eventually. I think.

It was Syrina's turn to sigh. "Alright, fine. Not much left to lose."

All at once she tingled all over, followed by an overwhelming burning sensation that started at the top of her head and cascaded down her body like magma. She slumped against the bank of copper piping her hand had been resting on, aware in the back of her mind that she could sense every detail of the tunnel. The agony coiled, squeezing thought from her mind. A high-pitched scream echoed up and down the hall, but then it faded and died along with the pain, and she realized it had been coming from her.

She clawed her way to her feet, coughing. "So much for subtlety." She wasn't sure if she'd said it out loud or just snarked it in her head.

Sorry about that. Are you okay?

"You tell me."

There was a pause. *I think so. I needed to put way less effort into that than I thought, so I went overboard. Sorry. But you can 'see' now, right?*

It was right. She could sense details in the valve-covered walls, grated floor, and pipe-covered ceiling both in front and behind her without turning her head. Her eyes still saw only blackness, but details formed in her mind. "This is pretty useful," she said, knowing the voice would know it for the understatement it was. Her throat felt raw and her body tingled and burned, but she felt more or less like herself again. "Maybe we should have tried this sooner."

You got by fine until now. Let's go.

———

She had to detour around two collapsed sections of the walkway and one blown out chunk of the Tidal Works, fallen across the tunnel in a single knot of wires and brass pipes, but the going wasn't as hard as the devastation in the city above implied. It took some time to find her way to the area near where N'talisan had shown her the Artifact, and when she got there, she was three levels below where they'd shaped the tunnel to the central chamber.

The glow lamps had begun working again a quarter-span after the collapsed machinery, but she'd grown used to the fierce tingling on her skin, and it was useful to see her surroundings without moving her head. Plus, the voice wasn't clear on how it could turn the effect off. Desperate sounds of workers echoed now, putting out fires. None were burning nearby, but the steam carried the stench of burning wood and slagged metal. One group had run past her, going the other way, but she'd pressed herself into an alcove in the passage wall, and they hadn't noticed her.

When she grew near to where N'talisan's tunnel opened up three floors above, she stopped. Syrina thought she'd need to find a route to climb up, but these sections had already been cleared of debris, and a path led in the direction she needed to go. A bad feeling tied her stomach in knots. Just nervous about what comes next, she told herself.

No. I feel it too. Something is wrong.

Well, shit.

At the last second, Syrina thought, "Oh, they're already here," before a massive eruption of steam blasted her backwards through the tunnel. She felt her flesh scald between the swirls of tattoos; an explosion of pain as bad as the one she'd felt earlier when the voice had increased her senses. *No.* She thought, the idea distant. *It's worse. It's not in my mind.* And it didn't go away.

She lay on the corroded grating of the passage, steam cascading over her. The pain had twisted itself into a burning, stinging itch, just as fierce as the raw agony had been, but she wasn't sure if it was because her tattoos were healing the damage or because she was in shock. She expected the voice to tell her which it was when she thought about it, but it seemed distracted.

Her surroundings were strange and blurry despite the lights, and she realized it was because she couldn't see. Not out of her eyes. Her face felt sticky. The steam subsided, and she stood, shaking. The tunnel spun beneath her.

You're okay, the voice reassured her, but it sounded unconvinced.

"It doesn't feel like it," she whispered back as she reeled down the tunnel in the direction she'd been going before, staggering from one wall to the other like a drunk going home after the bars closed.

The voice didn't answer, which she took as a discouraging sign.

The roiling steam stopped, but echoes of secondary blasts reverberated through the Tidal Works. Most of the distant sounds of repairs had fallen away, and the only noises now were the explosions and a throbbing whistle, slowly building like an enormous tea kettle nobody was taking off the stove. She couldn't tell where it was coming from except somewhere ahead, and against all her instincts, she plodded toward it. At least the spinning had subsided.

From the heat cascading from the passage in front of her, a shape emerged, framed in steam and smoke; small, with impossible speed.

No, not impossible. Syrina could move that fast too. She wasn't sure if it was the voice that had pointed that out through the clouds in her mind or it was her own thought.

The figure crashed into her, spilling her backwards and onto the ground once more. *How can she see me?* she wondered.

You're...damaged. Anyone could see you right now.

That sounded bad, but through the haze of her confused mind she couldn't quite place why. She felt the voice force the present back into focus.

She rolled to the side, out from under the Kalis on top of her, just as the other woman's rigid fingers punched a hole through the copper grate where Syrina's head had been.

The thought occurred to her that if this Kalis was taking the time to attack her, it was because she'd already accomplished whatever she'd set out to do. "The explosion, that sound." She paused in realization. "We're too late," she muttered under her breath as she somersaulted away from another strike, which she failed to avoid. Pain lashed through her lower back as the Kalis' fingers struck home, just to the left of her spine she'd meant to shatter.

No, the voice reassured. *If it was too late, she wouldn't bother fighting you. She'd just leave, or wait to die, or whatever. She might have finished what she set out to do, but it's not too late for us to stop it, and she's worried about it.*

Syrina decided that made sense as she rolled backwards again, this time avoiding a blow to her face. She realized she was dodging despite the other Kalis being in the Papsukkal Door. An explosion further away and somewhere beneath them ripped through the passage.

"How am I doing this?" she asked, reaching for her own Door and finding nothing.

Your senses through the tattoos. Her own tattoos don't matter to you now—you can see the space she's in without looking. The rest is just your training and reaction time.

Syrina reached for the Papsukkal Door again, and again, she found nothing.

No, you can't, the voice confirmed. *Your tattoos are busy doing other things, like sensing your surroundings and keeping you alive.*

That sounded decidedly bad. There seemed to be a lot of things lately she didn't like the sound of. She rolled backwards a third time, but the other Kalis clipped her shoulder. It was getting hotter.

"I'm losing," she pointed out.

I know. You have to go on the offensive.

"She's too fast."

No, she's not.

"*Well, okay,*" she thought, too exhausted now to say anything out loud. "*Thanks for the tip.*"

You won't win a straight fight.

Syrina didn't bother responding. Her limbs felt like rubber, and the intense, burning itch still threatened to consume every conscious thought. She wondered how the voice could be such a smart-ass at the same time it kept her focused.

The Kalis' assault was relentless. She'd stopped bothering to feint or even be cautious when she realized Syrina wouldn't reach for her own Papsukkal Door, and Syrina could feel the other woman's growing frustration at not being able to finish her. Still, she kept pushing, and Syrina kept falling back.

Until she couldn't.

She dodged to avoid a strike to her throat, which instead tore off the lower half of her right ear, and her back foot slipped into nothing. The tattered grates of the tunnel, which in this section Syrina recalled were just copper mesh platforms separating each level of the Tidal Works, were gone, ending in a jagged drop into blackness.

Well, that wasn't right, since for Syrina everything was blackness now, but the bottom was far enough down that even the increased awareness coming from her tattoos failed to find the bottom. The walls were a tangled mess of bent, hissing pipes and knotted copper wires until the floor resumed on the other side, forty hands beyond. She felt nauseous.

Her attacker saw the opportunity and pressed. Her blows became a blur of motion. Syrina sidestepped a few, but for every strike that missed, two more found home, and all she could do was twist again and again on the brink, preventing a killing blow.

Any single hit might not kill her, but she was dying. Her cheek, jaw, and nose were shattered, her ribs cracked, and her left arm snapped at the elbow within a few seconds of the Kalis' assault.

Without even realizing what she was doing until she was in the air, Syrina jumped. She didn't have the strength to make it all the way, but that wasn't her plan. She leaped at an angle, hitting the gnarled brass pipes a little less than halfway across the chasm, clinging to them with her good arm and praying to the Heavens she'd never believed in that they'd hold her weight.

The other Kalis, with the briefest of hesitation from within her own diminishing Door, leaped after her.

Syrina's racing mind had time to decide the other woman had no intention of leaving the Tidal Works alive. She only wanted to kill Syrina and ensure whatever she'd done couldn't be reversed.

Fine, then. As the woman jumped, Syrina wrapped her hand in a thick knot of loose cable, dragged herself up with her legs as far as she could, and kicked out.

The voice ensured that her timing was perfect. Just as the other Kalis reached Syrina's place against the wall, Syrina wasn't there, but swinging out by her good arm, her legs first extended back, then forward in a vicious kick to the woman's hands, right where they were finding purchase after they missed Syrina with an attack meant to drag them both down. It failed to dislodge the Kalis' hand from the broken pipe. Instead, it broke loose the whole knot of machinery just below where Syrina dangled.

The Kalis cursed and grabbed at Syrina's legs as the mass of metal crumbled and fell with a screeching groan that echoed over the noise of the dying Tidal Works, but Syrina was slick with blood, and the Kalis couldn't find purchase before the weight of the falling machines smashed into her chest. She vanished into the void with a grunt.

Syrina dangled by her hand knotted in the twist of cable and listened to the gong of the falling machine where it smashed into some precipice of stone lost to her senses. A second later there was a tremendous, wet boom as it struck the water.

Somewhere nearby, the hissing, screaming whistle of the dying Tidal Works continued to build.

23

ARCH BISHOP DALIIUS III

KIRIN INSISTED THEY DOCK IN N'DAL, FAR SOUTH OF
Tyrsh, and after an hour of half-hearted argument, Ka'id
agreed. She had acquaintances in Pom, but her Kalis had
pointed out that they didn't know where their loyalty to Ka'id
ended and their devotion to the Church began. While she
wasn't famous the way she'd been in Skalkaad, her face was
recognizable enough in the north part of the island that it was
inevitable someone would mark her return, and Kirin maintained they should play it safe until they knew who they could
trust.

Like the rest of the Isle of N'narad, N'dal had been
untouched by the war, but the population of fisher-folk, goat
herders, and sugarcane farmers were wary of strange ships
docking in their little harbor. It wasn't until it became clear that
the only two to disembark would be a debutante and her maid
on their way north that they became friendly enough. Still,
both Ka'id and Kirin agreed they should leave that same afternoon, rather than find lodging. They hired a covered camel
wagon nice enough to avoid further suspicion given Ka'id's

obvious status, but not so nice that it would draw the wrong kind of attention on the ten-day trip north to the capital.

Tension brewed in the tiny trading communities and coaching inns along the road. Travelers that far south had become rare in the years since the Grace's war had begun, but still thankfully not so uncommon that people would openly question an estate owner and her servant on the way home from checking her investments. As they neared Tyrsh, though, Kirin grew more nervous.

"Settle down," Ka'id chided. It was late afternoon. Autumn, now, but still warm enough that Ka'id sat on the driver's bench next to Kirin, her hand resting lightly on her lover's leg. "You're supposed to be the calm one, remember? My fearless guardian."

Kirin made an annoyed grunt, but softened it by giving Ka'id's hand a little squeeze. "I'm nervous because you're not. Even back in Eheene, before we were anything other than Ma'is and Kalis, I was nervous for you. You've never been careful enough. Not to mention we let Syrina free Kalis Jaya. It was a stupid idea and I'm still not sure why we went along with it. Jaya and whoever she's working for know too much about all of us now."

Ka'id looked thoughtful as she watched the approaching spires of Tyrsh, still several spans to the north. The trickle of farmers' carts laden with pickled fish and sugar cane and pilgrims going in and out of the city suggested the capital was still business as usual, but she thought she could taste a tension that hadn't been there when they left. "We're not too far from our cave," she noted, looking over to the sparse forest crawling up the mountains on their left.

"Don't change the subject."

Ka'id rolled her eyes. "Fine.

You might be right. Then again, this situation is unique,

isn't it? Things are spiraling out of the Syndicate's control. That's never happened before, and I'm sure they're not taking it very well. The war is looking less and less profitable from their perspective. They didn't just lose their cash reserves and capital in Eheene, remember—they lost control of the naphtha refineries. That's always where most of their income has come from. Now, to maintain this stupid war, the ones supposedly pulling the Arch Bishop's strings need to spend more tin than they're making just to keep up security, not to mention all their other expenses. There's also the funding of the excavations going on in the ruins for them to worry over, on top of everything else. They're not the only ones up there, you know. Mercenaries and vagabonds are pulling more profit out of that detritus than what's left of the Syndicate, what with everything else my former colleagues are forced to pay for."

"What's your point?" Kirin's curiosity sounded genuine as she glanced at Ka'id out of the corner of her eye.

"My point, my dear Kalis, is that the Merchant's Syndicate is running out of money for the first time in its venerable history, and I don't think they want this war to go on anymore. At this rate, they'd be better off just letting the Grace take Fom out of the fold so they can set up some lucrative trade deals with her. That would be my plan, given the situation. If I were a High Merchant." She gave Kirin a quick smile.

"You think the Arch Bishop is acting unilaterally?"

Ka'id shrugged. "It's just an educated guess. The Merchant's Syndicate has survived this long by being farsighted, and continuing this war doesn't make sense in the long term, or at this rate even in the short term. Those remaining High Merchants in Tyrsh might be more amicable to my return than when they threw me in the Bower House, including whoever Miss Kalis Jaya works for."

Kirin sighed. They would get to the city proper at the same

time the sun set. She didn't relish keeping an eye on Ka'id after dark. "That's a lot of conjecture to risk your life on."

"Maybe. I know how they think though. Even out of the loop as I've been these past five or six years, I can imagine how things must seem from their point of view. The High Merchant's Syndicate thrives on wealth and control, and they're rapidly losing both. Besides, I don't think we have time to spend months digging up anything else we could act on. No, as it stands, Kalis Syrina has her job in Fom, and we have our own part to play here." She paused. "Frankly, I'm glad we're here and not with her."

Kirin didn't respond, and Ka'id knew her well enough to take that as a silent agreement.

As the sun set over the western minarets, their camel clopped into Tyrsh.

———

Ka'id insisted they return to their townhouse in the Flowers District, and this time it was Kirin who relented. It would be less conspicuous than staying in a hotel if anyone recognized them, and there was little chance anyone was still watching the house after all this time, anyway.

Weeds choked the garden, and the lanterns along the path had no naphtha even if they'd wanted to light them, so they picked their way to the door in the dark. It was still locked. A layer of dust coated everything, including the wineglasses still sitting on the table—one dirty and four clean. Kirin began to wipe everything down with a damp cloth and generally tidied up. Ka'id told her not to worry about it, but Kirin pointed out it would look odd if the maid didn't do her job, in case anyone was watching.

Ka'id very much doubted anyone was, but she let Kirin

work while she washed the wineglasses and filled one for herself.

She leaned back at her seat at the table and sighed. "I'd almost forgotten how much I missed a good glass of wine." She frowned. "I suppose they're numbered now, since the Grace has taken it upon herself to uproot the best vineyards on Eris to grow those miserable vines. The short-sighted bitch."

Kirin paused in her scrubbing at the other end of the table to smile. "That language! I don't think I've ever heard you reduced to name-calling before."

Ka'id smiled back. "It's a subject I feel strongly about."

Kirin finally stopped her fussing and sat down in the chair next to Ka'id. She poured herself a glass. "I suppose I should enjoy it while it lasts too. My time with you in Tyrsh has made me soft."

Ka'id chuckled. "I don't think so. I hope not, anyway."

"Does that mean you still aim to go through with your plan?"

She shrugged. "I don't see any alternative. Still, we should get a feel for how the other High Merchants will react first. No point in going to all the trouble just to have them take us down."

Kirin raised her eyebrows over her glass. "'The other High Merchants?' Does that mean you intend to take your place again?"

Ka'id sipped her wine, looking thoughtful and not answering for a while. Then she sighed. "Maybe. To be honest, I'd given little thought to it either way until this very moment. I suppose we'll need to see what state the Syndicate is in when this is all over and go from there. Now, come. It's late. I'm sure our bed is as dusty as everything else in here, but it's still cleaner than a cave floor. We both have work tomorrow."

"Are your contacts ready with the documents?"

"I believe so. They've been paid up and ready for months now. All they need is the signal to start spreading the news."

Kirin smiled as they drained their glasses together and walked to the bedroom, hand in hand.

—————

N'nafal leaned back further in the winged leather chair he'd been reclining in since Ka'id had been led into his chamber an hour before. The Regent Building was a sprawling affair of offices and meeting rooms for a dozen interwoven corporations and holding companies. That N'nafal had his office on the top floor all but assured her he wasn't himself a High Merchant. No member of the Syndicate lacked that much subtlety.

"I wouldn't believe you, except that you've shown you have knowledge of certain events never disclosed to the public. I must therefore conclude you are telling the truth, or else you are somehow privy to enough confidential information that you've been able to create this elaborate falsehood for reasons that are as yet unclear. Under the circumstances and from where I'm sitting, the difference between those two alternatives doesn't much matter."

Ka'id sighed. She wished Kirin was here, but it didn't make sense that Ka'id would attend a meeting with her maid, and she wasn't willing to rouse suspicion if Jaya was watching, which she undoubtedly was. At the very least, she'd be lurking nearby somewhere, checking out everyone going in and out of her ward's office. Ka'id considered pointing out to N'nafal that his meetings wouldn't run so long if he'd just say what he wanted to say but decided against it. He would no doubt pontificate about the value of precise speech for twenty minutes, oblivious to the irony, and she was eager to get on with her plans.

Instead, she said, "Well, in that case I'll stop trying to convince you of my sincerity and get to the point."

N'nafal gestured for her to continue, but looked like he was about to say something else, so she pressed over him before he got the chance. "I can take care of the details myself. In fact," she raised her voice over N'nafal's objection and was thankful when he stopped to let her speak. "In fact, I would prefer it. What I need from you are assurances—as much as you can give —that your...superiors will neither get involved nor take offense at what we must do."

To her surprise, N'nafal paused a second as if making sure she finished speaking before he answered. "These things I can assure you, without even needing to discuss it with...well, anyone. You seem to know enough of my, shall we call them, connections, and I of yours, so I will get to the point without fear of revealing any more secrets best not revealed to those who are, as they say, not 'in the know.'"

Finally. But she dared not say it out loud, so she gestured with a smile for him to continue.

"The fear is not what you will do. I promise and assure you of that both, if in your mind there is a difference between the two."

Ka'id suppressed a sigh.

"It would thrill us, in fact, for you to do something about the Arch Bishop before things go further, given they have already gone too far by any measurement worth taking. No, no indeed. That is not the problem. The problem is the same as the reason none of my superiors or associates have done anything about him up to this point, when we first became aware, and even fearful, of the growing danger the Arch Bishop poses."

"Hmm. Yes, I wondered about that."

"Yes, well, the problem is, the Arch Bishop is very, shall we say, *convincing?* A skill they trained him in since a very young age, I am told, as I am sure you are aware." He gave Ka'id a meaningful look, and she nodded. "And as it turns out, atop his training, he has a natural talent for persuasion, such that it works very well—too well—on the very servants of those we both serve, you in the past and I in the present."

Ka'id blinked. "Are we being listened to now?" She glanced around the office and to the massive, layered bamboo door shut behind her.

N'nafal blinked back. "No. Not unless someone in the hall has their ear pressed against the door, and I can give you my word, if that were the case, they would be caught and I would know about their untoward behavior post-haste."

She sighed again as her facade of patience cracked. "Then please allow me to speak in plain language, to make sure I am understanding you right. The Arch Bishop has swayed the Kalis serving the High Merchant's Syndicate to his own cause, leaving the Syndicate without means to deal with his growing madness."

N'nafal's face had a look of horror on it, as if Ka'id had just revealed his innermost secrets to the Astrologers of Ristro themselves, which, to be fair, she'd already done, but he didn't know that. After a strangled pause, all he said at first was, "Yes."

But then he droned on about the trials they'd faced after Eheene, and Ka'id stopped listening. She knew about the Arch Bishop's training. That N'nafal did too meant she'd either been wrong and he really was himself a High Merchant, though she still thought that unlikely—or else the rest of the Syndicate had grown desperate enough to drag him deeper into the loop, and perhaps even groom him for ascension. She wondered what he thought of her, but for now it didn't matter. She also wondered if Ormo, in his grooming of Daliius, had instilled his obsession with Kalis into the Arch Bishop. Probably. Maybe Daliius had even been another one of his Kalis experiments like Syrina and the owl had been. Ormo had incorporated his obsession into everything he did, and it had made him the most powerful person in the world for a while, right up until it got him and a million or so other people killed. In fact, the more she thought about it, the more it seemed likely Syrina's former Ma'is had known Daliius could exert undue influence over the Kalis, maybe even had the foresight to train him specifically for it. Until not long ago it wouldn't have mattered; they were on the same side, after all, and still would be if Ormo hadn't died and left the Arch Bishop to grow a mind of his own. Ormo would have enjoyed a second layer of control over the other Kalis planted in Tyrsh. One the other High Merchant's wouldn't have known about.

But none of that mattered now, any more than what N'nafal thought of her. The point was, the Arch Bishop wanted to destroy the world, or at least the civilizations that struggled on its surface, and he had an unknown number of Kalis helping him do it.

She realized N'nafal had stopped talking and now watched her, his eyebrows furrowed into a single, black line. "Ah, yes," she cleared her throat. "Well, it stands to reason Daliius has sent at least some of his new underlings to Fom, yes?"

N'nafal hesitated, then nodded. "Most of them, even, I have heard. He has, after all, no reason to fear a conspiracy against him when he has gained control over all erstwhile tools of said conspirators, and by all accounts his madness has decreased his paranoia, rather than the other way around. In short, he believes he has already won."

"Good. That should make things somewhat easier, don't you think?"

He nodded again. Before he could say anything else, Ka'id stood to go, but then something occurred to her. "Kalis Jaya.

She was with you, back with all that unpleasantness, right? After I left the Bower House. How about her? Is she with Daliius now too?"

N'nafal frowned. "I don't know, I'm afraid, but I assume so. I believe they had sent her to reconnoiter the situation and she failed to check in a few days later. After that, I considered at interminable length the concept of—"

"Well then, I think my business here is finished. Too bad about Jaya. I liked her, you know, for whatever that's worth. But I need to get ready. I suppose we'll speak again, you and I, in once capacity or another. Or we'll all die. Until then!"

"Wait a moment! How did you know about Kalis Ja—

But Ka'id had already let herself out, closing the door gently behind her.

The townhouse was empty. Ka'id felt it even as she stopped on the overgrown path in front of the kitchen door. Her heart churned. They'd discussed whether to wait until Ka'id got back before Kirin went to the Cathedral of Light to check out the Arch Bishop's security, but decided together there was no point. She hadn't actually expected her Kalis to be there, but now she wished she'd stuck around to talk. Neither of them had expected that Ka'id would get information vital enough to delay a simple reconnaissance mission, but now Ka'id's lover was heading toward the man who'd already lured the rest of the Kalis in the city away from their masters.

Masters. If only their relationship had remained so uncomplicated.

But no, she corrected herself as she let herself into the kitchen and sat down in her chair, bottle of wine in hand. She regretted nothing, and she knew Kirin didn't either. She wasn't sure when their relationship had evolved from master and servant to lovers of convenience, and then to something altogether more, but she wouldn't trade it for anything. Even a return to her seat at the High Merchant's table. But now, she might have traded it for that, anyway. That, or nothing at all.

She drank deep, refilled her glass, and took a deep breath. She reminded herself that she hadn't survived this long by worrying about things she couldn't do anything about.

So instead, she drank and brooded about what to do, forcing her mind away from what she would feel like if she lost Kirin to the Arch Bishop. Her failure, even Syrina's failure in Fom which might lead to the end of their world as they knew it, was nothing compared to the thought of losing Kirin. Of facing the world alone.

She sat and drank and tried to force her mind to other things.

———

There was almost no security around the Cathedral of Light. It was disturbing. If Ka'id's theory was right, and she was usually right about that sort of thing, the entire area should have been either swarming with people protecting the Arch Bishop or trying to kill him. She knew she should go back to Ka'id and report it; her Ma'is was probably back at the townhouse waiting.

But if she left and came back the next day or even later that night without knowing why everyone was gone in the first place, the whole plaza might be crawling with Church military and Seneschal. Plus, who knew how many Kalis had gone over to the Arch Bishop's cause? Dozens had gone mercenary after Eheene, and it stood to reason more than one of them had hired themselves out to the Church of N'narad. It would be a lot easier keeping an eye out for them for them if she didn't have to avoid a hundred Seneschal at the same time.

Then again, if any Kalis had joined the Church, that was the sort of thing Ka'id might find out in her meeting with N'nafal.

No, she decided. It was better to act when the opportunity presented itself.

She finished her circle of the cathedral complex. Fifty regular soldiers marched in groups of ten on patrols they wouldn't be deviating from. Easy enough to avoid those. A few hundred regular worshipers milled too—far too few. Even this late in the afternoon, the central plaza normally teemed with faithful. She wondered again where they'd gone. It wasn't a holiday, and anyway, holidays were the sorts of things that filled the churches even more.

Well, it wouldn't pay to over-think it. If she was going to act, it would be better if there were fewer eyes around.

Kirin slid unseen across the square to the largest building in Tyrsh: The Cathedral of Light. The front doors were closed—another oddity—flanked on either side by two pairs of bored-looking footmen. She circled once more, looking for a better way in.

Around the side she found what she was looking for. A little path ran between the main cathedral and the slightly less-impressive Cathedral of Flowers. Thin stone arches stretched over it, carved with tiny knotted blossoms, polished until they gleamed in the shade between the buildings. Set into the wall of the Cathedral of Light was a short, steep stairway leading to a polished wooden door carved with the Sun and Eye. Service access to the basement. At the top of the stairs, a lone woman in chapel livery idled, looking even more bored than the men at the front door. No wonder. At least at the front door they had each other to talk to.

Kirin hesitated. She couldn't get past this guard without doing something about her, and if she did, there'd be no turning back. Was she ready to commit now, unilaterally? What would Ka'id think?

But that was a stupid question. Ka'id her Ma'is would be delighted if she succeeded and furious if she failed. And Ka'id, her lover? The thought came unexpected into Kirin's mind, but, she realized, not unwanted. At some point her faithfulness to her master, her simple fulfilling of Ma'is Kavik's needs in the days and months after she fled Eheene, had become something more. She'd sensed Ka'id's growing affection from the start, in those first days when they'd left the High Merchant's Syndicate and come to Tyrsh, fleeing Ormo. It had been nice to fill that need with the High Merchant—former High Merchant—she'd devoted herself to. But it had grown more than nice. Somewhere between Eheene and their settling in Tyrsh, the feeling had grown mutual. Imperceptible at first, since Kirin had already been as devoted to Ka'id as any Kalis to their Ma'is. More, since she'd chosen to steal away with her, rather than stay and serve the next High Merchant Kavik the way she'd been supposed to. The way the rest of Kavik's Kalis had.

And then she realized the feelings between them hadn't started in Tyrsh, but before, which was why Kirin had followed her from the Syndicate in the first place and never looked back.

So how would *that* Ehrina Ka'id feel about Kirin should she act now? The same if she was successful. Heartbroken if she failed.

But Ka'id understood risks that needed to be taken. It was one thing that Kirin loved about her. One of many.

She closed on the guard.

The woman wasn't paying much attention to her surroundings, and Kirin knocked her unconscious and eased her against the wall at the base of the stairwell. With a little luck, anyone who came across her would just assume she was taking a nap, as out of character for a faithful soldier of Heaven as that was. Still, less attention drawn than if she'd killed her, and less out of character than a temple guard disappearing from her post.

Kirin got lucky again when the woman had a key for the door. That wasn't always the case, and she didn't want to stand there fumbling with the lock, which looked formidable. She hadn't brought proper equipment for that.

Inside, she locked the door again behind her and found herself in a simple, large kitchen. Not used for preparing meals for the Arch Bishop or any of the other Church high-ups, but for the myriad of servants and retainers who held the place together. It was empty at the moment, which was lucky too, since tattoos or not, somebody would have noticed the opening door.

She'd visited the Cathedral of Light many times with Ka'id, and even met Arch Bishop Daliius once, back before the war, but she'd never been in the maze of passages below the nave, so she could only guess which way to go. Once she left the kitchen, she encountered several packs of nervous, gossiping retainers. They made her progress slow, as she ducked into empty rooms and dark alcoves to avoid them, but she could gather some information. The Arch Bishop had met with a High Merchant—in full regalia, no less—a few months before and had since become withdrawn and obsessive.

She and Ka'id already suspected he'd gotten something from the Merchant's Syndicate that had set him off, although it was interesting that an actual High Merchant had shown up at the Cathedral of Light, painted face and all. What Kirin found even more interesting were the whispers that Kalis had apparently walked the Cathedral halls with impunity for about a month before disappearing again.

Strange, that. According to everything they'd found until

now, the Syndicate no longer supported Daliius. What that High Merchant had given him before they'd cut ties were most likely more notes from Ormo's archives pertaining to the Tidal Works, which explained how he knew so much about destroying it. And while it would be just like the Syndicate in its bubble of paranoia to provide the Arch Bishop with a bunch of Kalis for security, they would have withdrawn them as soon as their relationship went sour.

That could have been exactly what happened, but Kirin had a feeling there was something more sinister going on. The timing between the High Merchants' cut ties with Daliius and the Kalis' presence here didn't add up. It sounded more like the Kalis had been here *after* the Syndicate abandoned the Arch Bishop. In most situations, she would have chalked the discrepancy up to the inaccuracies of gossip, but this time something didn't sit. She heard one of them say something about Kalis being sent to Fom. While that could be more rumor mongering, that was another quandary. The Kalis were common knowledge now, but that didn't mean the High Merchants would be careless enough with their favorite tools that commoners would know about their comings, never mind their goings. That led Kirin to believe the Kalis weren't with the Syndicate anymore, and whoever was controlling them—probably the Arch Bishop —didn't care who knew they existed.

And if *that* was the case, it left two questions. Why would so many Kalis abandon their Ma'is after generations of loyalty, and why did they all go to Fom?

She could make some guesses about the second question, but it didn't matter enough to dwell on at the moment because even if she was right, there was nothing she could do about it from Tyrsh. They were Syrina's problem now. The first question was more pressing, but Kirin was out of ideas.

Or the rumors were wrong and there were still Kalis all

over the complex who just hadn't found her yet, and she was about to get herself killed. But she didn't think so. There was a vein of consistency to all the idle talk, after spending three hours listening between all the mundane chatter. There was *something* going on.

And there was one way she could find the truth. As nervous as the rumors made her, it was too late to go back to Ka'id. The unconscious guard outside would know something had happened, and when she woke up in a few hours everyone else would know too. Kirin wouldn't have another chance.

She hid herself and listened for a while, until she decided she wasn't going to get any more information from chatting staff, then crept like a shadow up the stairs to the annex where the Arch Bishop kept his quarters.

The halls here were empty, and Kirin's sense of unease grew.

She was just starting down the wide corridor lined with portraits of former Arch Bishops and other saints when a voice said behind her, "I thought you'd all left."

Kirin turned. A vague form flickered in the doorway to the library, which was dark. She'd made a cursory glance in it and decided nobody was there. Careless.

The voice sounded familiar. "Kalis Jaya. You're still here." Kirin tried to play it off, but Jaya recognized her voice too.

"Kirin? You'd disappeared." Jaya's tone grew suspicious. "Why are you here? Not on behalf of the Arch Bishop."

Kirin's body tensed, but she kept her voice casual. "I still work for Ka'id. You? You were with N'nafal, or at least the person above him. What happened?"

Jaya's image shifted and grew harder to focus on. Kirin averted her gaze and tried to keep track of the shape of her in her peripheral vision. "I talked to the Arch Bishop about things." She paused. "You know, you should too. I know you're close to Ka'id. I never understood how a Kalis could grow so attached to someone who wasn't their Ma'is, but I get it now. Arch Bishop Daliius is a visionary. He's making the world a better place for us. For everyone."

Kirin's mind whirled as she sensed more than saw Jaya moving closer. "Rumor has it, he's trying to break the Tidal Works."

"That's right. You're well informed for someone so out of the loop."

"You know what will happen? It won't just cripple Fom."

"I know. He knows. The Syndicate turned on him when they figured out what the Tidal Works was and what would happen if he broke it. They wanted him to stop. He's not going to. The Arch Bishop has a vision. A true vision, not just the Syndicate's lust for power for power's sake. The Arch Bishop's future is a world without the Merchant's Syndicate. A world without the Church, even, or at least without the Church as it is now—a corrupt pawn of our former masters. A world where Kalis can rule, with no one to pull our strings. A world of peace."

Kirin blinked and took a few steps backward, trying to keep distance between herself and Jaya. She wondered if she could get through the Papsukkal Door in time if she had to. It had never been her strong suit. "That's stupid. The Kalis will die along with everyone else. Arch Bishop Daliius will die along with them."

"Some Kalis will die," Kirin heard the frown in Jaya's voice. "But most will survive. We're resourceful. We're better equipped to survive another Age of Ashes than anyone. Daliius, too. He's one of us, after all. Anyway, we're not doing it for us. We're not even doing it for him. We're doing it for Eris, and everyone on it. There's corruption at every level, in every institution, and it's festered for thousands of years. The only way to cure it for good is to start over. Most of the Kalis have already gone to Fom and sacrificed themselves for the cause."

Whatever had happened to Jaya, Kirin realized she wouldn't talk her out of it. Her mind spun through options and settled on the one that seemed the most likely to succeed, even though it was the one she was least likely to live through. *I'm sorry, Ehrina,* she thought. *I love you.*

"Will you take me to see him? Daliius, I mean."

Kirin had thought Jaya would refuse, whatever she'd said before. Her loyalty to the Arch Bishop was profound in its absoluteness, and words were cheap for Kalis. But Jaya sounded pleased, relieved even, when she said, "Yes, of course. Like I said, he can explain his plan better than I can."

There'd been no hesitation in her response, and a fresh wave of doubt rolled over Kirin as Jaya led her towards the nave.

———

Arch Bishop Daliius sat on the edge of the central dais, his back against the alter, staring at nothing. Other than him, and now Jaya and Kirin, the cathedral was empty. Unless, Kirin reminded herself, there were more Kalis lurking around, but based on what Jaya had said, she didn't think so.

He stirred as the two women entered from the eastern aisle, and found them in his peripheral vision. "Jaya," he said, his voice welcoming. "You've brought someone new."

Kirin wondered how he could recognize Jaya at a glance. She'd spent quite a bit of time with Syrina, but could still only recognize her by her voice. "I'm Kalis Kirin," she said as Jaya began to introduce her. Minor victories where she could find them.

"I've heard about you." There was surprise in the Arch

Bishop's soft voice as he rose, and to her astonishment, bowed. And something else sang in his voice too. Something that plucked at her mind.

She began to doubt the reason she'd come. She could feel Jaya's eyes burning into the back of her head. Kirin wondered if she could move fast enough to take out the Arch Bishop before either of them could react, and also found herself wondering if she wanted to.

Before she could resolve the conflict growing within her, the Arch Bishop spoke again and began to shuffle towards her. "I understand you are faithful to your master. Your new Ma'is, as it were. One once held sway over me, you know, and my life, too, was dedicated to the betterment of the Merchant's Syndicate. I spread the lies of the Church to keep the masses in sway, but I can tell by the way you move you knew that already. Your master, then, has been much more forthcoming about the reality of things than mine ever was, and now you are conflicted, confused. Just as we all once were."

He stopped, still twenty hands from where his voice held her in place. She didn't have any memory of halting her own approach, but she found she couldn't move. She couldn't do anything but wait for him to speak again. The excitement of anticipation welled in her chest.

Daliius must have sensed that he'd transfixed her, despite his inability to see through her tattoos with any clarity. He smiled. "Jaya must have told you something of our future together, or else you wouldn't have come. Not like this. Did she tell you everything? No? Good. I must admit, I always find it thrilling to share my vision with someone new.

"Think of the world as it is. Think of its flaws. Many, yes? Many indeed, and each one by itself seems insurmountable; together, overwhelming. Now, think of starting over again, with the visionaries of the Kalis taking their proper place at the head of a new civilization." He took another step, a beatific smile on his bland face.

Kirin thought about it. About the factions of the Church killing each other over...what? What had been so worth the countless lives already lost that the Grace even now continued her drive to separate Fom from the rest of N'narad? The notion that her corrupt vision was better than someone else's corrupt vision? She thought about the pirates of Ristro that preyed on both sides to fund their own crusade, which Syrina had told her had gone on since the Age of Ashes. They were no better. She thought about the Syndicate, creating the Church and its Heavens to keep the people of the world so focused on the false joy of death that they ignored the suffering they endured in life. The same people who gladly parted with every scrap of tin they could muster so their names could be written and forgotten in giant tomes no one ever read. It was all connected and had been even before the Age of Ashes had thrown them into this everlasting dark age; the same corruption that had driven Kavik, Ka'id, her Ma'is, her lover, from her rightful place at the Syndicate's table. The same corruption that had broken Syrina's heart and mind.

The world could be better. So much better.

The words of the Arch Bishop spun through her every thought, filling her with an elation she hadn't known existed, even in the arms of Ehrina Ka'id.

But that wasn't true, something deep in her heart pointed out. She *had* known such joy. She'd known it when Ma'is Kavik had come to her after the death of Carlas Storik and the collapse of NRI. She'd known it when she'd chosen her Ma'is over the Syndicate she'd been supposed to serve with her life, and Kavik had revealed herself—her true self—as Ehrina Ka'id. She'd known it those first weeks in the penthouse with the view of the very cathedral she now stood in, when she knew she would do anything for Ehrina, not because the woman was her Ma'is, but because she'd become so much more.

In that moment of clarity, when her lover's face stood over the swirling words of the Arch Bishop, she moved. She took three quick steps forward, not daring to take the second she'd need to step through the Papsukkal Door, and struck the Arch Bishop in the throat with the rigid blade of her hand.

He fell back, choking, a look of incomprehension in his eyes. Kirin fought down a well of regret so strong it took her breath away and wheeled in time to drop below Jaya's punch that would have shattered her spine. She stood up again and struck the other Kalis in the same motion, but too slow. Jaya caught Kirin's lower arm and twisted, splintering first her elbow, then her shoulder.

The explosion of pain blotted out the roiling emotions bouncing through her head, but Kirin ignored it long enough to clip the back of Jaya's leg with her foot, sending them both down, Kirin on top. She smashed down against Jaya's face with her good forearm as they fell against the marble tiles of the floor, and her broken arm, still gripped by Jaya, snapped in two more places, jagged ends of bone tearing through skin. The back of Jaya's head crunched, and her teeth shattered against Kirin's forearm, drawing blood as the other Kalis bit down hard, then went limp.

Choking with pain and confusion, Kirin staggered from the Cathedral of Light, the image of the Arch Bishop's shocked face competing with that of Ka'id's in her pain-clouded mind.

———

Ehrina Ka'id cradled Kirin's head in her lap, stroking her hairless scalp. The tattoos formed tiny ridges, almost imperceptible to the touch.

Her Kalis had appeared a little after dark, dazed and blank-faced, with tears in her eyes and her left arm sshattered in at least five places, hanging only by the skin and a few tendons at the elbow. Ka'id wasn't even sure if the tattoos could heal it enough to be functional again, though she knew they were trying.

She'd known what had happened, or at least the gist of it, long before Kirin had returned. Chaos reigned after one of the Arch Bishop's retainers had found him dead. Murdered, his throat crushed. A lone guard had been found unconscious at her post by the servant's kitchen door. No perpetrators could be found, but near Daliius's body they'd discovered a pile of ash and a few shards of burnt bone. Few knew what that meant, and those few all speculated that the attacker had herself been killed, though nobody could know for certain what had happened or who had killed his attacker. Suspicion boiled within the remaining ranks of the Merchant's Syndicate, along with no small amount of relief.

No, Ka'id corrected herself. No reason to alter the past from what it was. She hadn't known what happened. Not at all. She'd been beside herself, sure those had been Kirin's ashes scattered on the Cathedral floor, trying to convince herself otherwise through tears and pounding heart, until the moment her love staggered into the townhouse.

Kirin stirred, and Ka'id was glad. Not only because it was the woman she loved, but because their work wasn't over, and for the next part, she needed her Kalis.

Kirin's eyes fluttered open and locked on hers. "I love you," she said. Her tone was blunt, as matter-of-fact as if she'd stated she was hungry or the windows were dirty.

Ka'id's heart pounded with those words, and she smiled. "I love you too. Are you ready to go back to work?"

Kirin nodded, and Ka'id sensed a smile behind the tattoos. "My arm hurts."

Ka'id looked at where it still hung limp off the side of the couch, bent at impossible angles. The tattoos worked better unbound, but it hurt her to see it so. It was still mangled, but she thought it looked less twisted than it had been an hour ago. "Yes, it looks like it does."

Kirin grunted a little laugh. "I'm ready. Let's go."

———

"I object to this. We have no control over him. Over this 'Carlas the First.'"

"If it is not obvious you have already been overruled, Kavik, you have no place at this table."

"Now, now. Kavik is an idiot, but he makes an interesting point."

"Do you have something to contribute, Berdai? If you do, just come out and say it."

"My point is just what I said, Nyliik. This new candidate is unlike anything we've dealt with before. He's too clever, not attached to the Merchant's Syndicate in any meaningful way, and in my opinion, is altogether too much under the influence of this other one, this Ehrina Ka'id. His supposed adviser."

"They're rumored to be lovers."

"According to N'nafal, Ka'id claims to have once been a High Merchant herself."

"So you said, Kavik. And he is as much an idiot to spew such drivel as you are for believing him."

"It is too late. It's done."

The five robed figures with painted faces who gathered around the polished, oval table turned as one. The speaker shut the door behind him and took his place at the sixth and final seat.

"High Merchant Morn. You're late."

"We are all late," Morn stated. "This Ka'id has already put forth the priest Carlas's name to the Hierophants and the rest of the Council, who of course accepted it. Unanimously. They are even more anxious than we to put this entire affair behind them. He plans to call for immediate peace talks with Fom. That alone is enough to get him the votes."

"But—"

"There are no 'buts.' I told you, it is done. Before Ka'id even introduced her pet Carlas to the Church hierarchy, she made sure his plans for the Salvation Taxes had been disseminated throughout the city."

"His plans? What—"

"He intends what he calls a 'restructuring.' The Heavens, he claims, are no longer barred behind payments of Salvation Taxes to the Church. He says they never have been. 'A misinterpretation,' he calls it. He claims Heavens will judge people on their own merit, with their taxes to the Church of Tyrsh— that is what he's calling it, as if he'd already brokered peace with the Grace—their taxes to the Church of Tyrsh being secondary. 'Taken into account, but longer mandatory,' is how he put it."

"Absurd. The Church will be bankrupt. *We* will be bankrupt!"

"Nevertheless, it is, as you can imagine, a wildly popular idea. Even if they weren't supportive of Carlas because of his peace plans, the Hierophants and the rest of the Council could not oppose him without losing the people. Nor can we. Without the people, there is no Church."

"How long must have Ka'id been planning this?"

"Long enough. She must have had some pieces in place

before we put her in the Bower House. It appears we were right to suspect that woman, yet still managed to grossly underestimate her. But our mistakes are in the past now, and cannot be undone. As I said, it is finished. We have lost our Kalis and our ability to make more, we have lost our tin and our naphtha, and now we have lost our Church. We, the six of us here now, must rebuild under its shadow, until such time we can once more take our rightful place above it. Then, we can discuss removing this Arch Bishop Carlas and his accountant adviser. Before then, any action against them would be suicide—the last nail in the coffin of our venerable organization."

"Maybe..."

"Yes, Berdai?"

"Maybe we could expand our seats at this table by one. Invite this Ka'id to join us. We were, after all, once Fifteen. Could there not now be room for a seventh? Better to keep one like that close, where we could exert some modicum of control over her."

Morn rustled with the shaking of his head. "Impossible, I'm afraid. I already offered her a seat at the High Merchants' table. She turned it down."

24

BEGINNINGS

TIME BLURRED AS SYRINA DANGLED FROM THE BUNDLE OF cables. Her shoulder ached, and her other arm hung broken and useless at her side. The voice existed as a numbness throbbing through her body, keeping pain in check.

After moments or hours, she gathered her wits enough to drag herself upward and swing back and forth, gaining momentum until she released the wires and tumbled through the air to clutch the tattered rim of the far walkway with her good arm. She thought the wires would break as she swung, hurling her to her death far below, but they didn't. After hanging a moment, legs dangling over the abyss, she hauled herself up and lay on the hot, damp, metal grate, panting. Her breath made a bubbling, wheezing sound in her chest. Thuds and explosions reverberated in a directionless cacophony, and the high keening continued to build from somewhere ahead.

We need to go now. If you're just going to lie here, there wasn't much point exerting all that effort to get this far.

"Fuck you," Syrina said, but she lurched to her feet and staggered down the passage.

Another boom and gout of steam made her stagger back, but this time it was further ahead and she could wait a moment before moving on. A low, building squeal now competed with the keening sound, and some nearby section of the upper passages sagged and groaned. Some far away part of her mind wondered what was going on in the city above, and she realized she would never know. She wanted to regret it, but her emotions were something beyond her now. Her body and limbs felt strange and heavy, as if she wasn't so much stumbling as oozing. She wondered if whatever was left of her muscles were held to her bones only by the tattoos.

That's a morbid thought.

"Tell me I'm wrong." Syrina's whisper was harsh and thin, like she had gravel in her lungs. Her throat hurt.

Turn here. You can climb up. Almost there.

She was aware that the voice had changed the subject on purpose, but she obeyed with blind loyalty, desperate to get what needed to be done over with.

The pipes and joints she clambered up seared her feet, and her good hand stuck to them like her skin was made of wax. She avoided acknowledging the details of what her body had become in the churning heat of the dying machine and tried not to think about her growing suspicion that her face felt sticky because her eyes had boiled onto her cheeks. Through her tattoos, the world had become a swirl of outlines and vibrations, forging her surroundings in a way that was somehow both vague and distinct.

Another explosion threw her forward, and she screamed as her flesh blanched across her back. She couldn't remember the last time she'd made a sound because of physical pain before coming down here. In her training years, she supposed, but none of the pain she'd felt back then compared to the sensation of super-heated gas searing away her flesh and boiling the organs underneath. She couldn't breathe, and she fell forward onto her face with distant regret.

"I failed." She couldn't talk anymore, and the words seemed to be someone else's thoughts.

No. You're here. Get up. The wires above you, three steps ahead. Get us there.

She tried to move and couldn't, then tried again. She slid forward a couple hands on her stomach, feeling jellied bits of herself scraping off onto the twisted metal planks of the passage floor. Then she did it again.

The keening was all around, drowning her heightened senses from the tattoos into a white, static light filled with shadows, now growing ever dimmer. She groped upward, mind spinning, the world falling away. *"No Kalis ever lives to old age,"* she thought, not caring what the voice thought of the idea. *"There's no good or bad way to go for us. Just an end. The time we fail."* She remembered telling someone something like that once, long ago. Pasha. She'd told Pasha that. She wished she believed she would meet him now.

The voice didn't respond. Her hand touched something loose and rubbery. Somehow, she knew she was touching it, even though the nerves in her hand had been scraped and burned away. There was a strange sensation, like what remained of her blood sliding up her arm and through her hand, followed by an explosion of light.

———

At first, she thought she'd died, that one last blast of the decaying Tidal Works had sent her to one of the N'naradin Heavens she'd never believed in. But then came awareness. Not awareness of her surroundings, which remained cloaked in a featureless white nothingness that wasn't light, but wasn't anything else either. It was an internal awareness, which didn't make any sense at first, because although she was aware there was no longer pain, it hadn't been replaced by anything else. She'd never been so aware of the absence of awareness, which confused her.

Maybe I should open my eyes and look around, the thought occurred to her, but then she realized her eyes were neither closed nor open.

"Focus," the voice said.

It surprised Syrina to hear the voice use a voice, not in the back of her mind where it had been a constant presence, but outside, where she could hear it with her non-existent ears.

But then she realized that there'd been a place that had happened before, and everything started making sense.

With understanding, her surroundings came together, and the light sculpted itself into shapes and forms she could comprehend.

"That's right," encouraged the voice. "Don't use your senses. You don't have senses anymore. You can skip input and go straight for consciousness."

And somehow, that made sense too. Syrina looked around.

The voice stood in front of her like before, a gleaming mirror of herself. Unlike before, there was no quicksilver floor and ceiling stretching away in all directions to infinity. Just the general whiteness-that-wasn't-light. It gave her the impression it was only white because it wasn't anything else. And, she realized, her own body wasn't there at all, or even a representation of it. She'd become an awareness, floating before the image of the voice, and that was all.

"Try not to think about it. You'll get used to it, trust me. I should know, right?"

Syrina tried to relax and failed, but thought she might indeed get used to it, given enough time.

"Time is something we've got a lot of, now."

Are we in the Tidal Works?

The voice seemed to hesitate. "Kind of." It flowed away without getting further for a second. "There," it stated.

What?

"The Tidal Works—the real Tidal Works; the machines that have been keeping the Eye from tearing Eris apart every few months—are connected. All of them. Ten. Well, six now, but that should be enough. They just needed a sentient mind to keep them in check. Nine-thousand-some years is a long time for anything to run on auto pilot."

Wait. So that's what caused the Age of Ashes? The intelligence that was running the Tidal Works just...left?

"Left. Died. Switched off. Driven away by the precursors to the Merchant's Syndicate so they could seize control of whatever was left. There's no way to tell what happened, but yes."

You say there are six now? Four are gone, then.

"That's right. Three from the Age of Ashes, and one more from Kamahush. Good thing we stopped the one under Fom from shutting down. I doubt the other five could have held together very long."

But six can?

"Yeah." The voice hesitated again. "I think so. The AI that left an eon ago, it didn't have any help, and I do. I think we'll be okay, if we work together."

Help. The word fell like a stone out of Syrina's non-existent mouth.

The shimmering image of the voice smiled. "You're my voice now, kind of. I wasn't sure what would happen; if you would come with me or your mind would die with your body. I had a feeling, but I couldn't be sure. I absorbed enough of your...awareness, I guess you could say, that I could take part of you with me. Which is good, because like I said, keeping these machines going will be a lot of work. Not to mention the daystars. But at least you can watch the world go by with some of those, if we can get them working again. Me too, to be honest. I've grown attached to...out there, though it's embarrassing to admit. I'm not sure how the previous management felt about humanity, but those monkeys should be glad the new team gives a shit. Not that they'll ever know." It paused. "And as long as I'm being honest, I've grown attached to you. I wasn't looking forward to being by myself if I couldn't bring you along."

Wait, wait, wait. Syrina felt a stark clarity that she couldn't remember ever feeling before, but she also felt as dumb as an empty sack compared to the shimmering image of herself that she was talking to. *So, we're here for how long?*

The image shrugged. "As long as the Tidal Machines keep working, I suppose. Why? Is there someplace you need to be?"

Syrina looked around again at the general whiteness. She found she could pick out shapes, even form them in her mind, but then they would slip away again.

"Don't worry about it," the voice said. "Like I said, you'll get better at it."

From above there came a soft hoot, and a large, white owl drifted down on silent wings to perch on the voice's shoulder, which shimmered and rippled at its touch. The twin black feathers on its head curved up like horns or long, black ears. The owl hooted again. Its talons pinched, but not painfully, and its body was warm and soft. Syrina could feel it all, despite standing in front of it and not having a body of her own.

"See?" said the voice. "You're a natural in this place, just like I was in yours."

25

EPILOGUE

Ves stood on the deck of The Anna II, looking over the sea wall towards the jumble of gleaming towers and drab, grey architecture that was the city of Fom. Six months on, and he still couldn't get used to the absence of the permanent haze that once obscured all but the peaks of the Customs Towers.

"We sit here long enough, someone will notice." Mann's voice had grown old over the past few months, his speech now peppered with harsh, dry coughing that never quite went away. "Someone we don't want noticing, I mean."

Ves nodded, but he stood a few minutes more, looking at the strange sight of Fom without fog.

After the burning of the blackvine, he and Mann, along with two dozen freed indentured, had made their way over the ridge, intending on getting themselves lost in the city before the plantation owners organized themselves enough to track them down. Most of them ran the other way when they mounted the hill and saw the flash of fire under the clouds, and felt the near-constant rumble of the dying Tidal Works through their feet. Ves had considered it too, but Mann pointed out that if the

Tidal Works went up like Syrina said it would, it wouldn't matter how far they ran, and if it didn't, it would be easier to hide in the city. Ves thought about mentioning death by secondary explosion, which looked likely, but at the time that still seemed better than living in the wilderness on the run, waiting to be captured and forced back into indentured servitude.

They'd descended into Fom and tried to help where they could, though there wasn't much anyone could do beyond trying to stay alive. After a few days they wound up in the Lip, where at least there were no Tidal Works erupting beneath them. Things had gotten quiet for a few weeks after that, then terrible—bad enough that both of them thought it would be a matter of days or hours before everything ended for good.

Then came quiet, and the quiet lasted.

After a week, people started coming out from wherever they'd been hiding, while others trickled back from the mountains and villages along the delta to the north, where thousands had fled when everything started getting bad. They found Fom an unfamiliar place. Swaths of it lay in ruins or gone completely, tumbled into sinkholes where ancient limestone foundations had collapsed into the sea caves along with the shattered machinery of the Tidal Works. Without the machines, the fog and drizzle lifted, and the sun shone for the first time, bright and clear on the remains of the city.

The Tidal Works had become nothing but pockets of tattered metal and ceramic, sagging into the water in the depths of the caves. Most of the tunnels were full of blasted, ruined scrap, in places still ticking with millennia of stored heat. But near the center, in one vast chasm now free of the twists and tangles of the components that once surrounded it, a black obelisk jutted from the water, hundreds of hands high, twisted like a fat, squarish corkscrew and covered with fine, swirling grooves. Here and there, rubbery cables drooped, and a few chunks of twisted brass clung to its sides like baby karakh clinging to the backs of their mothers.

They didn't know how it had been possible for Syrina to accomplish...whatever she'd done. It looked impossible that anyone could have survived those last hours beneath the city, but Fom was still there, so she must have. None of them questioned whether it had been her. There was no reason to doubt who'd saved them.

Neither of them had felt an urge to stay. It had been easy for Ves to have his pick of the ships docked under the Customs Towers with everyone focused inward on rebuilding. He selected a small ex-military steamship—a tarfuel one, since still nobody knew how much they could rely on naphtha reserves—and recruited a skeleton crew from the villages along the coast, enough to get to Maresg. There, he'd found the rest, men and women eager to get out of the tree city nobody passed through anymore.

Even with peace hammered out between the now-independent Grace of Fom and the new Arch Bishop of Tyrsh in the following months, the life of a pirate was a pleasant enough one. Better now, since the militaries of both nations had better things to do than patrol around trying to kill each other.

And now here they were.

Ves rose from his reverie and walked with Mann back to the bridge.

———

"You going to take them up on their offer?" Mann asked. He and Ves sat eating their dinner of pickled goat and seaweed around Ves' new, elaborate desk in what Ves had taken to calling "the Captain's Stateroom," even though it was just a mid-deck cargo hold Ves had claimed as his cabin and office.

Ves laughed. "Hell no. I already got kicked out of the Corsairs once. I'd just get myself excommunicated again."

Mann shrugged. "The message said all would be forgiven."

"They forgave *me*. I'm not going back. Ash would come back from the dead just long enough to kill me."

Mann wanted to ask what had happened between Ves and the Astrologers all those years ago, but it wouldn't have been the first time, and he knew he'd get the same non-answer he always did. "They said if you don't come back, next time they see us, they'll attack on sight."

"Thank fuck." Ves took a long drink of rum, straight from the bottle. Even now that he had plenty of cups, he said he'd grown to prefer it that way. "Things are finally starting to get back to normal."

He passed the bottle to Mann, but the old man refused with a sigh that turned into another long string of stifled coughing. "I'm tired," he said after he could catch his breath.

"You're always tired." There might have been a hint of concern in Ves' voice.

Mann nodded with a laugh. "I've been tired since they threw me in the Pit and I met you. Before, even. Goddamn, since I can remember. Now I'm even more tired, but at least I finally have time to rest." He gave Ves a long, sober look. "When you get to be an old man, you'll be tired too." With that he stood, coughing into his sleeve. "Goodnight, friend. Don't stay up all night drinking. That shit will kill you." He gave a wave of goodnight, and went to his cabin.

———

Ves sat alone the next morning, sipping from a fresh bottle and waiting for Mann to join him for breakfast, but eventually he got bored enough to get up and go pound on his first mate's door. "Come on, old man," he called. "You even went to bed before me. It's time to get your ass up. I can't drink by myself all morning. They'll call me a drunk."

No answer.

"Shit." Ves tried the handle. It was unlocked. There was no reason for anyone to lock their doors on Ves' ship, because if any of his crew gave them one, he'd throw them overboard.

Mann lay on his back, eyes closed, face placid.

"Shit," Ves said again, and ran two steps to the bedside, knowing there was no point. Mann's skin was cold and waxy.

Tears welled in Ves' eyes, and he wiped at his face. "God-damn it. You could have at least waited long enough to say goodbye."

He sat next to his friend for a while, talking about nothing in particular, hating the idea of walking away, but he knew they needed him on the bridge. Eventually he rose, tugged the sheets over Mann's face, and went above.

He wanted to bury Mann where they'd buried Saphi and Anna, but it was impractical. It would take them almost a month to get to Skalkaad in the best conditions, and however he felt about it, it wouldn't do to keep a body on the ship that long.

In the bridge, Ves ignored the chatter and questions cast his way by his navigator and wheel man, a decent fellow named Cathar N'than—another refugee from Fom he'd picked up in Maresg. He scanned the charts spread on the table. "Yeah," he said, nodding to no one in particular. "It's not perfect, but what is? It's close enough."

To N'than, who was eyeing him with a face full of questions, he said, "Cut the engines. We're having a funeral."

An hour later he stood on the deck, Mann's frail frame in

his arms, wrapped in the same sheet Ves had covered him with. His body was light. Ves realized he must have been wasting away for months, even as he'd acted like he always had, right up until the end.

Now that all eyes were on him, he didn't know what to say. He looked at the faces of his crew, watching him with sympathetic eyes, and knew whatever words he came up with wouldn't be for them. They didn't know Albertus Mann. Not like he did. And now they never would. He looked down at the body and gently tugged the sheet back to look at the old man's face.

Mann's body was so light it was easy for Ves to cradle it with one arm, and with his free hand he scrubbed at his face, blinking away fresh tears. "I guess it doesn't matter much, but I can't get you to Saphi and Anna," he said, voice low enough his crew wouldn't be able to hear. Let them wonder. "S'okay. They'll find you alright if they can. Hell, maybe Syrina too. This isn't far from where I lost Ash though, so in the meantime, maybe you can meet up with him. You know, I always wished you two could have gotten to know each other for more than a few minutes. Your ghosts will have all sorts of shit to say about me." He paused and smiled through his tears. "Don't leave anything out when you tell him what we've been up to. Make me look good, will you?"

He took a breath like he might say something else, but then he just shook his head. "I'm glad I saved your ass from the Pit back then. Goodbye, old man." He sighed and let Mann's body fall into the sea.

He stood silent and blinking his tears for a few minutes, watching the waves, squinting against the sun glaring off the water. Then he turned. His crew still watched with serious faces. "Alright, back to work you fucks!" he yelled. "This goddamn world isn't going to rob itself."

He wiped his face again as he watched them scurry back to work and muttered under his breath, "Enough goddamn goodbyes for a lifetime."

———

The Arch Bishop, Carlas the First, took over the newly founded Church of Tyrsh even before they'd entombed Daliius in the Crypts of the Highest Heaven, but he did so with the unanimous support of the Hierophants and Council. He'd been a complete unknown until a few days after Daliius's murder, but even before they formally met him, they appreciated he didn't seem entwined, or even interested, in the intrigues and schemes that had plagued the Church of N'narad for centuries. He'd been a mere country priest with a crippled arm, from a tiny village no one had heard of, who'd risen from nowhere. The clergy were eager to put the both the war and the inconvenient details of Daliius's death behind them, and while the investigation into the murder might continue for years, nobody believed anything would come of it. They all privately agreed it was better that way.

Arch Bishop Carlas didn't have the strange, alluring charisma of Daliius, but he was far more even tempered and fair minded. When his first point of business was to contact the Grace of Fom and begin peace negotiations, only the most militant of the theocracy grumbled. The Grace had been effectively independent for centuries. The majority had grown tired of a war that seemed, in retrospect, based mostly on semantics. Not to mention, the citizens adored both the new Arch Bishop's casual demeanor and his take on Salvation Taxes. So much that the opposition feared any attempt to remove him would plunge the Island into a new civil war. They schemed, as he knew they would, but for now, that was all they could do.

Carlas's closest adviser was a woman named Ehrina Ka'id—an accountant, of all things, and a refugee from Eheene, though she'd been born in Pom, under the umbrella of the N'naradin Empire, so even her detractors were reluctant to openly call her a foreigner despite her decades-long absence. The two seemed inseparable, and in a matter of weeks rumors began circulating about their relationship. But with peace on the horizon and stability at home, only the most rigid puritans could bring themselves to care what the Arch Bishop and his accountant advisor did in their own time. It was, everyone said, between them and the Heavens.

Dear reader,

We hope you enjoyed reading *The Grace's War*. Please take a moment to leave a review, even if it's a short one. Your opinion is important to us.

Discover more books by R.A. Fisher at https://www.nextchapter.pub/authors/ra-fisher

Want to know when one of our books is free or discounted? Join the newsletter at http://eepurl.com/bqqB3H

Best regards,
R.A. Fisher and the Next Chapter Team

ABOUT THE AUTHOR

Robert Fisher has lived in Hiroshima, Japan with his wife and five-year-old son since 2015, where he occasionally teaches English, writes, and pretends to learn Japanese. Before that he lived in Vancouver, Canada where he worked in the beer industry and mostly just cavorted about, getting into trouble and eating Thai food. He placed fourth in The Vancouver Courier's literary contest with his short story *The Gift,* which appeared in that paper on February 20, 2009. His science fiction novella *The God Machine* was published by Blue Cubicle Press in 2011.

The Grace's War
ISBN: 978-4-86750-552-6

Published by
Next Chapter
1-60-20 Minami-Otsuka
170-0005 Toshima-Ku, Tokyo
+818035793528

6th June 2021

Lightning Source UK Ltd.
Milton Keynes UK
UKHW040728240621
386081UK00001B/148